Memories of a Mud Bee

A NOVEL

Madonna Ball

This book is a work of fiction. Names, characters, businesses, places, events and incidents are either the products of the author's imagination or used in a fictitious manner. Any resemblance to actual persons, living or dead, or actual events is purely coincidental.

Copyright © 2014 by Madonna Ball

HUMBLE
HOUND
PUBLISHING

www.HumbleHoundPublishing.com

ISBN: 0990754308
ISBN 13: 9780990754305

ONE

I didn't speak until I was almost four years old. I can't remember exactly how it was that I communicated before that though. I suppose I just pointed or shook my head yes or no instead of talking, like a mime. I hate comparing myself to a mime, considering that my brother Andrew and I despised mimes when we were children. We were deathly afraid of both mimes and clowns. Like most kids, we found their makeup and disguises deceitful. We didn't like the fact that their true expressions were masked. Also, mimes were always unnaturally thin and their black leotards seemed to cling to every part of their body that our eyes instinctively wanted to ignore. Their white faces and dismal expressions were unsettling. We could never understand the point. What was so fun about watching a morose grown man interact with some unseen object?

As absurd as I found mimes and their routines, I could relate. Like mimes, I felt trapped by some invisible force that kept me from gaining the attention I wanted from my family.

Years later my family claimed that my silence made sense, given the size of our family. They argued that there was no need for me to talk because everybody else just did the talking for me. Their argument seemed logical for years, but I came to understand that it wasn't exactly the truth. I don't blame them for not noticing me. I was small and quiet and found it difficult to assert myself. Truthfully, my family was probably just thankful that I didn't contribute to the noise and chaos that filled our home.

Our house was small and overcrowded, and it resembled all of the other houses in Riverton at the time. Most of the homes in this downriver community were two-family flats that were built in the early 1920s. "Downriver" is a term that the locals used to refer to the handful of cities located south of Detroit or more accurately, south of the Detroit River. The houses were covered in a depressing combination of aluminum and asbestos siding. Later, when we learned about the dangers of asbestos, we didn't think much of it. As kids we used to pick at the crumbling exterior of our house with a stick or our fingernails and pretend that the shiny specks embedded within it were gold or some other precious metal. My sister, Anna, admitted years later that sometimes she would even put flecks of siding in her mouth to see if they tasted like anything. The houses appeared big on the outside, but were small and boxy on the inside. They were so close together that they looked like they were only an arms-length apart from one another. Every once in a while I couldn't resist the urge to stick my arm out of my sister Ellen's bedroom window to see if I could actually touch our neighbor's house. Of course I didn't come close to reaching it, but it was fun to pretend there was a chance that I just might. A few streets over there were a handful of brick houses, which were owned by the older, wealthier residents of Riverton. Many of those homes still had working fireplaces. Sometimes when I was outside playing in the snow, the wind would carry with it the smell of a burning fire. That smell always left me feeling homesick for a family I'd never have. I was alone most of the time. I spent hours playing by myself either in my closet or on the side of the neighbor's house. The Petersons had lived in the house for over twenty years. When Mr. Peterson retired from Ford and their children were grown, they converted the upstairs to an apartment and rented it to various families for the remaining five or six years that they lived there. Mr. and Mrs. Peterson had recently moved back to North Carolina, and new tenants were due to move in soon. The backyard was fenced in, and in front of the fence was a small patch of grass and a single rose bush. I would sit there for hours playing with my dolls or just daydreaming.

That is where I was sitting the day Jana and Clyde Davis moved into the Peterson's upstairs apartment. I had no way of knowing that this chance encounter would serve as the catalyst that would allow my family to begin to heal.

TWO

I'd been staring at her for quite some time before I realized she was speaking to me. "Are you the welcoming committee?" Jana asked even louder the second time. The warm, yellow light of the sun circled her head and it was several seconds before I could begin to make out the shape of a face through the brightness. Her hair was long, blond and straight. It flowed down her back and framed her small face. I imagined that it felt like corn silk - soft, cool and smooth. Freckles dotted her long arms, legs, nose and cheeks. She wasn't wearing a stitch of makeup, and I quickly decided that if she had been, she would have looked ridiculous, kind of like a girl playing dress up. Her eyes, nose and mouth were delicate and childlike. I thought that she was pretty even with all of her freckles. I felt immediately as if I were in the presence of someone special. When she extended her hand, I wasn't sure if she wanted me to shake it or if she was offering to help me up. I clasped Jana's hand and pushed off the ground with my other one. With Jana's help, I sprung quickly up. Jana was taller than most women I knew. She was thin, which made me feel self conscious about my own soft, slightly round 8-year-old body. I smoothed out my shirt that was almost too small as I continued to size Jana up. She wore a long, strapless sundress and several long, beaded necklaces encircled her neck. My mom would have commented how Jana's strappy sandals were impractical, but I liked them and noticed that even her toes were freckled.

"You must be Mr. Peterson's little girl?" Jana inquired. She continued to talk about her move, ignoring the fact that I had yet not spoken a word. After several mesmerized minutes, I finally responded to Jana's initial question.

"Who? No! Mr. Peterson and his wife moved to North Carolina last year," I said.

"Oh, not that Mr. Peterson. I meant his son, Frank and his wife. What's her name again?" Jana asked.

"I didn't know that the Peterson's had a son and as for his wife, your guess is as good as mine." I replied.

"Well, they do have a son who is married with children and they're planning on moving into the main level of the house as soon as school gets out. I thought maybe they'd meet us here, since we're moving in today," Jana explained.

"Hmm," I said shrugging my shoulders nonchalantly.

"Well, we've established that you don't live here, so what are you doing here all tucked away like a little squirrel?" she asked playfully.

I wasn't comfortable with being put on the spot, so I simply introduced myself. "I'm just the neighbor, Suzanne.

I live next door," I informed her, pointing to our tired look-ing house. The siding needed to be replaced, along with the windows. Bikes and toys cluttered the backyard and as I looked over at it, I began to worry that one of us kids had better get the yard picked up before our dad got home.

"I like that name. It reminds me of the song." Jana hummed the first few verses of the song "Oh Susanna" before finally saying, "Well, Miss Suzanna, how about lend-ing us a hand."

Before I could ask who else was moving in with her, a young man came rushing awkwardly down the driveway with an armload of boxes and a longhaired dachshund trot-ting behind him. The man had the fast-paced walk of some-one who was carrying something far too heavy for comfort. She introduced us, "Suzanne, this is my husband Clyde. Clyde, this is Suzanne. She lives next door."

Clyde was tall and towered almost a foot above Jana. He had long chestnut hair and it was pulled back into a thick, tight ponytail. Long sideburns framed his handsome face. His eyes were brown and he had an easy smile.

"Nice to meet you, Suzanne," he said.

I nodded my head and said, "He's a funny looking dog. What's his name?" I adored all kinds of animals and had decided after our last field trip to the zoo that I was going to become a veterinarian or a zoologist when I grew up.

"This is Oscar and he's a longhaired dachshund," Clyde answered.

"He's so cute. I wish we could have a little dog, but my mom says that dogs are too much work," I said bend-ing down and stroking his long tubular body. Clyde assured me that Oscar was easy to take care of and said that I could come over and take him for a walk whenever I wanted.

While Clyde and I were making small talk about dachshunds, Jana was trying to figure out which key unlocked the door. She grew frustrated because there were four keys on her ring, but none of them seemed to work. After several minutes Clyde took his turn trying each key in the lock. He eventually found a key that seemed to fit, but the door still would not open. Jana pulled the key from the keyhole and placed the key ring onto Clyde's open hand. She waved her hands in a circular motion over the keys as if she was casting some kind of magical spell. She then picked up the key that fit in the keyhole and gently kissed it before trying one more time. When it didn't work, Jana and Clyde began to laugh over the absurdity of the situation. As I stood watching them, it occurred to me that Jana and Clyde were hippies. It wasn't just their clothes or their hair, but their demeanor. They were happy and relaxed. I decided that I would have to be careful not to talk about meeting them around our family, especially Dad. He had most recently waged a private war on all hippies, complaining daily about the changing dynamics of our neighborhood. "All the good families, who actually own their homes and take a little pride in their yards, are leaving and being replaced by those shifty, lazy hippies." He talked about them as if they were an infestation of rats.

I didn't share my father's sentiments, however. I was utterly fascinated by hippies and their lifestyle. They represented everything that our family wasn't. When they appeared on the nightly news in stories that covered anti-war protests, they came across as loving, open-minded people who were able to freely express their feelings. My parents didn't like the war either, so I never understood what their beef was with the hippies. And I'd had a few experiences with hippies that had me thinking this hippie thing was not all bad.

One day when I was walking home from school, a young hippie woman who had just moved into the neighborhood approached me. She wore a long, shapeless dress that hung from her body like a scarecrow's costume. Though in a hurry, she was still smiling and moving with very little urgency. "Hey, little girl, could you give me a hand carrying in these groceries?" she pleaded. "I'm gonna be late for work again and this time my boss will fire me for sure."

"Sure," I said.

I knew better than to talk to a stranger, and she was not only a stranger, but she was also a hippie, which made her even more dangerous, according to my dad. When the neighbors across the street, the Reichmann's, had moved in a few months earlier, my mom had sent me over to their house with a Bundt cake. When the hippies moved in, they got nothing but angry stares and the threat of an ass whooping from every man on the street if they got out of line. The wives were curious about the hippies and their bohemian lifestyles, but they wouldn't have dreamed of questioning their husbands, so they stayed away. I too was intrigued, and I refused to let fear stand in my way. I headed over to the van and grabbed several bags of groceries. "This sure is a lot of food," I observed.

"Well, we have a lot of people to feed," the young woman explained.

"Do you have children?" I asked.

For Larry, Olivia, Jack and Evan-
the loves of my life.
And to all of my brothers and sisters-
I wouldn't pay a penny to do it all over again,
but wouldn't trade any of you for
all the money in the world.

ACKNOWLEDGEMENTS

I would like to extend my deepest gratitude to Flora M Brown who held my hand throughout the entire publishing process. Thank you for answering my many questions and for your patience when dealing with my technological incompetence.

Thank you to Shaun Griffen who helped shape my story and fine-tune my words. You helped me find my voice.

My gratitude to my dear friends, Mary Riegle and Ellen Maschka. Mary, you have listened to my stories ever since our Euchre playing days at Michigan State and have never complained. Your support and encouragement has been more valuable than you will ever know.

Thank you, Ellen for sitting through countless lunches and phone conversations that consisted of me incessantly talking about everything that I needed to get done. You are a wonderful listener!

"No, but Stan and Sasha do. They have two boys, Spring and Wood. My man is John and I'm Joan," she said as she extended her hand for me to shake. "Sarah, Larry and their daughter, Forest, also live with us. Byron and John will only be staying until they can get their van fixed and then they're back on the road to tour with their band."

"Wow! That's a lot of people," I responded. "We have a lot of people living in our house, but we're an actual family." I thought it important to add the last bit about being a real family, but what I said must have struck a nerve with Joan because she launched into a speech about what it means to be a family.

"Well," she passionately explained, "even though we aren't technically related to each other, we're still a family of sorts. A family isn't just a mom and dad and kids. A family can include all kinds of people just as long as they all love and take care of each other." I stood silently mesmerized by Joan's passionate convictions. "I like to think of us as a family of friends who together help make the world a more beautiful place. You know, a world where everyone respects each other and looks out for each other." My silence must have been mistaken for lack of understanding, so Joan continued, "When people pool all of their positive energy together, great things can happen."

What Joan described didn't seem so bad to me. It actually sounded pretty cool. I feared that somehow she had heard about my dad's disdain for hippies, and that she would judge me for my dad's misconceptions.

When I entered her house, I felt like I had walked into a dream. There were plants everywhere. Some were hanging in baskets while others were in small pots lining the windowsills. The large potted ones on the floor looked more like trees than plants. I had never seen anything like it before. The only plant we had in our house was a philodendron left over from a funeral. Their house felt like a home.

There were no doors in any of the rooms; there were only long strands of beads hanging where the doors were once hinged. Music played in the background and the smell of incense reminded me of church.

A woman was resting on a couch nursing her child. The little girl looked to be two or three, and she stopped suckling long enough to say hi to me. I could hear the sound of men's voices as I approached the kitchen. Three of them were sitting around the table, talking and drinking coffee while the sweet smell of smoke from their clove cigarettes swirled around their heads. My dad smoked, but his cigarettes didn't smell like theirs. I discovered what clove cigarettes were when Anna and her friend got caught smoking them up in Anna's bedroom. She had learned her lesson after that because now she only smoked regular cigarettes so her smoke just blended in with the rest of the smoke in the house. Upon seeing them, I became aware of just how unsafe it really was to be in a house full of complete strangers. I didn't wait for them to acknowledge me. I placed the bags on the counter and turned tail. As I was walking out of the kitchen, Joan was walking in.

"Gotta go!" I casually called and walked out the front door and right into the dreaded Mrs. Daniels.

Mrs. Daniels was referred to as the neighborhood watchdog. She apparently had nothing better to do with her time than to sit on her front porch and monitor the comings and goings of every person who lived on our street. Her husband had died when she was very young, in her late thirties. They only had one child, who had been born with Down syndrome. His name was Brucie. Brucie suffered from various health problems, one of which was a chronic, snotty nose that dripped down onto his upper lip no matter the weather outside. He was a sweet boy and all of the kids had loved him. He'd spend hours blowing bubbles while the younger kids in the neighborhood ran around trying to pop them. Sometimes when the boys played ball in the street, they'd let Brucie take a break from shagging balls and let him take a turn at bat. He was strong as an ox and could send the ball sailing, but got confused when it came time to run. Brucie had died on the day of his thirtieth birthday. He went to bed one night and didn't wake up the next day. Mrs. Daniels was devastated. She had never remarried or moved from the home that she had shared with her husband and son. All of the kids in the neighborhood were afraid of her and suspected that she was some kind of witch because she was so crabby. She never smiled or said hi. She only frowned and barked out orders or made rude comments when we passed by her house. We tried to avoid her at all costs.

The men took pity on her and took turns helping her out with yard work and keeping up with the endless home repairs that came with residing in an older house. When Mrs. Daniels stopped driving, the women made sure to check in with her before they made a run to the grocery store and arranged carpools to get her to and from her appointments. People tried to be patient with her, but lately their patience was wearing thin. Over the last year or so she had grown more and more argumentative and demanding, complaining about everything and everyone. And here I had flown directly into her arms from within a house of forbidden strangers.

"Suzanne, what on earth are you doing in this house?" Mrs. Daniels asked.

"What are you doing here?" I answered her question with a question.

"I'm here to tell these people," she put a heavy emphasis on the word people, "that they'd better keep their music down and their riffraff friends off this street or I'm going to start calling the police."

Joan snuck past the two of us and hopped in her van. The van let out a weak cough when she attempted to start it. Mrs. Daniels and I paused, while we waited to see if her car would cooperate. One of the men from the kitchen walked out onto the porch to see who was at the door and another one came out to lend a hand with the stalled car. The guy standing at the door had no shirt on, which was the same as being naked as far as Mrs. Daniels was concerned, and she didn't hide her displeasure.

"Can I help you?" he asked in a pleasant voice. He was completely unfazed by Mrs. Daniels' disapproving stare. Mrs. Daniels lost her courage and remained silent.

She cleared her throat and said to me, "Come on, Suzanne. You're coming with me." She pulled me by the arm and dragged me down the street toward my house.

"Joyce, Joyce!" she yelled over and over again long before we reached the front door. My mom opened the door, panic stricken.

"Guess where I found your Suzanne?" Mrs. Daniels asked accusingly. "She was down at that cesspool on the

corner. You need to keep a better eye on her. Imagine, frat-
ernizing with those low brow, despicable people. I know
that you've got your hands full with all of those unruly
kids of yours, but you ought to do a better job. They run
around this neighborhood like a pack of wolves. Well, just
the other day -" My mom cut her off before she could finish
her sentence.

"Thank you for helping her home, Mrs. Daniels. That
was very kind of you. As for your advice, I would prefer that
you keep it to yourself. I don't need you telling me how to
raise my children. My children are not perfect, but they
are far from unruly and I resent you referring to them as
wolves. Now please get off my porch," my mom said without
ever raising her voice.

Stunned, Mrs. Daniels turned to leave.

"Oh, by the way, you'll need to find someone else to cut
your grass and to do your yard work because my oldest wolf
will no longer be of service to you," she added. My mom
took me by the hand and we walked into the house. I loved
how my mom stood up to Mrs. Daniels. My mom didn't tell
my dad about the incident, but she made me promise never
to go into a stranger's house again.

I had tried my hardest to keep that promise, but as I
stood with Jana and Clyde at the Peterson's door, my promise was forgotten. After several minutes of fumbling, when
Jana's key finally unlocked the door and she said, "Well,
come on in," in I went without a moment's hesitation.

Clyde had long ago given up trying to juggle his boxes
and had set them on the back steps. He wisely decided to
divide the boxes up between the three of us before heading

up the long, narrow flight of steps. When we got to the top, there was another locked door. Jana laughed when the door unlocked with the first key she tried.

"Come on in, Suzanne! Welcome to our humble abode!" Jana said, swaying her arms from side to side as if she were advertising a new appliance. The door opened into a large room that served as the kitchen and dining room. The walls were cream-colored and the windows were draped with curtains the color of butter. I observed that someone had taken the time to embroider them with small, delicate daisies. All of the curtains in our house were solid, plain colors, nothing fancy or feminine. I was entranced.

There was a wooden table in the corner of the room with four chairs placed around it. The three bedrooms varied in size. The larger room had an old commode in it and the smaller rooms were empty, except for an old fan and a beat up dresser. The bathroom was off the room at the rear of the house. This room was long and narrow and the two walls were lined with windows. It once was an upper level enclosed sun porch, but Jana quickly determined that it would now serve as their living room. She was delighted that there was plenty of space for their furniture and her indoor herb garden. All in all, the apartment was clean and well maintained. I could tell that Jana and Clyde were more than satisfied with the place.

"Well, should we go get the rest of your stuff?" I offered.

"There's not a lot left to get," Clyde explained, "The heavier stuff Jana and I will have to carry up later."

Clyde wrapped his arms around Jana's waist and she whispered, "It's everything I dreamed it would be."

Witnessing their affection made me feel uncomfortable. "Well, I should get going. My dad will be home soon and we'll be eating dinner," I explained.

"I'll tell you what," Jana suggested "how about you come over tomorrow after school for a snack and help us get this place set up?"

I eagerly accepted the invitation.

"You've got a real nice place here," I said.

"Thanks honey, we'll see you tomorrow." Clyde answered.

As I walked down the steps, I did something I rarely did. I smiled. I immediately added Jana and Clyde Davis to my perfect world and spent the next several hours imagining different scenarios that involved Jana, Clyde and me. For the rest of the night I was happy.

In my perfect world, my dad came home promptly at five for dinner and didn't crack open a beer. There was no fighting between our parents and we were all free to amble around the house without feeling like something bad might happen. With so many people in my real world family, it was almost certain that something would go wrong on any given day.

Our family was made up of eleven people: Danny, Ellen, Anna, Margo, Patty, Andrew, myself, Robbie, two unhappy parents, and the ghost of Little Owen, a child named for our father, who had died years before, and of whom we never ever spoke.

THREE

We didn't have a lot in terms of material possessions, and what we did have was never what we needed, exactly. None of the furniture ever seemed to fit in any of the rooms. It was all either too big or too small. Not one single couch or end table or any other furniture was ever selected based on the fact that it fit the décor or was aesthetically appealing. Everything in our house felt like an afterthought, including our relationships.

My interactions with my family seemed to occur accidently, random encounters between strangers who happened to be living in the same house. For all the years that I didn't speak, I was listening to and observing this seemingly random collection of people who were my family. I had a very active imagination and found comfort in a world that existed only in my mind. My inner world was safe and calm. The adults were never angry or sad and they loved me very much. But over the years I began to get lonely, no longer content with only my make-believe friends to keep me company. I longed for a real flesh-and-blood friend who knew me as well as my imaginary friends did. Making friends was difficult for me because I felt so different from other children my own age.

My quietness was frequently misinterpreted. People considered me shy or aloof, but I wasn't. I was just cautious and pensive. That's what my Aunt Susie always said. She was the one family member who believed that I was special, and told me that my wild imagination and my tendency to watch quietly was an expression of my natural curiosity about people and the world around me, and not something to be worried about.

She was right. From an early age I felt that my family was different than almost everybody else's I knew. I was fearful that if people found out about my family they wouldn't like them or, more specifically, me. My brothers and sisters didn't seem to have any problems making or keeping friends, but I suspected that was because they probably didn't talk much about our family.

This feeling of "differentness" turned me into an anthropologist of sorts. I studied families every chance I got. Though I never wrote a single observation down, I carefully stored my notes in my head so I could refer to them whenever I needed. I also didn't write them down because I didn't want anyone to read my personal thoughts. Nobody in our house ever had any privacy and someone would surely have read my notes. I frequently referred to my mental notes when contemplating what I would change about my life, if given the chance, and when comparing my imaginary perfect world with the real world around me.

I was an odd kid. Things that other children my age would never notice intrigued me. I was curious about how other families interacted with each other. Once when I was at the grocery store with my mom, I witnessed a man and a woman shopping together with their children. To start with, Dad wouldn't have been caught dead grocery shopping. He viewed shopping as woman's work. I had seen men in grocery stores before, but it was more than that. It was how the family behaved that I found foreign. They laughed and joked and seemed to be having fun as they wandered up and down the aisles in search of the items on their list. Periodically the dad would pick up speed and pretend that he had lost all control of the cart. The cart would zigzag from one side of the aisle to the next, causing the children who were wedged between the paper towel and the boxes of sugared cereal to squeal with delight. I followed them around the store pretending to shop. Every couple of minutes or so one of the children would reach for some random item on the shelf. Often times the parents said no, but sometimes they said yes, allowing the children to have some say in what was being purchased. I had never even thought to ask for anything I wanted when at the store. I already knew my mom's answer. She'd say, "You don't need that," or "You know we don't have the money for such things."

I knew from very early on that the first thing in our family I would have changed was our dad, Owen. In my perfect world he wouldn't drink, yell or have his southern accent. I didn't really mind the twang in his voice, but it was different and different was never good. There were other things about my dad that needed fixing, but if those first three things could be fixed, I figured everything else would probably just fall into place.

There were things about him that I liked very much. They were weird things to admire, but I found comfort in them nonetheless. The first thing was his smell. Most people smell like soap or fabric softener, but not him. His smell was unique. To me it was exotic, an eclectic combination of leather, tobacco, and metal or nails, with just a hint of Old Spice aftershave. The interior of his truck had the same smell, only stronger, and I thought it was fantastic.

He was a practical man and had a system for everything. For example, he kept his fingernail clippers and ChapStick in the pocket of his pants at all times. He was smart enough to know that if he kept these essentials in the medicine cabinet like most normal people, we kids would surely have lost them. Any time one of us had a hangnail or chapped lips, we had to wait for Dad to get home to take care of it. He'd reach into his pocket and pull out whichever one we needed at the time. He never let us go off with it, we had to use it right in front of him and then promptly return it to him when we were finished.

There weren't too many things about my mom, Joyce that I would have changed. More than anything I just wanted her to be happier and more attentive like other moms. I wanted her to spend time with just me, doing fun things like going to the Detroit Zoo or the park. Our only time together was spent going to church, which wasn't fun, or going to the doctor's office when I got sick. I got sick all of the time. Sometimes I tagged along with her when she had to run errands and there was nobody around to babysit me, but that wasn't very exciting either. She was all business when she shopped. She never wrote out a list of what she needed, but zoomed up and down the grocery aisles as if she was on a game show. She never browsed; with so many children, she didn't have time.

As for my brothers and sisters, I loved them, but they didn't really seem to love me. My oldest brother ignored me, and my sisters only seemed to love the two younger boys in our family. They never said that exactly, but I could tell by the way they always fawned all over them, though neither of them seemed particularly extraordinary to me.

There were so many things I imagined for all of us kids, but surprisingly what I wanted weren't material things like more toys and clothes or a nicer house. I desired things that money couldn't buy, like peace and quiet and the opportunity to be just happy, carefree kids.

My brother, Danny and oldest sister, Ellen were exactly a year apart. Anna, Patty and Margo were next in line. Margo came only eleven months after Patty and they both exhibited typical signs of *Middle Child Syndrome*, though in opposing ways. Patty was an extreme people-pleaser, while Margo was somewhat of a loner, marching to the beat of her own drum. Mom and dad must have been exhausted after the first five because they took a few years off before having any more kids. I followed their seventh child, Andrew, and Robbie came three years after me. Despite the cacophony of our large haphazard family many things remained unspoken, but one year in the late spring, just before the school year ended, things began to change.

FOUR

When I daydreamed about the kind of life I wanted, I never allowed myself to go too over the top when creating a new family. I feared that if God happened to be tuning into my thoughts at that exact moment, he would view my list as greedy. I learned in CCD that greed was one of the seven deadly sins. This caused me great concern. Mom was always preaching to us kids about accepting the gifts that God bestows upon us. She taught us never to question God, or anything or anyone else for that matter. So, when fantasizing about my family, I exercised some restraint. I didn't dare pretend that we were a family like the Brady Bunch, which is what I really wanted. Instead I pretended that nobody yelled or fought and that we all loved each other very much.

With all my mental lists, I created a perfect world in my mind and that's where I chose to live. In my world, everything had its place and made sense. I decided that confiding with anyone about this world would be too risky. Like everything else in our chaotic home, it would get destroyed, and my feelings and thoughts would be marginalized.

At home and at school, I kept to myself to avoid making any waves. I never asked for help, for fear of drawing attention to myself. Once when I was five, I caught a horrible summer cold. My nose ran excessively, leaving the skin directly above my lip red and chapped. Growing tired of the constant dripping, I shoved small pieces of tissue into each nostril, but this caused me to sneeze uncontrollably. I quickly determined that what I needed was medicine. I couldn't recall the name of the thick, purple syrupy medicine my mother had given us before, but was certain that I would recognize the bottle once I saw it.

I fished out the step chair from the back of the dark and dank kitchen closet. The closet stored everything except actual kitchen supplies: winter coats too worn out for anyone to actually wear, expired canned goods that were never going to be consumed and various other odds and ends that had been hastily shoved away, to be disposed of properly at a later date. The chair was heavy and awkwardly shaped, but I managed to drag it across the kitchen floor, positioning it directly in front of the cabinet above the stove.

It was a weird place to keep the medicine, considering that almost everybody had to stand on something and reach over the stovetop to get at it. When Margo was just six, she burnt the entire upper portion of her arm with a bubbling pot of spaghetti sauce. After the accident she couldn't even remember what she had been looking for in the first place. Instead of getting a chair, she had opened the oven door and stood on it. Margo was always slight of frame, so even with all of her weight on the door, it didn't immediately snap to a safely open position. She began bouncing on it and yelled to Patty when she came into the kitchen, "Patty, Look! It's like a diving board." She bounced up and down just once or twice more which caused the oven to inch forward ever so slightly. The pot on the back slid to the front and spilled out all over Margo's arm and chest. She howled like a scalded dog and Patty, not knowing any better, ran Margo over to the sink, placed her arm underneath the faucet and turned on the cold water. Her skin peeled off in sheets. When it healed it was no longer smooth and peachy colored; it was raised and puckered and red. Even after Margo's accident, it didn't occur to my parents to move the medicine.

So, in ignorance of the danger, I moved the chair, which did inch me closer to my destination, but I still wasn't quite tall enough to reach, even on my tiptoes. I scanned the kitchen in search of something else that I could place on the chair to elevate me even more. Next to the phone sat a large collection of old telephone books. Mom insisted on keeping all of them, so when new ones were left on our front steps every summer the stack grew. I always wondered why we kept them all - there was never a real need to keep any of them because, other than my dad, who talked occasionally to his family down south, nobody talked on the phone much. Everybody we knew lived within a few blocks of us, so we mostly talked to people in person. I grabbed three or four of the thicker books and stacked them on the chair. After finding my balance, I reached into the cupboard and began fingering the collection of sticky bottles. I eventually found the one I needed. After a few tugs, I was able to free it from the shelf. Just as I was pulling the bottle out of the cupboard, my sister, Ellen, wandered into the kitchen in search of a snack. She strolled past me not paying me any mind, as usual. I triumphantly made my descent down the step chair gripping the bottle like a trophy. The sound of the clicking cap refusing to come off finally caught Ellen's attention. She closed the refrigerator and released a long, exaggerated sigh.

"You need to press down firmly on the cap while twisting it in the same direction as the arrows in order for it to open," she informed me. Once the cap was successfully removed, I stood in the center of the kitchen, uncertain what to do next.

"I have a runny nose," I announced.

"Good for you," she said sarcastically underneath her breath. Without looking at the bottle or inquiring about my other symptoms, she instructed me to take one teaspoon. "Make sure you screw the cap back on properly before putting it away," she added, "That cupboard's a sticky mess."

Not knowing the difference between a teaspoon and a tablespoon, I selected a tablespoon from the rack of drying dishes. Before returning the bottle to its shelf, I decided to pour myself another dose. After all, I reasoned, my cold was extra bad. I immediately grew drowsy and crawled into my favorite secret place, my closet, where I fell into a deep sleep.

When I woke the next morning, my cold was gone. I had a metallic taste in my mouth and could feel my skin stretching when I yawned because of the crusty ring of dried saliva that had formed around my mouth, but I felt amazingly better. At breakfast, I was uncharacteristically chipper and told my mom that I was no longer sick. She was sipping her coffee and thumbing through the newspaper looking for coupons. She grunted at first in acknowledgement, but then lay her paper down and gave me a doubting look. She smoothed out the front of her housecoat and patted my hand and said, "Well, that's good dear, but I wasn't even aware that you were sick."

I frequently found it necessary to take matters into my own hands. Waiting for others to give me what I needed either took too long, or didn't work at all. I was careful never to reveal any of my family's business to the people at school, but it was difficult to be so private all of the time and sometimes I made the mistake of retreating to my make believe world while still in my classroom. When I checked out of reality, it was obvious to those around me. I didn't talk or move or get any of my work done. I would just sit there as if in a trance. People noticed, especially my teacher.

"Suzanne is a sweet girl," Mrs. Burns explained one day after school during a meeting with my mom, the principal and the special education teacher, Mrs. Row. "She never acts up and as far as the other children - well, she doesn't *not* get along with them, but doesn't really interact with them either." Not quite sure what my problem was or how to fix it, it was decided that my inability to pay attention and make friends meant that I needed extra help. "When Suzanne completes her work, she receives all A's. She's very articulate when she chooses to speak and we all agree that she's creative," Mrs. Burns continued. Not sure what the problem was, it was decided that I would receive extra help from Mrs. Row who was not only a special education teacher, but also held a master's degree in child psychology. Seeing Mrs. Row everyday was like a dream come true for me. I couldn't believe my luck.

Each morning from 9:15 to 10:30, I left my regular classroom with Mrs. Burns and traveled down to Mrs. Row's room at the end of the hall. The room was only about a third the size of a regular classroom or office, but it was inviting. There were two small round tables with primary colored chairs. The walls were lined with bookshelves and covered in posters. One was of a man climbing a mountain that read, "Dare to Dream Big!" Another one had a kitten dangling from a tree branch and read, "Hang on Baby." There were several other posters and plaques with similar sayings that were meant to be supportive and encouraging. The best part of the room was the big, overstuffed beanbags and throw pillows that were strewn across the floor and in front of the bookshelves. We were allowed to curl up and quietly read if we completed all of our work or were waiting for Mrs. Row to finish up with somebody else. I was always done with my work early because I didn't have any trouble in reading or math like the other kids did. I'd carefully select a book off the shelf and burrow down into the beanbag and read. It didn't take me long to make my way through the collection of books that Mrs. Row had to offer. Every couple of days Mrs. Row would write out a hall pass so I could walk down to the library and select some more books or periodicals to read. We didn't have many books at home, so going to Mrs. Row's room and reading was my favorite part of the entire day.

When I wasn't talking to Mrs. Row about the books I was reading, we talked about my feelings. Mrs. Row would ask me very general questions and then remain silent while I did all of the talking. Each day she selected a different topic for us to explore: hobbies, favorite school subjects or people I admired. I would get so engrossed in these conversations that I was always shocked when Mrs. Row informed me that it was time to head back to the regular classroom.

When the topic of our family eventually came up, I was speechless. "Suzanne, honey, tell me about your family? What do you like to do with them?" Mrs. Row prompted. I was totally stumped. I should have seen that question coming, but I wasn't sure how to respond.

"Well, I kind of have a big family," I ad-libbed, "Our dad grew up on a plantation way down in South Carolina."

Mrs. Row raised her eyebrows in surprise and commented, "I didn't realize that. Well, isn't that interesting."

I immediately began to worry that Mrs. Row might think that I came from a long line of racists, so I further explained, "Oh, don't worry. My dad's family never owned any slaves in the day. They were one of the few families in the area that actually took in black folks. His family gave them a place to stay and together they worked the land, side by side. They split the money they earned raising tobacco fifty-fifty. Even Steven." Lying was easier than I thought. I continued my tale, telling her that our dad had grown tired of farming and decided to give the railroad a try. "That's how he met our mom - while riding the rails. He's rarely home and we mostly see him on the weekends." I hoped that the second lie served as an explanation for why my parents never attended any of the school functions.

I felt a little guilty lying to Mrs. Row, but rationalized it by telling myself that I was partly telling the truth. My dad's family did grow tobacco at one time, only they were dirt poor. I wasn't sure if Mrs. Row believed my story, but she didn't probe any further into my family history.

FIVE

When Dad didn't arrive home by five, worry descended upon the household. Nobody vocalized his or her concerns right away out of respect for those who might not have noticed the time just yet. Later, Dad's empty chair at the head of the dinner table spoke volumes. The optimists clung to the hope that there was a perfectly normal explanation for his tardiness, but the pessimists recalled that there was only one time in the history of our family when he came home late and wasn't intoxicated.

Two summers earlier, a man Dad worked with was killed on the job site. He was more than just another guy on the job though; he was one of his best friends. It was a freak accident, the kind that couldn't have been prevented and nobody could have imagined. Dad, being the foreman on the job, had to fill out reports, talk with the union rep, calm down and send home the rest of his crew. Being the man's friend required Dad to be the one to deliver the news to his buddy's wife and kids. Once home, Dad refused to discuss the details of the gruesome death while we were still awake. Once we were all in bed, he painfully recalled the details to Mom, who immediately threw up. Our parents had a difficult time explaining to us kids a few nights later at the vigil why the casket had to be closed. Throughout the course of the evening we repeatedly overheard mention of a wrecking ball. By the end of the night, my older brothers and sisters were able to connect the dots and understand why we couldn't look upon the face of Dad's deceased friend.

So it was clear, the naysayers were right to worry when Dad wasn't home at his regular time. With each passing minute, the Pollyannas were forced to admit that Dad was most likely once again out trying to "tie one on." The energy of our combined worry manifested itself as an emotional magnetic force that bound us together as the evening wore painfully on. We played board games, watched TV or listened to music - anything to get our minds off the impending arrival of our dad. If by seven o'clock he was still a no show, it was inevitable that we wouldn't see him until much later and that he most likely would be totally drunk.

Eventually our silent worry was replaced with debate over the state he'd be in when he finally graced us with his presence. Either way, we knew he'd be drunk. Sometimes, he'd be in a relatively happy mood, arms filled with greasy take out boxes. More times than not, though, he'd come in like a swirling tornado destroying everything in its path. Mom learned within the first couple of years of marriage that it was impossible to keep anything nice in our house. Her few cherished possessions - their wedding china, the mismatched wine glasses that once belonged to her parents and the few remaining pieces of her great grandma's tea set brought from Quebec - had long ago perished. We kids had very few things that we could truly call our own. The younger kids wore hand-me-downs from the older kids and the older kids got most of their clothes from garage sales or Goodwill. The few toys we received for Christmas were usually broken by Easter and if by chance we were given a gift that commemorated a special event - First Holy Communion, an award from school or a special birthday present, we refused to express any sentimentality over it out of fear that it too would be destroyed during one of our dad's explosive episodes.

Dad never had much as a kid either. His family was poorer than ours and he frequently went to bed with an empty stomach. His family ate mostly rabbits or squirrels and the vegetables his mother and sisters canned up. But once in a while, if there were a little extra money, his dad would come home with a roast. It was never very big, but it was a treat. His mom would boil potatoes with real butter and cook up a pot full of green beans with a piece of fatback in it. Dad cherished that memory and spoke of it often. It was one of the few stories from his childhood that we ever heard. He equated a full stomach with being happy and wanted to share that feeling with his own family, but his alcohol-fueled, misguided efforts often went awry.

Some nights before his last drink, he'd ask the fry cook at the bar to whip up an order of food to bring home to us kids. He'd come in just as loud as ever and yell up the back steps, "You kids get on up and come down here and see what I brought home!" All of my brothers and sisters would get up, already knowing what his surprise was. If they were lucky, after gorging themselves on deep-fried chicken gizzards and ribs, Dad would let them go back to bed, but sometimes he'd round them up and herd them into the living room to listen to music. He'd dust off his favorite country records and play the same songs over and over again while they pretended to enjoy it.

If already in bed, I would not get up for these late night feasts. I'd hunker down under my blankets and force myself to think good thoughts.

I didn't bother making an appearance, since nobody seemed to notice that I wasn't present anyway. I hated the way the stringy rib meat always got stuck in my teeth, and how the entire house smelled of stale beer and pungent cocktail sauce. I loved to eat, but not in the middle of the night or with my dad, especially if he had been drinking. I was afraid of Dad. It wasn't just the yelling and cursing, or him busting up the house that scared me. It was the way he looked when he was drunk. His eyes would get red and glossy and wild. His skin, which was tanned year round from working outside and from being part Cherokee, took on a more reddish tone. He looked like a devil when he drank. A previous year Andrew had dressed as a devil for Halloween. Mom dyed an old pair of long underwear red and made a set of horns out of some leftover pieces of aluminum foil. She smeared rouge all over his face and penciled on a thin moustache with eyeliner. It was a cool costume and though I thought my brother looked scary, I didn't think it was cool when Dad looked this way. Too real.

Our sister Margo hated the music and the bar food as much as I did, but she played along - she had to. The older siblings had long ago formed an unconscious allegiance. They would deal with our father together, no matter what. It sickened Margo to watch the rest of them gobble up the food. She thought they were a bunch of sell-outs who could be bribed with chicken gizzards. Anna and Danny were the biggest offenders of them all, seeming to view this simple food as a culinary extravaganza. They'd pick the ribs clean, sucking the marrow out of the bones. They tossed back the gizzards often two or three at a time as if they were eating popcorn. To appease our dad, Margo would slowly nibble on the crunchy breading, which was pretty tasty, but she stopped there. The little ball of meat on the inside was like chewing on a rubber band, and it made her gag. No amount of cocktail sauce could mask its texture. For Margo, it was more than just not liking the food though. What she despised more than anything was how everybody went along with his charade. There wasn't a person in that house who didn't begin to panic as Dad's drunken scenes unfolded. Pretending was exhausting and after an hour or so, everybody was ready for sleep, especially our dad.

He'd pass out wherever he happened to be and we'd all stumble off to bed. It wasn't uncommon for Mom to wake in the middle of the night to find him asleep on the bathroom floor or sitting in a chair with his upper body sprawled out across the kitchen table.

But if he didn't come home in good spirits, he came in like a rabid dog, snapping and growling at everything and everyone. The exorbitant amount of time he'd need to spend trying to manipulate the locks and deadbolts left him so agitated that he'd kick in the back door like a drug enforcement officer raiding a dealer's house. Mom tried every cleaner available, but none could erase the permanent outline of his boot on the door. As nerve-wracking as these loud performances were, we were thankful for the warning. It gave us time to batten down the hatches and prepare for act two of the grand drama.

If Ellen were still reading in bed, she'd quickly turn out the lamp and pretend to be asleep. Most parents would be ecstatic that their children loved to read as much as Ellen did, but not Dad. "What the hell are you reading about now?" he'd yell. "Don't you got anything better to do with your time?" His implication that she was somehow lazy infuriated Ellen. If she wasn't at work or doing schoolwork, she was taking care of us kids or completing chores. She read in her spare time or late at night when everyone else was asleep. Once she could no longer hear him shuffling around downstairs she'd crawl out from under her blankets and resume reading.

On these bad nights, our father's dramatic entrance gave Anna the time she needed to fan the cigarette smoke out her bedroom window after high-tailing it to the bathroom to flush the evidence down the toilet. "Dad's the biggest hypocrite I know," Anna complained to the rest of us when our parents weren't around. "He smokes, and everybody knows that mom smokes, even though she doesn't really do it in front of us."

"She smokes?" Andrew once asked surprised. "When? Where?" He wasn't all that disturbed by the fact that she smoked, but couldn't wrap his brain around the fact that he wasn't aware of it.

"It doesn't matter where. Mostly in the basement when she's pretending to do laundry, I guess. The point is, they both smoke and when I got busted last week for smoking in the girl's bathroom at school, they both acted as if I just robbed a bank or something. Such hypocrites," Anna huffed.

Andrew didn't concern himself too much with the goings on of the household. Like me, he was an expert at keeping a low profile and tried his best not to do anything that would make dad angry.

By the time Dad finally made it inside the house after kicking in the door, everybody was on high alert. He'd slam cupboard doors and stomp around just enough to make certain that the entire household was aware of his presence. Making the long trek up the staircase was tiring, but he managed. He went from room to room and whichever poor sap sat up in bed and made eye contact with him, or made the rookie mistake of asking what he was doing, was done for. He'd pull whoever it was out of bed to complete some random task, such as refolding the clothes in his or her dresser drawer or organizing the clothes hanging in the closet. Once Patty tried to get sneaky by only folding the top layer of her clothes and leaving the rest of the clothes underneath it unfolded. She quickly learned not to do that again. One night when he was conducting one of his random bedroom tidiness checks, he stumbled across Patty's trick and was furious. He tore through her drawer pulling out every article of clothing that she owned including her underwear and undershirts. After busting the screen out of the bedroom window, he tossed the clothing out. She had to scramble outside into the dark to collect her wardrobe off the ground before morning. Some nights he'd wake everyone up to clean the basement or to sort through the toys. If a broken toy were discovered, he'd make us throw it away.

Sometimes the owner of the toy would protest and explain that he or she was still using it even if it didn't work properly. He didn't bend, in the trash it went. He would then lecture us on how we needed to take care of our things or about how he never even had toys growing up. Sometimes he would just force someone to stay up half the night talking to him. These conversations usually started out okay, but then he would remember some event or time when he had been wronged and all hell would break loose.

If he couldn't engage anyone upstairs, he'd head back downstairs to mix it up with Mom. They'd argue for half an hour or so before she'd give up and announce that she was going to bed. Sometimes he was too tired to protest, but other times he refused to let her call the shots.

The night before Jana and Clyde moved in was a night when we didn't get lucky and Dad didn't come in bearing gifts.

SIX

We worried all through dinner and later as we cleared the table and washed the dishes. By 6:30, Dad was still a no show. Once certain that the kitchen would pass our dad's scrutiny, Anna suggested that we listen to the new album that she and Ellen had jointly purchased. Those who reached the living room first were able to secure a comfortable spot on one of the couches or loveseats, but latecomers had to be content to sprawl out across the worn, carpeted floor. I enjoyed these sing-a-longs as much as the rest of my brothers and sisters did, but preferred to participate from a safe distance. I snuggled down on my parent's bedroom floor, which was right off the living room, all tucked away and out of sight in the space between the bed and the wall. I shuffled my stockinged feet back and forth across the wall as my head clumsily swayed from side to side. Here in the dark was the closest I had ever come to actually dancing.

Patty was the first to reach the living room and therefore earned the right to be the deejay. When the music began to play, we blocked out the popping and cracking that resonated from the stereo speakers and focused only on the light-hearted voice of Roger Miller.

Chug-a-lug chug-a-lug
Make ya wanna holla hidy hoe
Burns your tummy don't you know
Chug-a-lug chug a lug.

Our records were in rough shape, scratched and tired. Every one of them skipped, but we wouldn't have dreamed of throwing a single one away. Music consoled all of us children, especially the older ones, who had longest endured the emotional and mental stress of living in our household. The records that we collected and the songs that flooded the airwaves of AM radio during the early 1970's were contemplative and often sappy, but they captured the angst that we all felt. I guess we took comfort in knowing that people outside our immediate family had also known loss. We could relate to these artists because they too had overcome hardships or were stuck in relationships that brought more sorrow than happiness. A lot of the music we listened to could also be silly or nonsensical. Those songs allowed us to blow off steam and to act as if we didn't have a care in the world. The universal power of music allowed us to express our thoughts and emotions without uttering a word or confronting the real issues that plagued us.

After some time, Anna and Patty grew tired of simply listening and singing. Enthusiastically, they jumped off the couch and began dancing and acting out the words to the songs. Ellen smiled, but only watched as our sisters, "acted the fool," as our father was accustomed to saying anytime we kids actually cut loose and had a little fun. Ellen was rarely silly and seldom partook in the younger siblings' shenanigans.

From the time she was born, Ellen had seemed more mature than her age. When Danny, Ellen, and Anna were little and played make-believe games, Ellen always assumed the authoritative role. If they were playing school, she was the teacher. When they played house, she was the mom, while Danny and Anna eagerly played the roles of the obedient but silly children. There was never any mention of a father in their games... just a sweet, loving mother who cooked, cleaned, and happily took care of the children.

Margo was not the least bit amused by our sisters' musical pantomime act, or their choice in music. She glared at them, arms crossed in protest, her face tattooed with a scowl the moment Patty started playing that *hillbilly* music. Margo despised our father's music, and couldn't understand why any of us would voluntarily listen to it after all of these years. Hadn't we all been tortured enough? This distraction they we were trying to create was all on account of him in the first place.

When the back door slammed, everybody stopped dancing and singing and remained quiet, waiting to see if it was Dad. After a minute or so, Danny came do-si-doing into the room with a pork chop in his hand and a big smile on his face. Relief filled the room, and we resumed our program. Danny motioned for Ellen to get up and dance with him, but she refused. Robbie, who by now was bouncing up and down on the cushions, jumped off the couch and onto Danny's back, laughing uncontrollably as Danny spun him round and round in circles. Margo gave up her seat on the couch, and thumbed through our music collection in search of something else to play. She stacked the 45s on the turntable, and when the first one dropped, Ellen had a change of heart. She coaxed Andrew away from his baseball cards, and the two of them danced as Danny and Anna serenaded them.

Nobody heard Dad's truck pull up in front of the house. He usually parked his truck in the garage, which he accessed from the alley, but he'd missed the turn and didn't want to go back around the block. Whoever was supposed to secure the doors had dropped the ball. Dad appeared from out of nowhere and stood in the foyer watching us.

"What the hell kind of rotgut are you listening to?" he asked. Danny set Robbie back down on the couch before he answered Dad's question.

"Just some music. We were just getting ready to go to bed," he lied.

"That's not music; that's shit," Dad yelled. He stomped over to the record player and yanked back the arm. Before the record could stop spinning, he snatched it up and sent it careening through the air, smashing it into the wall. He then made a beeline to the crate where the rest of the music was stored, and pulled out several albums – except those that were his – and did the same thing. There were many casualties before Anna attempted to reason with him.

"No, Dad! Please stop!" she pleaded, as he was about to send the Beatles' *White Album* across the room. "Why do you have to be so mean?" Anna asked.

Danny turned to Ellen and said, "Take the kids upstairs and get them to bed."

With the album still in his possession, Dad got within an inch of Anna's face, "So I'm mean, huh?" he asked.

Anna didn't back down. "We're just listening to music and having a little fun. Why do you always have to be so unreasonable?" Dad tossed the album onto the couch and grabbed Anna's shoulders and shook them wildly. When he finally stopped, she stumbled back a few steps.

"Damn it, Dad, that's enough. Just relax," Danny yelled.

Dad grabbed Danny by the shirt collar. "You little shit! Don't you tell me to relax in my own house. I'll do whatever I damn well please," he yelled.

"Okay, okay," Danny assured him. Dad let him go and then smoothed out the front of his shirt in an attempt to make nice. The living room was empty except for the three of them. Ellen had gotten the other kids upstairs, but had forgotten about me. I was no longer on the side of the bed in the other room, but was now on my feet, hiding behind the bedroom door. I held my breath, too afraid to breathe, and remained perfectly still. I'd have to wait for exactly the right moment to make my escape.

Dad calmed down, but appeared confused, uncertain of where he was or what he was doing. He stumbled around a bit looking for a place to rest. Danny took advantage of his confusion and motioned to Anna that they should clear out, but Anna didn't move. Her eyes darted in the direction of our parent's bedroom, and she mouthed, "Suzanne is still in there."

"You two are cut from the same cloth," Dad said regaining his composure and interrupting Danny and Anna's plans. "You're both a couple of smartass hardheads who know everything. Now pick up this mess," he barked. He plopped down on the couch and shut his eyes while Anna and Danny sifted through the remains of our beloved records. Just when they thought he might be out, he opened his eyes and surveyed the room. "Where the hell is your mother?" he bellowed.

"She's down at Mrs. Thompson's house," Anna begrudgingly told him. When he gave no indication that he understood what she was talking about, she sighed and added, "It's ceramics night, remember?" Dad seemed satisfied with her answer, and then shut his eyes again. After several minutes a slight whistling sound escaped his nostrils and mouth, which was slightly ajar. Dad had a deviated septum so he sounded like he was gasping for his last breath when he slept, especially after a night of drinking. His broken nose was a result of a fight he had with a boy when he was in high school.

Anna noticed the bedroom door move slightly as I peeked around it, checking to see if the coast was clear. Anna gave me the okay, but then abruptly held up her hand to stop me when she heard keys jingling at the front door. Several seconds later, Mom appeared, carrying in her arms four freshly painted ceramic plates. Each plate depicted our grandparent's cottage up north as it appeared during each of the four seasons. They owned eighty acres of land about an hour east of Traverse City, and they had been going up there since Mom was a little girl. The addition to the cottage was almost complete, and our grandparents would live up there permanently as soon as it was ready. The plates were symbolic of a sweet time in our mother's life, a time when she knew only happiness, no sorrow. She'd worked on them diligently for the last several months, and was proud of her creation.

The sound of the door had jerked Dad awake before she entered the living room, and when she spotted him sitting on the couch, she secured her plates in her arms before forcing a smile on her face. "Hi Owen. Did you just get home? Have you eaten anything yet?" she asked.

"No, I figured there wouldn't be a damn thing to eat since it was your night to get together with all those cackling hens you call friends," he answered. Mom held her tongue and didn't dispute his accusation. She always cooked dinner, even on the nights she played bingo or attended one of her Downriver Dieters Club meetings.

The women were supposed to weigh in weekly, but she only managed to attend the meetings once or maybe twice a month if she were lucky. Dad thought it was a waste of time.

"You want to lose weight? Stop eating so damn much and get outside and work in the yard instead of lounging around the house all the damn time," he'd preach with his tenth beer in one hand and a cigarette in the other. It was true that she had been a member for five years and managed to only lose and regain the same three pounds, but she didn't just go to the meetings to lose weight. She went for the camaraderie of the other housewives in the neighborhood.

"Well, if you're hungry, we can warm you up something to eat," Mom suggested.

Dad contemplated her offer for a minute or so before finally saying, "I reckon I could eat a little something." Danny and Anna didn't wait for Mom to ask for help. They fled to the kitchen and began preparing him a plate while Mom started tidying up the living room. Danny grabbed several pieces of cornbread from the breadbox and crumbled it into a deep cereal bowl. He then retrieved a large chunk of a Vidalia onion from the refrigerator and gave it a rough chop before sprinkling it over the cornbread. Anna began to warm the soup beans in a pot to pour over the cornbread and onions. She arranged two pork chops on a jellyroll pan and placed them in the oven to take the chill off. She was glad he'd agreed to eat. Getting food in him was important, *almost* an antidote, after he'd been out drinking. She prayed he would eat and just go to bed. Dad made his way into the kitchen and commented on how good the beans smelled. He liked home-cooked food that was simple, nothing that was overcomplicated or fussy. We were the only family in America not eating casseroles. Dad despised them. Before he reached the kitchen table, he stopped and out of the blue called out to Mom, "How much money is in our savings account?"

"I don't know right off the top of my head," she answered from the living room. "I guess I'd have to check and see." She went to their bedroom to search for their latest bank statement. She noticed me standing behind the door and gave me a quizzical look. I held my index finger up to my pursed lips and shook my head. She looked confused at first, but then got the picture that I was hiding and continued her search.

"Yum, nice and hot. Here ya go!" Anna tried to sound cheerful as she presented him with the food, but he brushed her off and headed back towards the living room.

"Son of a bitch!" he yelled as he walked into the bedroom, "Can't you keep track of what we have, or do you just make it your business to spend all the damn money?"

Mom set her plates down on the bed and sifted through the top drawer of the dresser they shared. The drawer was lined with labeled shoeboxes filled with important documents. She had one box for their bills, one for us kids, which stored our birth certificates and immunization records, and one that stored all their warranties and owner's manuals. Only one box wasn't labeled, and it was filled with a hodgepodge of things. The problem with her system was that she didn't always use it. When she was too busy, she'd just toss the paperwork into the drawer and tell herself she would file it later. Only "later" meant "every few months." So it usually took a little effort to locate anything.

Dad stood behind her and looked over her shoulder. He began to criticize how unorganized everything was. Before she could put her hands on the statement, he pushed her aside and pulled the entire drawer out of the dresser and dumped its contents onto the bed. After he'd emptied it, he carelessly dropped the drawer onto the floor.

"For Pete's sake," she cried. "Do you have to make such a mess?"

"I'll show you a mess!" he yelled. He reached for the closest thing he could put his hands on, which was one of her plates. He threw it, not aiming for anything in particular. It crashed against the bedroom door. I flinched when it hit, but still managed not to give away my position.

"No!" Mom sobbed as hot tears streamed down her face. She scooped up her winter, spring and summer plates before he could destroy those too. "How can you be so thoughtless?" she asked.

Dad ignored her pleas and rifled through the second drawer of the dresser. As the two of them continued to argue, I decided that it was now or never. I sucked in my stomach making myself skinny enough to slide out from behind the door without disturbing it, crouched down onto all fours and crawled out of the room. Once I'd safely cleared the living room, I stood up and ran all the way up to my bedroom and hopped into the bed I shared with Patty, still fully clothed. When Patty offered me her hand, I took it. Neither of us said a word. We didn't need to. We found comfort in knowing the other one was there.

It didn't take long for Dad to grow tired, and suddenly the bickering stopped. A couple of minutes passed. Patty's breathing became slow and shallow, and I could tell she was sleeping. I loosened my hand from Patty's grip and rolled over onto my side. I too began to relax and let myself drift back to my earlier thoughts. I had been daydreaming about what it would be like if Don Cornelius himself handpicked me, from hundreds of members of the studio audience, to be one of the featured dancers on the main stage of the *Soul Train* set. Our family loved *Soul Train*, but only got to watch it if Dad wasn't home. He thought everybody on the show was immoral and on dope. Anymore, he thought that everybody was on dope.

The emotional martial law imposed upon us children was permanent, but it did not restore the order our family needed. We grumbled here and there to one another about our circumstances, about our dad who was a tyrant, but accepted that a full-blown coup d'état was out of the question. We wanted to rise up and protest against him, but years of being scolded and hushed every time we attempted to express an honest feeling or thought left us feeling defeated. Truth equaled confrontation, and confrontation meant our dad might have to admit guilt or attempt to change, and that was out of the question. I used to imagine that if someone made a film documenting our lives, the soundtrack would be comprised of one gut wrenching, depressing song after another.

SEVEN

I woke the next morning with my encounter with Jana and Clyde still fresh in my mind. I replayed meeting them over and over in my head. How I was going to get through the entire day at school, I wasn't sure. Before I ventured into the kitchen, I peered out the window to make sure that Dad had really left for work. Standing in the Peterson's backyard was Clyde. He was wearing athletic shorts and an old pair of basketball shoes. He did a series of stretches and then jumped over the back fence and took off running down the alley. How I wished I could run right along with him. I couldn't stop thinking about yesterday's invitation to visit. I wandered into the kitchen looking for something to eat. My mom was standing at the sink. "What would you like to eat?" she asked, never turning in my direction.

"I'll just eat some cereal. I'm not that hungry." I lied. I couldn't tell my mom why I was too excited to eat. As I poured my cereal, I thought about how different our mom was from Jana. The two of them had absolutely nothing in common. Jana was tall, blond and young. Mom was short, had mousy brown hair, and wasn't exactly old, but certainly was not hip and cool like Jana. Jana smiled easily, while Mom hardly smiled at all. Mom was pretty though. Sometimes when my parents were busy, I'd sneak into their room and thumb through their old photo albums. In all of the pictures when my mom was a young girl living at home, she looked happy. She was athletic as a young girl and there were several pictures of her horseback riding and running track.

I loved my mom and knew that she loved me, but I also knew that we would never have the kind of relationship that the mothers and daughters on my favorite TV shows had. Sometimes before I started school and it was just me and Robbie at home I would catch my mom kind of staring off in space while she was doing the dishes or snapping beans for dinner. She'd have a dreamy look on her face and when she caught my gaze, her mood would change and she'd look like a child getting caught doing something that she shouldn't be doing. She looked like Andrew when my mom would tap on the kitchen window that faced the backyard when she'd catch him peeing on one of her flowering bushes. (Andrew liked peeing outside, and did it every chance he got.)

Danny, Ellen and Anna walked into the kitchen as if they were walking through quicksand. Danny had the cereal box in one hand and the milk jug in the other. As he began to throw his head back to take a swig, Anna slapped him on his back yelling, "Don't even think about it you swine!" He set the jug on the counter and filled his bowl almost to the top. As he poured the milk, the cereal began to spill onto the counter.

"Watch what you're doing. There's not much cereal left," Ellen pleaded.

"Oh well," Danny laughed, "you're getting fat. You can afford to skip a few meals."

"Just forget it!" she yelled. Ellen flipped Danny off, kissed Mom on the cheek and reminded her that she had to work after school before walking out the door.

Anna opted for toast rather than taking the remainder of the cereal. As she waited for her toast, she slipped into the bathroom off the kitchen and admired her braided hair. Both braids were secured with ribbon that perfectly matched her uniform. Ellen had brought the ribbon home from Kresge's Department store, which was where she worked. Ellen was always doing sweet things like that for the rest of us. It was a miracle that she ever came home with a check. Sometimes we'd stop by the store after school and Ellen would treat us to a bag of Swedish Fish or something small from the lunch counter. Anna ate her toast and dusted the crumbs off the front of her sweater. Just then, Patty, Margo, Andrew and Robbie joined us in the kitchen. Robbie made a beeline to Anna. Anna scooped him up as Robbie wrapped his legs around her waist. As she hugged him, she inhaled deeply.

"Why do you always smell like dough, like a loaf of bread?" she teased.

"I don't know," Robbie giggled and added, "Time to climb the mountain." She set him down on the floor and bent her knees. Robbie climbed up her legs until he reached her waist. At that point, she flipped him over. They did this over and over until Robbie got dizzy.

When it was time to leave, she set him down in his high-chair, "I have a game after school. I'll see you later tonight," she told Mom. As she began to walk out the door, Robbie started to sob. Robbie adored Anna, but she knew better than to stop and try to console him. After a couple of minutes he would settle down and find comfort in his thumb.

It was the last year that Patty, Margo, Andrew and I would be at the same school. Patty and Margo would be starting junior high in the fall. After inhaling our food and saying our morning prayers, the four of us said our good-byes and also left.

It made Patty and Margo furious that our older brothers and sisters didn't have to get down on their hands and knees behind the couch and say three Hail Marys and three Our Fathers before going to school like we younger ones did. This ritual of praying before school began shortly after Andrew started school. Almost every morning before heading out the door, Andrew would breakdown crying, not wanting to go. Mom could never get out of him why, but said that praying would help him get through the day and, surprisingly, it did. He no longer cried at school or before going to school, but Mom still insisted that we pray each morning.

Once we were free to go, Patty and Margo would hook up with the Barton girls, who lived across the street, and Andrew would take off with a pack of boys from his class. I was content to walk to school by myself, especially today since it gave me time to think about my afterschool date with Jana.

EIGHT

Jana was hopelessly optimistic, never acknowledging the fact that her childhood had been over before it ever really began. Jana's mother left her when she was two, leaving her father, Thomas to raise her on his own. For the next eight years, Thomas served as both father and mother to Jana, making it his mission to raise a daughter who would be oblivious to the fact that she was motherless. He savored every moment spent with Jana and his role as her only parent.

Jana was at summer camp the night Thomas died. It had been her first time away from home and Thomas had been reluctant to let her go. In the end, his desire for her to experience a normal childhood trumped his own fears associated with giving her a little independence. A month was a long time considering that they hadn't spent a single day apart, but somehow he managed to let her go. It was almost two weeks before he received his first postcard from her, but the wait had been worth it. As he read it, he was struck by how different she sounded. Jana sounded like an actual child, a carefree and happy little girl. She was having the time of her life.

Thomas was a police officer in the same small town where he grew up. It was a quiet, sleepy town that rarely experienced any type of real crime. Aside from the occasional call regarding a lost pet or a complaint concerning some kind of sophomoric prank carried out by a few high-spirited high school boys, most of his days were uneventful. He rarely worked in the evening, but with Jana being gone, he had agreed to do a few weeks of afternoons. His shift was within ten minutes of being over when the call came in. Two men had robbed a convenience store and were spotted on their way out of town in what was presumably a stolen car. Thomas spotted the car and pursued it, immediately calling for back up. He threw on the sirens, signaling them to pull over and was surprised when within seconds, their car stopped. The assailants were two young men who looked barely old enough to shave. When Thomas walked up to the car, he thought they looked like they were high on adrenaline and were relieved that the whole event would soon be behind them. He actually felt bad for them. For a brief moment he contemplated letting them go. He wanted to shout, "Get out of here! What were you thinking? Don't do it again! You're both young, go live your lives!" But of course he didn't. He waited for backup to arrive and then proceeded to arrest them. Thomas was in the process of handcuffing one of them while his partner was putting the other suspect in the back of the patrol car. A semi-truck driven by a man who had been awake for the last twenty-two hours, crossed over onto the shoulder of the road, killing all four men.

Thomas' widowed mother was too old to care for Jana, so Jana was sent to live with Thomas' sister and her husband, who lived in an affluent area of Baltimore.

For years following her father's death, people shook their heads with pity and disbelief when hearing her story. This always puzzled Jana because she didn't think of her story as tragic. She barely remembered her mother, so how could she miss someone who she never really knew? As for her father, she knew that he loved her and even though he wasn't physically there, she knew he was there in spirit. His presence surrounded her. She could feel him. He was always with her, guiding her decisions and comforting her when nobody else could. She convinced herself that the love they shared was more than what most living people experienced. Every year, on the first day of school, she had sensed him walking with her to the bus stop and into her new classroom. When she danced her first dance with a boy, she could have sworn that he was there, counting, so that she would stay in sync with the music. He was there when she graduated high school and on the day she met and fell in love with Clyde. Jana knew the power of love to heal and to sustain you, when times were good, and when they were bad. And it was this knowledge that Suzanne felt radiating from Jana like sunlight.

NINE

Thanks to Mom, there was no need for anyone else in the family to ever set an alarm. She started her day every morning, Monday through Friday at 5:30 a.m., dragging herself out of bed, to begin the mundane task of getting Dad off to work. This process should have been relatively uncomplicated for it entailed nothing more than packing his lunch and making coffee, but it wasn't. He rarely ate breakfast and drank only one cup of coffee before he left, leaving some in the pot for his thermos, which he took with him to work every day, regardless of the temperature outside. She didn't rouse Dad from bed every morning until 6:15. For only these forty-five minutes each day, she was completely alone with her own thoughts.

Dad was a simple man, but he possessed a complicated spirit. His work ethic was impeccable and as much as he hated his job at times, it would never have occurred to him to take a day off. Relaxing and taking it easy was not in his nature, even if it meant he went into work slightly drunk from the night before. Routine and structure were his religion; it was what grounded him. Before leaving his bedroom each morning, he would put on one of the three blue work uniforms that he owned. The uniforms were made of a sturdy cotton blend and each long-sleeved shirt had his name, "Owen," stitched in gold lettering. He would then head to the bathroom to splash cold water on his face and to brush his teeth before making his way to the kitchen. He viewed showering in the morning as impractical. He preferred to shower after work each night, when he felt he actually needed one. He didn't punch the clock until 7:30, but he insisted on getting to the yard by 7:00. "You never know when something could come up," he lectured. "I'm not gonna be one of those assholes who come strolling in late every other day because of a flat tire or an accident on the expressway." Getting there early gave him time to drink some more coffee, read the paper, or shoot the breeze with the guys (though he didn't particularly like them). He made it a habit to arrive anywhere he went just a little bit early.

So, at the same time every morning, mom made sure his mug of coffee was waiting for him on the table, next to his ashtray and pack of Pall Mall cigarettes. It was usually in the middle of enjoying his first cigarette of the day that he would begin quizzing Mom. The conflicts that inevitably broke out each morning between the two of them were what woke us each day. We'd jolt awake and lay silently, waiting in trepidation for what the next twenty minutes or so might hold for each of us.

Trappist monks with their vows of silence had nothing on us Williams children. After years of sustained silence, of never expressing our feelings, we settled into our roles as emotional mutes.

Once awake, we snuggled down into our beds and waited. Sometimes we refrained from rolling over into a more comfortable position out of fear of being heard. If we were lucky, Dad would simply spout off about some trivial thing or perceived wrong. His list of complaints was extensive and varied from day to day. He was constantly contradicting himself. One day he would complain about the crappy lunches that Mom packed for him, but if she'd stocked up on snacks that he liked, he'd object and accuse her of spending too much money on groceries. He could drone on and on about bills that needed to be paid, and if they were all caught up on their bills, he'd fret about future expenses that were sure to come. What we kids dreaded the most was when he chose to address a supposed infraction committed by one of us. His mind was like that proverbial steel trap and he could recall the exact time, place, and nature of each offense. On the mornings when he ignored Mom, one of us kids was forced to step into the ring to be his sparring partner. Each of us would lie in bed trying to recall the events of the previous few days, imagining what we might have done to offend him. This was a losing proposition, since something as basic as breathing too heavily while eating could set him off. He had a long list of inexcusable behavior. It included, as follows: dipping our cookies in milk, coughing at the table, using lights or watching TV during the day, especially in the summer when it was hot, being on the phone when he came in from work, having zits (which was a sign of poor hygiene), laziness or being promiscuous, forgetting to do a chore or not completing the chore, or having the finished job not measure up to his impossible standard. One thing was for certain, none of us wanted to be on the receiving end of his verbal lashing.

Once he finally left for work, we were left feeling one of two ways: guilty because someone other than ourselves had been mentally assaulted, or anxious because we had been selected for punishment, which meant that it was time to begin plotting how to avoid being his victim the next time.

When we were under attack, Mom said nothing. She knew that interfering would incite him even more and simply worsen his tirade. Deep down, I think that she was thankful that she was spared. In our house, it was every man for himself, survival of the fittest.

When it was time for him to leave, his ranting would finally end, the back door would slam, and the sound of Dad's work truck screaming down the back alley was the signal that everyone could commence breathing again.

After years of the same routine, Mom was tired but she didn't dare complain. She remained silent in her struggle to accept the decision she had made years earlier to be his wife. When she absolutely couldn't take it anymore, she confided in her priest, who instructed her to continue "offering it up to the Lord." We knew she wondered what else God could possibly want from her.

TEN

It had taken Mom only a few months to realize that she had made a terrible mistake in marrying Dad. She did truly love him, but she did not know until later how damaged he was. The couple of beers he drank around her when they were dating relaxed him, made him sociable. But after they were married, he rarely stopped after a couple. Two beers quickly turned into twelve, and he then turned into a different person. He became ill-tempered and cruel. When he was drunk, his aggression flowed as easily as the drinks. Every thought that was in his head, every pain that was never expressed came spilling out of him. His anger flowed over her, and later over our family, drowning us all in fear and sadness. We knew it was his past that was killing him, but he couldn't figure out how to live in the present.

My parents dated for a little over a year before they got engaged. Their interactions when together were limited to casual outings, which were often supervised. One of my mom's many cousins or sisters was always tagging along with them. Sometimes they even double dated. Dad didn't mind, because he liked being surrounded by people. When they went out with others, his drinking was less noticeable. The two of them would have a beer at the ballpark and sometimes he'd have two or three, but Mom never viewed his drinking as excessive. Her parents weren't teetotalers, but their drinking was limited to an occasional glass of wine around the holidays or an ice-cold beer at the church cookout in the summer, so she was not accustomed to considering alcohol a problem.

Dad wasn't used to all of the rules that went along with dating a Catholic high school girl, but he followed them. Mom was different than the girls he had dated before. She was refined and formally educated, a lady, and being a lady meant that nothing more than kissing was allowed. Her Catholicism and devotion intrigued him.

Dad was dragged to a few bible revivals growing up, but organized religion had never been part of his upbringing. When they talked about marriage, he agreed that he would convert, because Mom would only marry a Catholic.

They met at the Riley Boarding House, where dad lived. She worked there twice a week, every Tuesday and Thursday after school. It was an old Victorian house filled with boarders who came to work in one of the automotive factories in Detroit. Mrs. Riley was in her sixties and had a difficult time keeping up the house on her own. Mom cooked, cleaned, and did laundry or anything else Mrs. Riley needed her to do. When they first started running into each other, Dad paid her very little attention. He thought she was a cute kid, but far too young to date. He was five years older and had many female companions.

He worked as a welder at The Great Lakes Engineering Works and when he wasn't working, he was at the bar or hanging out with the guys at the garage. He was by no means an intellectual, but he was naturally smart. He knew about things that Mom didn't, like farming and machinery, and he was hard working. Mom's father admired that quality in Dad, and so did Mom.

Dad was ruggedly handsome and strong and women often compared him to Gary Cooper. People were surprised by his southern accent and soon counted it as one of his many charms.

Mom was paid well and with those wages and the money she earned working at a jewelry store, she had managed to save a nice little nest egg for college. She was raised in a traditional Catholic home with her mom and dad and six siblings. Her dad worked at the steel mill and her mom stayed home and raised the children. Nobody in her family had ever gone to college and for years she boasted that she was going to be the first. She loved science and dreamed of being the next Marie Curie. Our grandma worried about her ambitious dreams. It wasn't that she didn't think that she was smart enough; she was afraid that by pursuing an education and a career that she would be forced to forgo being a mother.

The nuns at her school, especially Sister Edith, praised her intelligence and encouraged her to pursue a higher education once she left Holy Family Catholic School. Sister Edith taught Science and Latin and mom felt lucky to have had her for both classes. The other sisters did not care for

Sister Edith because they viewed her interactions with the students as too casual. Mother Superior always reminded her, "We are not here to be friends with the students and should not treat them as our equals. Our job is to develop their relationship with God, not with us. Children learn better when they fear you, not when they like you." Sister Edith disagreed, but kept her opinions to herself.

Sadly, after meeting Dad, Mom's desire to attend college slowly faded. I never understood why she couldn't do both - why she couldn't love Dad and go to school. But she fell in love, gave up her dreams of college and dove head first into having children. Mom saw the world only in absolutes. She wasn't very good at finding the happy medium. She either loved us or ignored us, but never consistently made herself available, except if it came to one of the boys or Dad. She bent over backwards to please them, but in the long run she never got the gratification that she thought she would being just a mother.

Our parents got acquainted one evening during dinner at the boarding house. The Riley's didn't make it a habit of inviting boarders or the help to eat dinner with them, but they were childless and felt our parents were like the children they never had. Mr. Riley was a plumber and he and Dad hit it off right from the beginning. They had a lot in common: beer and tinkering. Several dinners followed, and soon Mom and Dad fell into the habit of sitting out on the front porch swing of the boarding house talking after she finished her work. It was during those chats when Mom first learned the watered-down version of dad's childhood. He didn't go into specifics, but Mom came to understand that his upbringing was very different from her own.

Dad's abusive father raised him and his twelve siblings alone after the sudden and unexpected death of their mother. Dad was only six when she died, and everything that was good and kind in their home died with her. His father, Doward, wasn't an innately bad man, but generations of poverty and isolation in the mountains left him with very little to be happy about. Years later when he was asked about his childhood, our dad would say nothing other than that times were different when he was a kid. He'd say children then were tougher, immune to the pain that the softer children of today would have felt not having a mother. But truth be told, we all knew he never got over losing his mother.

He'd describe his mother to us proudly, telling us how physically strong she was, and explaining that she could work alongside any man in the fields, but that she had the gentlest hands when consoling her children. She never learned to read, but she was creative and inquisitive. She loved to paint and once, when returning home from a rare visit with her family in Indiana, she stopped in a shop that sold books and rare keepsakes. There she found a book of postcards with replicas of the paintings of Renoir, Monet, and Van Gogh. That book was her most prized possession and she kept it safely hidden in the bottom of her bureau drawer. She studied that book as the Baptists in those parts studied their Bibles, committing every picture to memory as if memorizing verse. She knew nothing of the artists' lives, but they inspired her to be an artist. She painted on anything that she could get her hands on. When she didn't have paint - which was often - she sketched. She mostly drew nature scenes or still lifes. Her children eagerly anticipated bedtime because it was then they might find one of her paintings or sketches tucked under their pillow. There were thirteen of them, so they had to be patient.

Dad still had the last painting she had given him. It was a picture of a small cluster of huckleberries hanging on a vine that she had painted on the back of a torn envelope. When he had found it under his pillow years earlier, the berries were a vibrant shade of blue. The berries were almost entirely faded and the envelope was soft and thin by the time he shared it with us. It was clear to us that when she died, her book and the little happiness that he possessed disappeared. It took him years to feel genuine happiness again. Meeting Mom and starting his own family did bring him joy, but it was always overshadowed by the loss of his mother's love, and by his father's abuse. For a while he had managed to carve out a somewhat happy life for himself and emerge from these early trials, but we came to understand that when his baby son, our brother, Little Owen died, the best part of him died with him.

For generations his family had been born in the mountains of North Carolina, raised in the mountains, and in the mountains was where they stayed. Dad wanted something better. He wasn't sure what it was, but he was certain that he didn't want to spend the rest of his life behind a mule pulling a plow. He had earned a high school diploma, but his education had been sketchy. It was standard practice in those parts for children to miss school when it was time to plant or harvest tobacco. He went to school when he could and learned to read and write, but unlike Mom, he was far from college ready.

What he lacked in formal education, he made up for with life experiences. On the night of his high school graduation, and against his dad's wishes, he and two of his best buddies packed the few personal belongings they had and headed for Detroit. Once they arrived, they went their separate ways. Owen spent a year working as a laborer for Ford, but then was drafted into the army. He was stationed in Korea, but saw no action. His family back home joked that he had experienced enough action on the day he was born and throughout his childhood to last a lifetime. They liked to believe that God had graciously spared him.

ELEVEN

Our dad, Owen was his mom's last baby. Her pregnancy with him was uneventful, like all of her previous pregnancies. She prepared meals, canned, tended to the children and assisted her husband in the fields when it was time to harvest the crops. Sarah savored the sounds and smells of the mountains surrounding her and preferred to be outdoors than confined to the house. If it weren't for her telling people, nobody would have known she was expecting again. She always wore loose, handmade cotton dresses and never wore pants. A womanly figure she did not have. Sarah was short, barely over five feet tall. Her hands and feet were the size of a child's and her hips were narrow, even after bearing nine children.

On the day of our dad's birth, Sarah's labor began much the same way as the falling snow. The flakes were light and billowy, beautiful at first, but as each hour passed, the snow fell faster and the flakes doubled in size and mass. The light dusting on the ground quickly became a thick, dense blanket of snow.

Sarah woke at dawn as always. After stoking the fire, she began to prepare breakfast. She wasn't particularly hungry that morning and figured that her appetite would grow upon smelling the food, but it didn't. Her lack of appetite was soon accompanied by nausea. A couple of the younger kids had been sick earlier in the week with some kind of stomach ailment and she was certain that she had caught whatever they had. She nibbled on a leftover piece of cornbread from the night before while the rest of the family ate breakfast. Her husband Doward decided that the children would stay home from school that day. After finishing the morning dishes, she decided to tackle a mountain of laundry that needed tending. She shook her head while sorting the socks, trying to imagine how they all could have developed holes at the same time, and sat down to begin mending.

Our dad's oldest sister, Susie followed Doward's instructions and quickly dressed to head out to the canning house to retrieve some provisions before the storm worsened. On the way out, she noticed for the first time how pale and tired and uncomfortable Sarah looked. She decided it was more important to tend to her mom. She selected the fluffiest pillow she could find from the loft and placed it behind her mother's lower back. She wrapped her in a small quilt. Sarah gave her oldest daughter a thankful smile and then motioned for the basket of socks to be returned so she could continue her work.

Her relief was temporary. The dull pain that had settled in her back travelled down the length of her left leg. This pain, along with the queasy stomach, plagued Sarah well into the late afternoon. By dusk she could no longer deny that she was in labor. With a little more than four weeks to go to full term, she wasn't prepared for a baby just yet. Sarah could be stubborn and she made up her mind not to send for the midwife until the hard labor began.

Doward and the children ate dinner in silence and went about their nightly routine. Only when the contractions quickened and the pain intensified did Sarah instruct Doward to fetch the midwife. By then, well over a foot of snow had fallen. As Doward pushed open the front door of the cabin, the blistering wind and snow drifted in with him. He informed Sarah that the roads were too dangerous for travel. There was no way his flatbed truck or the wagon would be able to pass through the winding mountains to retrieve the midwife. To make matters worse, the doctor who tended to the people scattered throughout the mountains was a traveling doctor and his whereabouts were rarely known. Sarah assured Doward that the baby would be safely delivered with the help of the older girls. It wasn't ideal, but this was her tenth delivery and if she experienced no complications, she should be able to talk the girls through it. She recalled countless stories of women who had delivered their own babies. She gave directions to the girls as calmly as she could between each contraction.

Susie boiled a large pot of water, saving some of the water to sterilize her mother's sewing scissors. With the help of her younger sister Martha, they stripped the only set of sheets off the bed and carefully folded and put away Sarah's wedding quilt. Her bedding was replaced with old, moth-ridden blankets, which should have been discarded years ago anyway. With the help of Doward, Sarah made her way into the bedroom. The girls helped their mother change out of her clothes and into a nightgown. Once she was settled in, Susie and Martha shooed the younger kids away and positioned themselves on either side of their mother's bed and waited. The labor progressed quickly and Sarah informed the girls that it was time to start pushing. Susie pulled back the blanket as Sarah inched forward into an upright position. Sarah spread her legs and instructed the girls to push her legs up and out. She clamped her arms around each leg, leaned forward and bore down. She let out a soft cry of frustration and pain, then collapsed back into the pillow. Her bare legs flopped open and closed as she writhed in pain. Martha blushed upon seeing her mother's female parts. "You're not a little girl anymore," Sarah said. Martha avoided her mom's eyes and instead looked down at her feet. Sarah grabbed her hand and added, "You're not a little girl, but you'll always be my baby girl. I'm sorry darling that you've gotta see your mama like this."

"It's okay, mama. I like helping you," Martha assured her.

They wiped the sweat from her brow and endured having their hands tightly rung every time another contraction assaulted their mother. The pushing was not productive and went on for far longer than with the other births, and Sarah became concerned. The sun was almost up and Doward too grew worried as he impatiently smoked his pipe and waited for his next child to be born. His own sister had died during her last birth and he worried that once again he would need to find another mother for his children. Without informing

Sarah or the girls, he bundled up and left in search of someone who had more experience than the girls.

Nearly two hours later, Sarah delivered her baby. With the final push, Sarah collapsed, leaving the girls alone with their silent, slightly blue baby brother. Susie firmly held him in her arms while Martha wiped off the white film that covered his entire body. The two of them quietly debated what to do with the umbilical cord that still connected their brother to their mother. At that moment, Doward came in, looking as if he'd been sprinkled with powdered sugar. With him was Virgie, an elderly woman who lived in a holler, about a mile down the road.

She immediately took charge and cut the cord and passed the baby to Doward. Sarah had lost a lot of blood, but Virgie had seen far worse. Doward stood gazing at his son, who was struggling to take his first breath. He was uncertain what to do. Virgie instructed Doward to place the baby on the bed and to begin rubbing his chest while the girls rubbed his hands, feet, arms and legs. Doward was frightened. His hands were so big and his son's abdomen was so small. The palm of his hand completely covered his chest. Using only two fingers, he began to rub where he assumed his heart was located.

After several seconds, he still did not respond. In one swift motion, Virgie scooped him up off the bed and began to firmly and vigorously rub his back. Still not getting a response, she began to slowly breathe air into his mouth while Doward rubbed his chest, trying to persuade his little heart to beat. Owen eventually let out a weak cry and began to breathe on his own. Virgie declared him a miracle, but cautioned Doward that she had never seen a baby that fragile at birth go on to live. She wrapped him tightly in a blanket, set him in a shoebox and placed the box down next to the potbelly stove to warm him up. She prepared a sugar tit - a spoonful of honey dropped into a piece of clean cloth that was twisted and secured with twine in the form of a bulb and used as a pacifier - and instructed the girls to periodically place it in his mouth until he was strong enough to nurse from his mother.

She then turned her attention back to Sarah and began to push down on her abdomen, working the placenta from the uterus.

Almost ten hours later, Sarah woke to the sound of her baby crying. She opened her eyes to see old Dr. Lewis standing over her taking her vitals.

"Wasn't sure you were ever going to wake up, little lady," he told her. It took Sarah a few moments to remember that she had given birth. She lunged forward, trying to sit up, before landing back onto the bed in a heap. Dr. Lewis assured her that the baby was fine even though his entrance into the world had been difficult.

"I want to see him," she insisted.

Doward walked into the bedroom holding the box. She looked into the box and was startled by his appearance. His hair was black and thick and wild. It sat on his head like a coonskin cap. His eyes were the brightest blue she had ever seen and his skin was tangerine orange. The doctor assured her that his coloring would take on a more normal appearance in a few days. She gently lifted him out of the box and cradled him in her arms.

"Well, hello there little fellow. You just about scared your mama to death. For someone so little you sure did make everyone work," she smiled and cooed for a few minutes more, before growing suddenly exhausted. Susie took her little brother from her mother's arms and urged her to rest.

Before she closed her eyes she managed to ask, "What should we name him?" She was hoping to name him after her own Pa, but before she could suggest it, Doward revealed the name he had already picked out.

"We'll name him Owen after my great grandpa. He was a good man. Strong as an ox and luckier than any son-of-a-bitch alive," he announced proudly.

Throughout his childhood and adolescence Dad saw his fair share of sickness and mishaps, but he always bounced back. He was like a cat with nine lives, his mother used to say. It was the people around him, the people he cared about the most, who weren't so lucky.

TWELVE

Jana began working at Eddie's Market when she was 16. She worked a couple of hours every day after school and on the weekends. Her friends thought she was crazy to work as much as she did. Her Aunt Margie and Uncle Walter were never able to have children of their own and from day one they provided her with everything she needed. Jana didn't work for the money; she worked for the sheer pleasure of being around food. Her favorite part of her job was educating the customers on what they were buying. She could suggest the best cut of meat for whatever was on the customer's menu for the night or assist an uncertain housewife in selecting a wine that would best accompany the fish that she had just placed in her shopping cart. There were many customers who planned their trip to the market based on whether or not Jana would be working that day. Jana also loved to cook and was the only teenager in her neighborhood who enjoyed gardening. Her aunt and uncle happily agreed when she asked to put in a small garden in their backyard. Uncle Walter wasn't crazy about having his yard torn up, but he had never seen Jana as excited about anything as she was about the prospect of having a garden of her own. She marked off a small area where the garden would be, but each day the area grew bigger and bigger, eventually taking up half of the backyard. She spent hours tending to her plants and when they yielded far more than what the family could use, she supplied their neighbors with fresh produce.

Her aunt and uncle grew concerned when it got to be her senior year and Jana said nothing about college. She was an exceptional student and they always assumed that she would go. They visited several universities, but after much consideration, she decided not to head off to college right away. She'd continue working at the market and start school the following fall. When she was offered a management position, she eagerly accepted it and talk of college never came up again. And then one day, Clyde walked into her life.

Clyde stood in line for what seemed like forever waiting to order a sandwich. Most of the guys he worked with were content with a burger and a beer at one of the local watering holes, but Clyde grew tired of eating the same greasy bar food. He had spent the last few weeks working in this area and was certain he could locate a more suitable place to grab a quick lunch.

People who shopped at Eddie's tended to come from the posh neighborhoods surrounding it, and on the fateful day that Clyde decided to come in, the other customers were a little taken aback by his appearance. He wore tattered, dirty jeans and an orange work vest. Once inside the market he regretted not putting his shirt back on under his vest. His hardhat rested under his arm, he wore his hair in a ponytail and long strands of hair escaped his rubber band and had to be tucked repeatedly back behind his ear. Even with his face covered in dust and grime, he was the most handsome man that Jana had ever seen. She noticed him immediately when he walked into the market. He stuck out like a sore thumb.

She took the opportunity to study him while he waited in the deli line. She was in the produce section on the other side of the store and when he looked in her direction, she gave him a shy smile and a little wave. He casually turned around to make certain that her acknowledgment hadn't been intended for someone else. A short, elderly lady with blue hair was behind him and she was too busy fidgeting with her checkbook to be interacting with anyone. When he turned back around, Jana was no longer standing in front of the basket of muskmelon. He scoured the store trying to locate her and just as he decided to relinquish his spot in line, he discovered that she was walking straight toward him.

A casual observer might have concluded that they were two old friends being reunited after many years. When his number was called, signaling that he could place his order, Clyde was no longer in line. He was with Jana, picnicking on the lunch that she had prepared for herself, on the back end of his truck. By the time they were finished eating, he sensed that Jana too had known real loss. He could feel the presence of Jana's father even though she had not yet mentioned him. Clyde too had been orphaned, leaving him able to spot other foundlings immediately. Though Jana was loved dearly by her father and knew of her mother's existence, she still struggled with issues of abandonment.

Aunt Margie and Uncle Frank were not surprised when less than a year later Jana announced that she was marrying Clyde. They clung to the hope that she would one day find her way to college, or maybe even culinary school, but they accepted that with Clyde was where she wanted to be. After the wedding, it took only a few weeks for them to make all of the necessary arrangements to move.

They said their goodbyes and with only what they could fit in the back of Clyde's old pickup truck, they headed for Detroit. Clyde got hired at Ford Motor Company through the help of an old friend from his days at Boys Town. Jana and Clyde were two orphans in search of a life of their own choosing, determined to no longer let their lives be lives of circumstance.

THIRTEEN

Being at school all day, imagining my first real visit with Jana was painful for me. Time passed slowly and I was even less engaged than normal. At 3:30, Mrs. Burns instructed us to clean our work areas and get ready for dismissal. I haphazardly packed up my stuff and lined up. When the bell rang, I bolted out the door, not bothering to wait for Andrew, Patty or Margo, as I usually did. I ran the four blocks home and crashed through the back door, throwing my belongings at the bottom of the landing. "Hi Mom!" I called out, "I'm going outside for a while. I'll be home in time for dinner." Mom mumbled something inaudible and I was back out the door. I hopped over the fence, ran to the back entrance of the Peterson's house, and rang the doorbell.

Jana was standing in the sun porch looking out the window and called out, "It's open sweet pea, come on up!" I opened the door and jogged up the steps. The door at the top of the landing was open and I could hear music playing. I walked into the kitchen and was amazed at how the apartment had been transformed since the day before. It looked as if they had lived there for years.

"Wow! This place looks great. Clyde said yesterday that there wasn't a whole lot left to get out of the truck," I said.

"Today was trash day. When Clyde went on his morning run, he found a lot of cool stuff that people were getting rid of," Jana replied, very matter of fact. "One man's trash is another man's treasure," she added. I walked from room to room examining all of their treasures.

"Well, it looks like you are settled in. You really don't need me," I said.

"Of course I do! I still have a couple of boxes to go through and besides, that was just an excuse to get you back over," Jana said. "But before we do that, tell me about yourself." I pretended not to hear her. Jana handed me a stack of plates and what to me seemed like fancy cloth napkins and asked if I could set the table.

Flowers were arranged in a cobalt blue vase in the center of the table. I noticed that they were cut from my mom's hydrangea bush that partly hung over on the Peterson's side of the fence. My mother never cut flowers from any of the flowering bushes that were in our backyard, so I was glad that Jana had discovered them.

As I began to set the table, Jana walked over to give me the silverware and stopped to smell the flowers. "Smell them, Suzanne. Don't they smell heavenly?" she asked. I stopped what I was doing and smelled them. To be honest, I couldn't smell a thing because my nose was all stuffed up, but I lied and said they smelled really pretty. As I went to place the napkin next to the plate, I hesitated because I wasn't sure which side of the plate it went on.

"Other side, honey," she said.

"Oh yeah, what was I thinking?" I lied. I hadn't the faintest idea which side the napkin or any of the silverware went on. The cloth napkins were a first for me. My family didn't really use napkins, cloth or otherwise, when we ate so I was doubly impressed. Meals weren't too formal at our house. Our kitchen table barely fit in the room and we were short on spaces for everyone to sit down at the table together. Anna usually stood at the countertop and ate when everybody was home to eat a meal. She never complained, but she really resented having to be the only one to stand at the counter to eat. "What the hell, are we down south in Mississippi where they have a white counter and a colored counter? I feel so segregated," she would gripe only later, to the rest of us, never to Mom and Dad. We felt that Danny should have stood at the counter because he was the oldest and a boy, but he never did. The boys in the family were treated like crown princes, while the girls were treated like handmaids.

When I finished setting the table, I walked over to the counter where Jana was chopping up some kind of green herb and sprinkling it over a bowl of something I had never seen. It looked liked baby food, soft and mushy. It didn't look very appetizing, but I smiled and said, "Yum!" when Jana caught me looking at it.

Jana looked beautiful. She was wearing another long dress, but today she was barefoot. Her hair was in a twist and secured with a clip that resembled a seashell. The apron she had tied around her accentuated her tiny waist. Every time she moved, the bracelets on her arm traveled up to her elbow and made a jingly sound.

"I like your hair, Jana. It's pretty," I told her.

"Would you like me to do your hair like mine? I think it's long enough," she offered.

"Oh, that's nice, but you don't have to bother. You're cooking dinner," I said. I didn't tell her that I'd been doing my own hair ever since I could remember. Once in a while my sisters did it if we were going somewhere special and Mom wanted me to look presentable.

"It's no bother, Suzanne. Follow me," she instructed. She took me into her bedroom. The room looked like it belonged in a castle. Everything was draped in ruffles and soft pastels and she even had a canopy bed. The bed and matching furniture was white and painted with gold swirls throughout.

"Wow! You're so lucky to have a canopy bed. I've always wanted one!" I cried.

Jana just laughed and said, "Clyde doesn't like this furniture. Can you blame him? It's what was in my room back home. The bed is barely big enough for the two of us, but Clyde slept on a friend's couch back in Baltimore so this is all we've got. When we save up enough money, the first thing we're going to buy is a new bedroom set," she explained as I walked around their room in awe. "Hopefully Clyde will luck out and find something salvageable on trash day that we can refinish and use in the meantime, and then we'll just have to buy a new mattress," Jana added. "Let me talk to Clyde, but maybe we can let you have this set then, or at least buy it for real cheap."

"That would be nice, but there is no way my mom and dad could afford this. Besides, I share a bed with my sister,

Patty and there just isn't enough space in our bedroom for all of this. Too bad, though," I said.

I sat down on the stool that was placed in front of her vanity and marveled over all of the knick-knacks that covered it. She had an actual glass perfume bottle - the kind with the little stopper that kept the perfume from spilling out. All the sophisticated women in old black-and-white movies had them. They'd pull the crystal stopper out of the bottle and dab it behind their ears before heading off to the theater or some other fancy place.

When I opened her jewelry box a little ballerina began to spin around in circles, pirouetting to the sound of a song I had never heard before. Jana came up behind me and began to brush my hair. Her hands were so soft and warm. When she came to a snarl, she didn't just yank through it like my sisters. Jana was gentle. She pulled out a spray bottle from one of her vanity drawers and squirted some kind of solution onto my hair. Whatever it was smelled citrusy, like oranges. She waited a couple of seconds and then continued to comb my hair out. The comb slid through my hair easily. She set the comb down and ran her fingers through either side of my hair and gathered it all in the back.

"Hand me a couple of those bobby pins, sweetie. Your hair is quite a bit shorter than mine, but I think that I can still make it work," she told me. She twisted my hair up and secured it with a clip similar to hers and then used the bobby pins to capture the short hairs that wanted to escape. I looked pretty good with my hair up, I thought.

"Let's see what else we can do," she sang out. She took the stopper out of the glass bottle and dabbed it behind both my ears. Her perfume smelled different than my mom's. My mom had received a small bottle of perfume for her last birthday from all of her sisters. She made such a big fuss about receiving it because it was really expensive, but I didn't think it smelled very good. It had a stupid name. Who'd want perfume named after a T.V. channel - *Chanel Number 5?*

"I like this perfume. What's it called?" I asked.

"It's not perfume, it's patchouli," Jana informed me. "Doesn't it smell good?"

She removed the lid off a round glass jar that had lotion in it. "Here, turn around and face me," she instructed. She placed several dots of lotion onto my face and then gently began to rub it in. She finished me off with a smear of petroleum jelly across my lips to make them shiny. "You look beautiful, Suzanne," she told me.

"Thanks, Jana! So do you."

We walked back into the kitchen just as Clyde came walking into the apartment. He was holding another bouquet of flowers, but these he had purchased at the florist. Jana looked at him lovingly. "These are for my favorite girl," he said as he presented them to her. She nuzzled his neck and then kissed him on the cheek and thanked him for the flowers.

"Don't you girls look pretty," he teased. "I thought you were supposed to be working this afternoon."

Jana instructed Clyde and I to sit down as she brought the food over to the table. "We have cucumber sandwiches, hummus and pita bread and a tomato bisque soup. Dig in!" she urged. The menu sounded foreign to me and I was reluctant to dive in. Jana laughed and explained, "Clyde and I are vegetarians. Try it! I think you'll really enjoy it, Suzanne."

Because our dad was from the south, every meal prepared by Mom consisted of some kind of meat, potatoes prepared in one of two ways (fried or mashed), and a variety of vegetables seasoned with bacon grease.

I tried the food while Clyde told us all about his first day of work. He worked on the assembly line and though most people would view his work as tedious, Clyde made it sound utterly fascinating. Clyde took a break from talking and ate, so Jana explained how Clyde was starting classes the following week to become a boilermaker. I'd heard of a boilermaker and wasn't sure what they did, but pretended to be impressed.

"What does your dad do, Suzanne?" Clyde asked.

"He is a welder," I answered, but then quickly changed the subject. "This hummus is delicious and I love these cucumber sandwiches." She was right, I had prepared myself to dislike the food, but it was really tasty.

"A welder, huh? You need to introduce me to your dad. I'd like to bend his ear," Clyde responded. The words had barely escaped his lips when I heard the shouting. I knew immediately who it was. At first I pretended not to hear it, but when the argument escalated, I could no longer ignore it. I looked down at my lap and willed it to stop. Clyde and Jana exchanged glances, because it wasn't difficult to determine where the voices were coming from. Clyde got up from the table and casually closed the window.

"It gets a little cool when the sun goes behind the clouds," he explained.

Before anybody could say anything else, I was up on my feet. "I have to get going, I can't stay. I just remembered that I have something I need to do." My cloth napkin was caught up in my feet as I stumbled to the door. I picked it up and ran down the steps.

"Suzanne, wait!" Jana pleaded, but it was too late, I was already gone.

Clyde and Jana must have sat in their kitchen for the next thirty-five minutes listening to my dad's explosive rant.

As usual when a fight ensued between my parents, Danny was forced to intervene. Poor Danny often served as the decoy when our dad began to get into it with Mom.

As I hurried down the stairs towards home, I heard the back door of our house fly open and my dad storm out, a trail of profanity flowing from him. My dad liked to swear.

FOURTEEN

I was mortified. How could I ever face Jana and Clyde again? That evening, I sat in my closet recreating the events of the evening, as they would have happened in my perfect world. After we finished eating, Jana would have suggested going to the Dairy Queen to get a *Jack and Jill*. As we walked home slowly, eating our ice cream, Clyde would continue to talk about starting school and Jana would talk about putting in her vegetable garden. I would suggest that we stop at Carney Park and as we approached the entrance to the park, Clyde would playfully call out, "Last one to the swings is a rotten egg!" We'd play at the park until the last of the sun had set and then walk home enjoying the soft, spring breeze.

I was overcome with exhaustion and fell asleep on the closet floor. That is where I stayed until I woke at 3:00 a.m.

At first I couldn't figure out where the voices were coming from. I could clearly make out my dad's voice, but it took several seconds to recognize the other voices. The voices belonged to my mom, Jana, Clyde and a fourth voice that I had never heard before. I opened the closet door to discover that nobody was in my bedroom. As I walked down the staircase, I heard whispers coming from the kitchen. Everybody else in the house was up except for Robbie. Andrew was sitting on Ellen's lap. By the expressions on their faces, I knew that something bad had happened.

It wasn't until everybody saw me walking into the kitchen that they realized that I had not been present during the craziness of the last hour or so.

"Where have you been?" Patty asked.

"I fell asleep in the closet," I answered truthfully. I was a deep sleeper and over the years I managed to sleep through many dramas big and small that frequently played out in our household.

"What kind of freak falls asleep in a closet? What are you—some kind of vampire," Danny asked disgustedly.

"Leave her alone, Danny. Suzanne, if I could fit in the closet, I'd be right there with you," Anna said.

I gave Anna an appreciative smile before asking, "Why are all of you up, and who are all those people in front of our house?"

"You really don't have any clue about what's going on, do you?" Danny asked. I shook my head no.

"Well, count your lucky stars that you were asleep for this one," Ellen said and squeezed Andrew's hand even tighter to reassure him. Ellen proceeded to fill me in on what I had missed.

When Dad wasn't at work or at home making everybody else's life miserable, you could find him at *Lucky's*. *Lucky's* was a little bar-and-grill located not too far from our house. A retired police officer named Lucky owned it, and his old police friends and the guys from the neighborhood were really the only ones who ever went there. There were many nights when Dad was given a police escort home because he was too drunk to drive, or so inebriated that he couldn't even walk home. This night was one of those nights.

It took two of them to walk him to the front door. There was no doorbell, so they just knocked very loudly. Danny came to the door and let them in.

"Alright, Danny where do you want him?" Officer Richardson asked.

"Just put him on the couch," Danny answered, not even looking at Dad.

"Okay, Owen. Here ya go, buddy." They dropped him on the couch. One of them reached down to place an arm that was hanging over the side of the couch up onto his chest.

Danny said, "Don't bother. His ass will be on the floor in a couple of minutes." The police officers left and Danny went back to bed. Dad had apparently slept for about an hour or so, but then had woken up. He was cold and had to use the bathroom. After relieving himself, he stumbled to the refrigerator to get something to eat. He was famished. He had failed to eat before storming out of the house after the fight earlier that evening. After drinking ten or twelve beers, he now felt shaky and queasy. Who knows if it was because he couldn't find the leftovers, or if he didn't like what he found, but whatever the case, he went ballistic, taking his anger out on the food in the refrigerator.

He started with the powdered milk that wasn't thick and creamy like the buttermilk he liked, but was a sickly watered-down white. Mom secretly mixed regular milk with the powdered milk when money was tight. For years she thought that she had everybody fooled. When we inquired about why the milk was in a pitcher instead of its original container, she would lie and say that the carton must have sprung a leak. Her lie worked on us younger kids, but the older kids knew better. They never let her secret out, but suggested sarcastically that she might want to shop at another store that sold milk that came in higher quality vessels.

Dad hurled the pitcher; the milk exploded upon impact and dripped down the wall. Next he tossed the left over spaghetti sauce from that night's dinner. The bowl cracked in two and the congealed sauce plopped into a pile on the floor. He managed to empty the entire second shelf in less than a minute.

"Damn it, Joyce, there's not a damn thing in this house that's worth a damn to eat," he yelled. When Dad was mad, he swore more than usual. Anna joked that he needed a dictionary for potty mouths because he would often use the same cuss word repeatedly. The sentences that he put together never made sense. Anna imitated him perfectly, "What son-of-a-bitch drank the last of the milk and put the son-of-a-bitch carton in the son-of-a-bitch refrigerator?" Danny and Ellen would howl and roll on the floor when she impersonated Dad throwing one of his tantrums.

Mom emerged from her bedroom and entered the kitchen with confidence, her head held high. She almost slipped on the food that now covered the floors and walls, but managed to stay on her feet. By then Dad had moved on to the pantry. She didn't acknowledge him or his mess, but just strolled past him to the refrigerator as if she was surveying its contents in preparation for a trip to the grocery store. "Why is it so fucking hard for you to make anything that I want to eat?" dad yelled. She continued searching for something to give him.

"I can make you an egg sandwich?" she offered.

"I don't want a fucking sandwich. I eat fucking sandwiches every fucking day for lunch. What else do you have? How is it that you go shopping every other day and there still isn't a fucking thing to eat? What do you do with all of my money?" he screamed.

She stopped looking and slammed the door. "Make yourself something to eat. I'm going back to bed," she informed him.

"You're not going any damn where," he said as he trailed behind her, "I asked you a question," he yelled even louder. She didn't answer or stop, but kept walking through the kitchen and in the direction of their bedroom. He grabbed her by the arm and swung her around.

"By God, let go of me!" she screamed.

She was in her socks, which made it easy for him to drag her by the arm across the linoleum floor. He let her go, but she cowered against the stove. "Don't you walk away from me! I'm so sick and damn tired of you always walking away!" He shoved her so hard into the stove that when she hit it, the oven door bounced open.

Hearing the commotion, Danny woke with a start, his bedroom door flew open and he too was in the kitchen. He ran up behind Dad and looped both arms through his arms in an attempt to restrain him long enough for Mom to get away.

He caught Dad by surprise, "What the hell?" Dad protested and struggled to free himself. It didn't take long for him to break free from Danny's grip. He swung around quickly and lunged for Danny. After one or two steps, his feet flew out from under him and he came crashing down onto the floor. "Son of a bitch!" he yelled.

When Dad was angry, he had a wild-eyed look about him. When he was drunk and angry, he resembled a ferocious animal trapped in a net. He sprung off of the floor and started after Danny once more. Mom escaped, ran out of the kitchen and right out the front door. Sometimes she just sat out on the steps and waited for him to pass out or cool off. Other times she ran all the way to her parent's house and left us to fend for ourselves for the night. I used to worry that she was never coming back and that we'd be stuck with just our dad to care for us. I too wanted to run away and even tried to one time.

I didn't get too far, only a couple of blocks. A drunkard, who was probably oblivious to my presence, came stumbling out of the alley and crossed my path. I panicked when I saw him because, in addition to mimes and clowns, I had a fear of hobos. I ran back in the direction of home, but took an unplanned detour to the park. I sat on a swing for about an hour trying to kill some time. I naively believed that when I arrived home my family would be overcome with joy. They would realize just how much they loved me and would promise to treat me better. When I entered the house and announced my return, my family hadn't the faintest idea I had ever left.

"You little son of a bitch," Dad screamed at Danny. Danny balled up his hands in anticipation, but he was not fast enough and received a fist to the left side of his cheek. He swayed, but recovered quickly.

"I hate you, I fucking hate you!" Danny screamed. While Dad was shaking off his stinging hand, Danny delivered his own blow. Dad fell hard to the floor and Danny jumped on top of him. The two of them rolled around on the floor with their fists flying. Although Danny was pretty tough, Dad was still stronger and managed to flip him over and pinned him to the floor by his throat.

By now, everyone else was in the kitchen, too. "Get off of him. You're going to kill him," Ellen pleaded. She ran to the basement landing and grabbed the broom. She quickly returned and proceeded to hit dad over and over again, trying to knock him off of Danny. Dad jumped off Danny and forced the broom out of Ellen's hands. Before she could comprehend what was happening, Dad had Ellen pinned up against the wall with the broom handle pressed up against her neck. Danny was still on the floor trying to catch his breath when Anna showed up with Dad's twelve-gauge shotgun. She placed the barrel firmly up against the back of his head.

"Let go of her or I swear to God, I'll blow your head off," Anna warned. Dad had trained all of us kids to shoot a gun. He owned several and kept them locked in the gun cabinet. The key was stashed under some old blankets that were stacked on the closet shelf. For such a hotheaded and impulsive man, he was also strangely cautious and never stored the ammo with the guns. The shells and the bullets were hidden in Mom's sock and underwear drawer. The gun that Anna so confidently held wasn't loaded, and Owen knew it. Owen dropped the broom as he turned around and faced Anna. "You really think you're something, don't ya?" he asked.

"No, but it'll be over my dead body that I let you hurt my mom or any of my brothers or sisters," she answered, aiming the gun straight at him.

Margo and Andrew were hovering on the landing and Patty was standing with the phone in her hands. She had called the police while Dad and Danny were rolling around on the floor. Hearing the sirens, Anna lowered the gun. Danny quickly took it out of her hands and returned it to the gun cabinet before the police got there. When the police officer came to the front door, Dad answered it.

"What the hell do you want, Jim?" he asked. Jim was one of the cops who hung out at *Lucky's*. His partner was over at Jana and Clyde's, talking to Mom, who had taken refuge there.

"Come on, Owen. You know damn well why I'm here. Now, let me come in." Dad stepped aside and let Jim into the foyer.

"We got a bunch of calls from your neighbors that there was some kind of disturbance going on over here," Jim told him.

"Well, there's a bunch of goddamn nosey people living on this street. There isn't anything going on in here. Just a little squabble with the kids," he lied.

"Owen, one of the calls came from your house and another one came from your wife who is over at your neighbor's house as we speak. She sounded a little shaken up on the phone," Jim explained. "I think that it would be best if you came into the station with me and let things settle down a little bit."

"Hell no!" Dad exclaimed.

"Owen, I'm not asking. By the looks of things," Jim looked in at the mess in the kitchen, "everybody needs a little time to cool down and get some sleep. Come on buddy, tomorrow this will be behind you and everybody will be feeling better." Dad was exhausted. He decided that it would just be easier to go. Jim turned to the kids.

"You kids alright?" he asked. We remained silent, but then Danny finally answered that we were all okay. "Go on now and get some sleep. We'll send your mom over in just a minute." He looked over at Patty and Margo and gave them a wink. His daughter Violet was in their class. The two of them walked out the front door and the other police officer came walking over with Jana, Clyde and Mom. It wasn't all that cold out, but Jana had wrapped a thick wool blanket around Mom's shoulders.

"Well, thanks again for being so understanding. I'm sorry that these were the circumstances under which we had to meet for the first time," she said to Jana.

When Mom came into the house, Margo, Patty, and Robbie went back into their rooms. Danny was standing at the refrigerator drinking from a jug of milk and Ellen and Anna were cleaning up the mess.

"Girls, I got this. You're all going to have to get up in a couple of hours and go to school. Why don't you try to get some sleep," she suggested. Danny put the milk away and kissed Mom on the check before returning to his room. The girls ignored what she said and kept on cleaning. Mom walked into the living room to lie down on the couch. She needed to shut her eyes for just a minute before tackling the mess. She didn't notice me sitting in the other chair. I quietly got up, covered my mom up with the blanket and went up to my own room. Patty was already sleeping, so I slipped into bed and tried to go to sleep.

Nobody spoke as we got ready for school later that same day. There was nothing to be said, no words could right this all too familiar drama. For years Mom attempted to provide some kind of explanation or excuse for Dad's behavior, but she eventually gave up trying to make sense of it for us. We had all given up too. One by one, we walked out the door, each silently reciting the guardian angel prayer we hoped would keep us safe.

For the next several hours at school, we would be able to relax a little and let our guard down. When Margo walked by Mom, she stopped briefly as if she were going to say something, but then just touched her hand and kept walking.

I had slipped out unnoticed and headed down the street with my head down. When I finally looked up, I noticed that Jana was walking towards me. It was too late to cross over to the other side without it seeming rude.

"Hey Suzanne," called Jana "do you mind if I walk with you for a while?" I didn't answer, so Jana took that as a yes. We walked for a couple of minutes before Jana spoke. "Suzanne, please don't be embarrassed about last night. Clyde and I would never judge you or your folks." I remained silent. Jana clasped her hand around mine and we walked in silence, hand in hand, all the way to the gate of the school. I looked at Jana shyly, wanting to thank her for walking me to school, but the words were trapped inside my mouth. I swallowed hard and felt a large lump forming in my throat. I felt as if I were choking. I began to panic and the memory of the time I choked on a large piece of steak one night during dinner flooded in.

Andrew had been the first one to notice that something was wrong.

"What the heck's wrong with Suzanne?" he shouted. Everybody stopped eating and looked at me. I was sitting there perfectly silently, with a pained look on my face. I began pushing down on my neck with my fingers as if I were giving myself a massage.

Everybody panicked once they realized what was happening. My dad reached across the table with one hand and yanked me off the old church pew that served as seating on one side of the table. He turned me over his knee and dislodged the chunk of meat by whacking me repeatedly on the back. After the meat popped out, my dad turned me around and hugged me. He hugged me so tight that I felt like the prey of a boa constrictor being slowly squeezed to death.

"Dad, I can't breathe," I was barely able to squeak out. He let go of me and gave me a good long stare. I was scared. Then I threw up. I projectile vomited right onto my dad. Puke ran down the front of his shirt. We all waited for him to explode, but he didn't. He went into the bedroom and took off his work shirt.

When he sat back down at the table he was wearing only his white undershirt and said, "Now go on and eat your steak. You'll be fine."

My throat burned and the bitter taste in my mouth made me gag. I feared that I would choke again and just stared at my steak.

"I said eat that steak, Suzanne. If you don't eat it now you'll never eat it again and life ain't worth living without a good piece of meat. Don't let that old fear call the shots."

I did what I was told and ate every bite. When I was done eating, I snuck outside and sat by my rosebush and cried.

Now, standing in front of the school with Jana, I felt ashamed. I began to walk away, unable to face Jana any longer. She reached out and pulled me towards her. It didn't register what Jana was trying to do. She wrapped her long, skinny arms around me and hugged me tightly. At first I was stiff, unsure how to respond. Eventually my arms found their way around Jana's tiny waist. I felt myself melting towards the ground. As my knees began to fold, so did Jana's. The earthy smell of her patchouli and the surge of emotion made me dizzy.

I was the first to break from our embrace. I looked at Jana, expecting her to say something else about last night, but she didn't. She smiled her sweet smile and said, "Well, have a good day at school, Suzanne!" I gave her a little wave and scurried to join the other children waiting in line for the bell to ring.

FIFTEEN

That day was an early dismissal day because of the carnival that Holy Family Catholic Church held each year. Everybody in the city attended the carnival whether they were Catholic or not. Jana decided to explore the neighborhood and return to the school in time to meet Suzanne when she got out. It was a brilliant spring day, the sun was shining and the wind was perfectly still. The scent of new life hung in the air. The blooming spring flowers mixed with the smell of fresh cut grass, created a fragrant bouquet. As she walked up and down the streets, she observed that the houses were old, but well maintained. Freshly washed clothes hung on the clotheslines. The well-manicured yards made her think of her dad. He had loved being outside, especially this time of year. He had spent every free moment working in the yard or tending to his garden.

She had inherited her love of nature and gardening from him. His presence was strong today and she knew that he was there because of Suzanne. Jana's heart had felt heavy since meeting her. She saw a lot of herself in Suzanne. Although this little girl had not been orphaned as she had been, Jana recognized the pain that Suzanne masked. She strolled through the neighborhood for well over an hour, until she stumbled upon *Novak's Market*. It was small but quaint, and Jana was surprised by the selection of produce and novelties that the small store offered. As she examined the produce, her thoughts kept drifting back to the events of the night before. Deep in thought, she hadn't noticed that Joyce was standing across from her until she heard her speaking to Mr. Novak.

Joyce was an attractive woman. She had a nice figure for a woman in her mid-thirties who had delivered nine babies. She kept her hair short, like many other women her age. She achieved her soft curls by setting her hair every other night in pin curlers. She was too young to wear the muumuus that many of the older ladies at her church wore, but felt that she was too old for the long, flowing dresses that Jana wore. Joyce usually wore cotton pedal pushers or dress slacks with a sensible button down blouse. She never left the house without first applying her frosted peach-colored lipstick and without placing her crumpled, slightly used tissue in the front of her bra.

"Hello, Joyce! How are you?" Jana asked. Although they had just met hours earlier, Jana suspected that Joyce would probably fail to recognize her since it had been under such traumatic circumstances. But even in everyday interactions, others frequently felt that Joyce was preoccupied with more pressing issues. Mr. Novak returned to stocking his shelves. He was a sweet man who always greeted his customers when they came into his store. He was relieved when customers ran into someone else they knew so that he could get back to work. Mr. Novak, or Tomas, as his Czech customers called him, had been in the country for about ten years. His children spoke almost perfect English, but he still found it difficult to have lengthy conversations with his English-speaking customers.

"I'm fine, Jana. Just a little tired," Joyce dutifully responded. The two women stood waiting for the other to say something to break the awkward silence.

"If you need any help with the kids today, Clyde and I would love to help out," Jana finally said.

"Owen is already out. His brother-in-law picked him up earlier this morning. I think he went into work. I'm going to stay with my mom and dad until the dust settles," Joyce said before quickly adding, "He's pretty low key after one of these major episodes. The kids will be fine."

"Okay, but if you need anything, we're right next door," Jana said as she rubbed Joyce's hand.

"You're a sweet young lady, Jana. Thank you for being so kind," Joyce said. Both women stood waiting for the other to end the conversation.

"You know, sometimes things aren't what they seem," Joyce offered as an explanation to a question that hadn't yet been asked.

"And sometimes things are exactly as they seem," Jana gently responded. Joyce turned her head into her shoulder and began to cry. Jana inched closer, as Joyce leaned into her. Joyce continued to weep. Jana understood that Joyce's crying was about more than the events of last night. She didn't ask, but just let her cry. Mr. and Mrs. Novak walked over, but said nothing. They each placed a hand on Joyce's shoulder, and then turned and walked into the room in the back of the store. Joyce wasn't sure how long she had stood crying in Jana's hair, but when she was done, she pulled her tissue from her bra, blew her nose, and walked out the front door. Jana browsed awhile more at Novak's and arrived back at the school just as the dismissal bell was ringing.

SIXTEEN

I was the last child to walk out the door at the end of the school day. I scanned the blacktop looking for Patty, Margo, and Andrew. The three of them were each talking to their own group of friends, finalizing their plans for the carnival. I was heading in their direction when I spotted Jana making her way through the clusters of students.

"What are you doing here?" I asked, surprised.

"I came to pick you up from school. Clyde is meeting with a friend tonight after work. I thought that it would be fun to go to the carnival together - that is, if you don't already have plans to go with anyone else," Jana replied.

"I don't really like carnivals. I'm scared of all the rides and the smell of the greasy carnival food makes me sick to my stomach," I answered apologetically.

"That's funny! I don't really like carnivals either. What else do you like to do? Today is your day, it's all about you," Jana told me.

"Well," I carefully thought, "I like going to the park."

"The park it is then!" Jana exclaimed. "Let's go back to my place and pack a picnic just in case we get hungry later," Jana suggested. "On second thought, maybe you should check in with your mom just to make sure it's okay."

When I got home, my mom was packing an overnight bag for herself and Robbie. I walked into her room and asked if it was okay if I went to the park with Jana.

"Sure. Why not? She seems like a nice girl. But don't you want to go to the carnival with all of the other kids?" she asked.

"Not especially. I don't really like carnivals," I explained.

"I didn't know that. What kind of kid doesn't like carnivals?" she asked. She zipped up her bag and looked at Robbie and said, "Are you ready, kiddo? We're going to stay the night with Grandma and Grandpa."

"I love Grandma and Grandpa! Yahoo!" he chanted as he ran in circles.

"Have fun, Buddy," I said.

"Thanks, sis," Robbie said and he gave me a quick squeeze.

"Suzanne, after the park, why don't you come over, too? Andrew went to the carnival with his friends and I told him to come to your grandparents afterward. Margo and Patty are having a sleepover at Violet's house," my mom explained.

"Are Ellen and Anna coming home tonight?" I asked.

"Yes, so is Danny, but I'm sure that it won't be until much later," she said.

"Is dad coming home?" I asked.

"Well, of course he is," she said casually as if the previous night had never happened.

"Well, we'll see. Maybe I'll just hang out with Jana until the older kids get home," I replied.

"Okay, Suzanne, but don't wear out your welcome. Jana and Clyde are a real nice couple and I'm sure they have better things to do than hang out with you," she lectured.

I said goodbye to my mom and skipped over to Jana and Clyde's place.

"Come on up, Suzanne!" Jana yelled.

I laughed when I saw Jana standing on the landing. "You look like a pack mule," I teased. Jana's face was buried behind the provisions she had packed for our afternoon at the park. "Why don't I give you a hand," I offered.

"What we need is a wagon," Jana quipped. "Does your family have one?"

"I think we have one in the garage. I'll go check," I volunteered. A few minutes later I returned with a rusty wagon filled with dry leaves and covered in spider webs. Jana wiped it clean with an old rag and we loaded up our supplies.

SEVENTEEN

The bright orange vests of the arborists and the sound of the humming chainsaws and wood chippers served as a painful reminder of the park's failing health. "Maybe we should try the other side," Jana suggested, "There doesn't seem to be as much going on over there." As humble as this little park was, it was one of my favorite places, and one of the very few places I felt safe.

We settled on a quiet spot under a large tree near the wading pool and tennis courts. Seeing the pool made me eager for summer break and swimming. It didn't matter to me if the pool had "more pee than water in it," as Patty claimed, or that the water only came up to my knees. I loved the warmth of the sun on my face when I'd lie back in the water and watch as my hair floated around my head like sea-weed. Picking off the dried, blue specks of paint that stuck to my body when I got out of the pool was just another part of the experience. When I'd sit on the grass on my towel and eat my box lunch, I'd imagine I was at a resort.

Dad would have been angry if he had known we took box lunches because everybody knew that the city provided box lunches for the "poor" kids. Our family was poor, but we weren't as poor as the families who got free lunch. In Dad's mind, he made a good living, but just had too many children.

Jana unfolded the blanket and spread it out across the grass. I tried to entice a few squirrels over our way with a discarded piece of candy bar I found in the grass. From a small basket Jana pulled out an assortment of dips, two Mason jars filled with lemonade, a couple of sandwich bags filled with crackers and chips, and two peanut butter and jelly sandwiches. She placed the assortment of snacks in the center of the blanket, kicked off her sandals and sat down. I gave up trying to engage the squirrels and turned my attention to Jana saying, "It's a shame what happened to these trees. They look so pathetic covered in all that white paint." Trees throughout the city had been infected with Dutch elm disease, but the park had been hit especially hard, resulting in the removal of many trees. Jana closed her eyes and ran her hand across the bark of the tree. The grooves in between the raised pieces of bark were clogged with paint. "Why didn't the city at least use brown paint?" I asked, "Wouldn't that have looked more natural?"

"It's terrible what happened to these magnificent trees," Jana replied, "but it's all part of life, part of the natural world. You can't have life without disease or death." Jana stood up, dusted off her hands and wrapped her arms around the trunk of the tree as far as they could reach, giving it a hug. "These trees are trying to heal and maybe this paint will prevent the other trees from getting sick. Let's not focus on the negative, but instead enjoy them just as they are, paint and all," Jana suggested. I got up and tried hugging the tree, but my arms wouldn't reach all the way around. Together Jana and I circled our arms around the tree and gave it a big hug before finally sitting down.

We sat in silence for several minutes enjoying the sun and the solitude before I asked, "What were you like as a little girl, Jana?" Jana paused and gave careful consideration to my question before responding.

"Well, Suzanne, believe it or not I was a lot like you," she answered. "I was quiet and inquisitive and I didn't mind spending time by myself. Unlike you, I didn't have any brothers and sisters. My Aunt Margie and Uncle Walter were sweet, but they weren't my playmates. Most of their friends' children were older than me. I had to be creative and entertain myself."

"Why did you live with your Aunt Margie and Uncle Walter?" I asked.

Jana explained how her mom had left and that her dad had died. She didn't really remember a lot about her mom. The only real memory she had was of her mom having taken her to get her picture taken. Before her dad died he used to tease Jana saying, "Jana, you've got an active imagination. You were just a little over two when your mama took you to get your picture taken. There is no way that you could have remembered that."

But Jana did remember. It was warm out, maybe in the spring, possibly the summer. Jana's mom had given her a bath and then dressed her in a new sundress that was covered with strawberries. They drove to the local photographers and before entering the shop, her mom stopped at a carousel. She dropped in a nickel and placed Jana on the back of a white pony with a red saddle. As Jana slowly went round and round, her mother clapped her hands and hummed along with the music. When the carousel stopped, she took several pictures of Jana, who was smiling from ear to ear. It occurred to Jana several years later that she had never come across any of those pictures. When her dad died, her Aunt Margie gave her a cigar box full of pictures and mementos that had belonged to him. The formal picture that was taken after they left the carousel was in the box, but there was not one picture of her sitting on that white pony. Her dad had always been thankful that Jana could not recall any other events from that day, because it was that same day, with no note or any kind of explanation, that her mom had packed up her stuff and left them.

For the next hour or so, Jana shared all kinds of stories about her childhood. My favorite story was the one she told of how she met and fell in love with Clyde. Jana described life in Baltimore and how they had decided to move to Michigan after they got married. I was enthralled. Even though I didn't like sharing information about myself, I found other peoples' stories intriguing. Jana was a good storyteller and I loved a good story. I could have sat and listened to her stories all day.

"Well, now that you know everything there is to know about me, why don't you tell me your story, Suzanne?" Jana asked. She grabbed a few crackers and then rolled over to make herself more comfortable.

"Me?" I asked. I was confused. Jana's question seemed a little absurd, but I didn't want to be rude, so I answered, "I don't have a story. I am only eight."

"Sure you do," Jana said "everyone has a story. Sometimes our story begins long before we're born, but it's still ours," she assured me. "Our stories define us as people, as individuals. Two people can be in the same story, but their individual experiences, their own emotions and thoughts are what make the story theirs. We can share a past, but we can't share how that past shapes us. That's up to each of us to figure out on our own."

I remained quiet, thinking about my family. "Don't you see?" Jana asked, "You have the power within you to decide what role your past will play in your future. You don't get to choose how you come into this world, but you can decide how to live out your life once you're here."

I tried to digest what Jana had just said. It made sense, but I still wasn't sure that I had a story. My family had a story, but I always felt excluded from it. I guessed that Andrew and Robbie probably did too.

"It's okay, Suzanne. Why don't you tell me about your family," Jana insisted. I kicked off my flip-flops and settled onto the blanket.

"Okay, but I am not sure what you want to know. Where do I start?" I asked.

"I find that it's always best to start at the beginning," Jana encouraged me.

That was easier said than done. I thought about our family history in the same way I thought about the history of man. Instead of B.C. and A.D., I categorized our family's past into two distinct eras, B.O. and A.O. That stood for, "Before Little Owen's death" and "After Little Owen's death." Andrew, Robbie and I fell into the, "After Little Owen's death" era.

For me, it seemed clear that his death was what shaped the story of our family, though the details surrounding his loss were fuzzy. Little Owen had died many years earlier, yet it was taboo to talk about it. What I knew of his death was learned from listening to people's conversations when they thought I wasn't listening.

For the next several hours, underneath the branches of the dying tree, I told Jana about my family. I spoke more in that one afternoon than I had in all the eight years of my life.

EIGHTEEN

Even though I knew Danny the least, I thought that since he was the oldest he was the most logical person to start with. Describing Danny was going to be a challenge and I worried that Jana might find it odd that I really didn't know my own brother. I decided not to dwell on the unknown; I'd focus instead on what I did know. Jana looked so eager to hear what I had to say and I didn't want to disappoint her. She had been so open and honest with me when talking about her family and it felt so good to share my story with her.

I often caught Danny staring at me. Not just staring-more like analyzing me. He did the same thing with Andrew and Robbie, but I doubted they ever noticed. It felt like he was observing us, trying to decide whether it was safe to engage with us or not. Danny's behavior reminded me of Marlin Perkins when he observed the animals featured on his weekly show, *Animal Kingdom*.

I loved *Animal Kingdom* and every Sunday I patiently waited for 7:00 p.m. for the show to air. Though the animals mesmerized me, I was even more intrigued by the show's host. He quietly yet patiently observed the animals in their natural habitats. And even when they weren't doing anything particularly exciting, he spoke as if they were. He was articulate and passionate about animals and to me he was amazing.

Danny was definitely like Marlin Perkins, a quiet observer. He was cautious around us three youngest and treated us as if we were priceless heirlooms-just looking, never touching. Danny was the oldest in the family and the one who had the most memories of Little Owen. He had waited patiently for years for a little brother. He loved my older sisters, but he had thought that it would be cool to have a brother, an ally.

When Little Owen died, Danny grew up fast. The first few days after his death, Danny was asked to do the craziest tasks by many seemingly sane people. He was only ten, but our aunt asked one night if he could drive her to the store so she could pick up some groceries. After many sleepless nights, the family doctor had prescribed pills to help Mom relax and sleep, and then some medication to help her get up and function in the mornings. He left the pills and instructions for taking the medication with Danny. He pulled him aside and warned, "Don't let her take too many. Sometimes women in these situations can lose their heads and take too much. These pills can be deadly." Danny was too young for such responsibilities, but being the oldest meant having things thrust onto him whether he was ready or not.

Danny was usually the first one to appear from his room each morning once our dad left for the day. All of us kids were responsible for completing chores around the house, but Danny was given the brunt of the work. He had so many more demands placed on him than his friends. For starters, he was not allowed to come and go as he pleased. When not at school, he was either working at the hardware store or mowing the lawns of almost every divorced, elderly and widowed woman who lived on our street. Sometimes they paid him, but sometimes they didn't. He was athletic, handsome and well-liked. Adults viewed Danny as responsible, a refreshing change from most teenagers at the time, who donned long hair, smoked weed and had no regard for authority or respect for their elders. In addition to his athleticism and good looks, Danny was a chameleon. He could quickly assess any situation and morph into the character he was required to play. He was a natural performer. His peers liked him because he was a sharp-tongued rebel who routinely pulled the wool over adults' eyes. Danny was the go-to guy when you needed booze or a forged parent signature.

But mostly people liked him because he made people feel safe and he had the gift of putting people at ease. The best thing about Danny was that he never asked for anything in return. He was an attention seeker who thrived on earning everybody's approval. But of course, the approval he earnestly and secretly sought after the most, and never achieved, was Dad's.

Although Danny more than earned Dad's praise, Dad refused to give it to him. That was the hardest thing for Danny to come to terms with - Dad's unwillingness to give people what they needed, even when he could more than afford to. Danny wasn't responsible for Little Owen's death, but he couldn't prevent it either and so he felt guilty. After Little Owen died, the distance between Danny and Dad became even wider. Danny couldn't do anything right and Dad spent even less time with him.

Danny was born ten months after our parents were married. He was granted the luxury of being the baby for only one year. It was the only time in his life that he was doted on by Mom and Dad, the only time he was not burdened with responsibility or guilt. The rest of us followed one after another for the next ten or so years, which forced him to resign his childhood and to take on the role of the big brother much too soon.

When Danny was 14, our Grandma Maddie (our mom's mother) gave him a photo album for his confirmation. It was a tradition that she had started with her own children and one that she decided to continue with her grandchildren. Danny was less than enthused when presented with his, but he politely accepted it and pretended to be excited. Other guys he knew received a little cash for their confirmation or were presented with one of those fancy bakery cakes decorated with thick, white, glittery frosting and a cutout paper cross. Danny didn't receive a cake or cash. As soon as mass was over, a few pictures were taken of him with his sponsor and our family went home. Once home we plopped down in front of the T.V. while Mom went to bed and Dad cracked open a beer. Danny went to his room and began thumbing through his album before going to bed. The black and white pictures were of Mom and her family. There were only a few pictures of Danny. In every picture Danny noticed that he wore either a scowl on his face or looked as if he had been crying. He concluded that the person taking the pictures was either clueless about photography, or he was just a miserable, worrisome kid. He suspected that both theories were probably true. Danny never remembered being allowed to be just a regular kid. He was constantly being reminded that he was the oldest, the one who needed to look out for everybody else, the one to make the sacrifices and the one to always do without.

To make matters worse, he and Ellen shared the same birthday. Mom only made one cake and Ellen was always the one who was allowed to pick out the cake that she wanted. "After all," Mom would remind him when he was still young enough to care and to complain about it, "She's your sister and you are older. I'm sorry, Danny but that's just how it is when you're the oldest. I know - I was the oldest. God rewards those who make the most sacrifices." If that were true, Danny believed that God owed him big time.

Jana was a thoughtful listener and remained quiet as I spoke about my brother. I stopped talking to eat some more food. This provided Jana with the opportunity to inquire about Little Owen's death.

"Suzanne, how did your brother, Little Owen die?" I didn't answer right away. "He died in an accident. I don't really know any of the details. I've tried asking, but all it does is make people sad or angry," I answered truthfully.

"Well, have you ever tried asking one of your older sisters? Sometimes sisters are easier to talk to than your mom or dad or brothers," Jana suggested.

"Hmm, you don't know my sisters. They're all so moody and they really don't care a thing about me. They love Andrew and Robbie because they're boys. I guess they figure that if they love them enough, then they won't die like Little Owen did," I answered.

"Suzanne, that's nonsense. Loving someone doesn't keep him or her from dying. If that were the case, both my dad and Clyde's parents would still be alive. Your sisters do love you and so do your parents," Jana assured me.

"I wouldn't be so sure. My parents used up all of their love on Little Owen," I said.

"You're wrong again, Suzanne," Jana continued, "Love doesn't work that way. They love all of you very much. They don't love any of you any more or less. None of you can take Little Owen's place because there was only one Little Owen. I love Clyde and my aunt and uncle, but that doesn't take the place of the love I have for my dad. Like I said, love doesn't work that way." Jana said. I looked at her in disbelief. Jana could tell that I wasn't ready to hear that. Someday, I would understand what Jana was trying to tell me, but not yet.

"Tell me about your sisters. I haven't really met any of them yet. From what I can tell you all look so much alike. I always wanted a sister," Jana said.

"Okay, but let me finish eating first. I am super hungry," I said shoving another cracker in my mouth.

Jana smiled, "Me too, but then again, I'm always hungry."

NINETEEN

Ellen came into our family one year to the day after Danny. People assumed that she was older than Danny because she had a seriousness about her that Danny lacked. Although Ellen, Anna, Patty and Margo were relatively close in age, they weren't as close as one might suspect. My four sisters couldn't have been any more different.

Ellen was fiercely private. She spent hours in her tiny room reading, and when she wasn't reading, she was working. She had friends, but lately she spent less and less time with them because they all had boyfriends. Ellen didn't have a boyfriend. There were many boys who were interested, but she had eyes for only one boy and he was off limits.

His name was Antoni Kowalski. Before entering high school, Ellen had been in the same class with Antoni every year since kindergarten. His mom and dad came to the United States with their families shortly after World War II.

His parents grew up in Poletown, in East Detroit and married quite young. For years they tried to have children, but could never conceive. After years of doctor visits, rosaries, and novenas, they took their doctor's advice and gave up. By then they were in their mid-forties and were too exhausted to think about adoption. On the day of her forty-sixth birthday, Mrs. Kowalski learned that she was pregnant.

Antoni was referred to as her "miracle baby" and everybody treated him as such. He was the baby Jesus in the Nativity Play for three years in a row at Holy Family Parish. By the third year, many parishioners felt that enough was enough. The little boy who played Joseph couldn't even carry him, and so instead he rode in on the back of a miniature donkey borrowed from a petting zoo. When the holy family approached the crèche, Antoni climbed off the donkey's back, walked to the crib and lay down in the trough where his legs hung over the sides. Many of the new moms were outraged that he was allowed to play the part again. People politely smiled as Mr. and Mrs. Kowalski beamed with pride. Many of the other, more cynical parishioners joked about the absurdity of a child that age and size playing the baby Jesus, "Better hang onto that donkey for the upcoming Passion Play. Antoni could reprise his role as Jesus when he rode into the city of Jerusalem," they joked.

Whether it was all of the praying everyone did for Antoni's conception or because of all the attention showered on him once he was born, Antoni was truly special. He was handsome, kind and deeply religious. Right around the time of his First Holy Communion, he announced that he was going to become a priest. His parents were so proud, but couldn't bear to send him away to a seminary school. They dutifully promised the Lord that their son would be his when he graduated high school. Ellen was head over heals in love with Antoni, but she never told anyone. She prayed every day that he would change his mind about becoming a priest and clung to the hope that someday she and Antoni would be together. For now, she had to be content just being his friend.

Antoni was someone that Ellen could depend on. He knew about her father's drinking and after Little Owen died, he was the only person who could console her. Antoni was very wise for his age and comforted Ellen with prayer and the promise that Little Owen was in heaven with the Lord.

Sometimes they would even pray together, but lately Ellen avoided Antoni because of the shame she felt from her own private prayers. Ellen, much like Danny, longed for independence. She loved her sisters, but resented always having to take care of them. She retreated to her room as much as possible. She was counting the days until she could leave and take care only of herself.

Anna was the third oldest and probably the one who was the closest to Danny. She and Margo shared a bedroom and Anna hated it. She felt that it was totally unfair that Ellen had a room of her own. Mom reminded her that Ellen's room was really nothing more than an oversized closet with a window, but Anna didn't care. Worse than having to share the room, the bed, and the closet with Margo, was being woken up every night by her screaming. Margo suffered from terrible nightmares.

Each night, like clockwork, Margo would sit upright in bed and scream as if someone was killing her. When it first started happening, everyone in the house would come running into the room. The room that Patty and I shared was separated from Anna and Margo's room only by a door jam, no door. The previous owners of the house had removed it and it sat in the basement covered by a sheet. Margo's screaming happened so frequently (sometimes even twice a night) that nobody came into the room anymore. Anna would silence her sister by jabbing her in the ribs and telling her to be quiet. The most annoying thing about her screaming was that Margo would fall right back to sleep within seconds. Ellen, Anna, Patty, and I would remain awake for what seemed like forever.

Anna was the most outgoing of all of the girls. She was wildly popular at school and was the captain of the pom-pom squad. When Holy Family School finally closed their doors, we had to transfer to the local public schools. Anna couldn't have been happier. She hated the uniforms and all of the silly rules. She held the record for the most uniform violations and had also gotten detention for smoking in the bathroom a couple of times. She could understand being written up for her uniform, she admitted to hiking her skirt up several inches higher than the regulation height in the student handbook, but found the detention sentence hypocritical, considering our priest was a smoker and even stood outside after mass smoking cigarettes.

Danny jokingly referred to her as, "The United Nations," on account of her eagerness to search out any and all students who were foreign, a different race or a religion other than Catholic. She liked people who were the most unlike our family. She was in heaven going to public school with all of the kids from all over the city, and Anna viewed religion as a waste of time. "After all," she would remind everyone when Mom wasn't within earshot, "What has God really ever done for us? He stole our baby brother; he strapped us with a dad who's a drunk and a raging lunatic, and placed us in this poor ass family where we are forced to live like hobos. I don't know about all of you, but as far as I'm concerned, he gave us the shaft."

"Anna, you shouldn't say things like that. God can hear you and you are being blasphemous," Patty would warn her.

"Ooh, I'm scared. What else can he do to me that he hasn't already done? Grow up, Patty. Why don't you and Antoni run off together and become the next Maria and Captain Von Trapp. You'd have to fight Ellen for him, though. But she's such a sissy. She'll never tell him how she feels about him. She'll stay pining away for him in her bedroom for the rest of her life. You're all so pathetic."

"Very funny, Anna! The only problem with your little scenario is Antoni wants to become a priest and Captain Von Trapp wasn't a priest. Your little joke doesn't even make sense."

"You're an idiot, Patty. My point is that you and Antoni are wasting your time with all that God crap. The two of you are perfect for each other," Anna would argue.

Anna always felt guilty after fighting with us. She loved us all very much, but couldn't stand how we never stood up to our dad. She viewed us as weak.

Anna was fearless when it came to Dad. Everybody else thought she was crazy and that she had some kind of death wish. She defied him constantly. He would tell her to be home as soon as the game she was cheering at was over, but she would come strolling through the front door four hours after the game, with beer on her breath as if she was right on time. He'd ask where she had been and without missing a beat she would reply, "There was a party after the game and my friends and I went for a little bit. What's the big deal?" Dad would go through the roof.

One night she came home reeking of marijuana. When he asked her if she was smoking dope, she answered him truthfully and then added how smoking weed was actually better for you than drinking alcohol. Her honesty and lack of fear is what enraged him the most. Anna paid dearly for her forthrightness. Over the last couple of years she had endured several beatings and survived them all. She was knocked down a flight of steps, thrashed into a china cabinet, and beaten with a belt.

When Dad couldn't find his belt, he'd use anything he could get his hands on - a broom, a cane, a flyswatter, a newspaper, it didn't matter - whatever he could grab would work. The backs of her legs were so badly bruised at times that she was forced to miss cheering at some of her games. It didn't matter how much he yelled or how badly he beat her, as soon as Anna was able to leave the house, she was back to doing whatever she wanted to do, damn the consequences.

As Jana listened to me talk about my sisters she wondered if they were all as observant as I was. "Do you talk about all of this stuff with your sisters? What do they say about your dad and his behavior?" she asked.

I stood up from the blanket and straightened out my shorts that were too tight and were creeping up my backside. "We don't really talk a lot. What's the point? We can't do anything about it anyway," I theorized.

"Boy, there are so many of you. I don't know if I can keep you all straight," Jana said.

"Well, we're all really different, that's for sure. Just look at Patty and Margo, people mix the two of them up all the time and they're complete opposites of each other," I informed her.

Patty and Margo were eleven months apart, but were in the same grade because Patty was held back in kindergarten. Joyce dressed them like twins and they were the only girls in the family who didn't have to share clothes. That was because there was such a big difference in their size. Patty was short and a little stocky. Margo was almost two inches taller and lithe. She had the body of a ballerina and even carried herself like one. She would have loved to dance, but taking any kind of class that required tuition was out of the question. There simply wasn't any extra money for stuff like that. If we couldn't participate in the activity through school or if it wasn't a free class offered at the community center, we didn't do it.

When Margo and Patty were younger, they slept in the small room off the kitchen. It was one of two bedrooms on the first floor of the house (the other being our parents'). It was tradition that the baby stayed in our parents' room and the next two youngest stayed in the room closest to them. It was easier for Mom when one of the younger ones woke in the middle of the night sick or from a bad dream. The girls liked being close to our mom and dad when they were little.

The early morning hours, between three and four a.m., was Margo's favorite time of the day. The house was quiet except for the faint hum of people breathing. Margo had never been a good sleeper. She fell asleep quickly, but often woke three or four hours later plagued with fear. Sometimes she woke up in other parts of the house, but had no memory of how she got there. Mom said she was a sleep-walker, as though this were a perfectly normal thing. Margo never recalled walking to different places in the house, but she had a strange feeling that she flew around the house at night and sometimes to places that she didn't recognize. She never told Mom about her flying theory (though she told the rest of us about it) because she assumed that she had been dreaming and thought nothing more of it. Sometimes she woke up in the middle of the night soaking wet with sweat. She felt anxious and worried and would have a difficult time falling back to sleep.

Shortly after Little Owen was born, she discovered that her insomnia now brought with it an unexpected gift.

It was during those bouts of insomnia that her ritual with Little Owen began. Margo loved her baby brother from the moment she saw him. Their eyes locked when our mother first gently laid him in her lap. No one else had noticed, but Margo felt a bolt of electricity had just surged through her body. In that single, short gaze, Margo knew that the two of them were soul mates that would forever share a very strong bond. Later she learned this connection they shared was so strong, not even death could sever it.

The crinkling of the plastic crib sheet was the first sound Margo waited for each morning. Once in a while, he would twist and turn a bit and it would turn out to be a false alarm, before finding his thumb. The gentle sucking of his thumb would allow him to fall back asleep for at least another ten or fifteen minutes. To be safe, Margo would not go to him until she heard his familiar, soft cry. His cry sounded like the call of a mourning dove far off in the distance. Having had so many children, it took a little more urgency and volume before our mom awakened.

Upon hearing his cooing, Margo would then have to act with precision and skill to get to him without waking anyone up. First, she had to untangle herself from Patty. Once she escaped her bed unnoticed, she would have to make it in and out of our parents' bedroom without waking them. She wouldn't have gotten in trouble for taking care of him. Our exhausted mother was thankful for the help. Margo just wanted to have him all to herself.

Margo tiptoed through our parents' open bedroom door and across the room to the changing table. There she gathered the items she needed for Little Owen before crossing over to his crib. The list of supplies was long, but necessary: two cloth diapers, a pair of plastic pants, a fresh undershirt, baby powder and diaper cream.

As she approached his crib, her heart would begin to fill with excitement. She felt nothing but pure, uncomplicated love for her little brother. She would look down upon him adoringly, but not for long. She'd lower the side of the crib so she could scoop him up quickly so that his cries did not grow any louder. Lifting him was hard, considering that she was so little herself, but she managed. She'd clumsily lift him up and out of the crib using a little potty chair as a stool. She had to be careful not to drop him or any of his supplies. He wasn't very heavy, but his head was still floppy, which made it difficult for her to carry him. Once she had safely retrieved him from the crib, she carried him down the hall and into the family room. Margo would then spread a blanket on the floor and set him down lovingly. As she knelt over him to change his diaper, he would reach up and pull her long, sun streaked hair. This always caused her to smile and Margo would stop to take in the tender interaction that their secret morning rendezvous allowed. Little Owen would smile up at her and her heart would melt. She would lift him up into her arms. Lost in love, she didn't notice the absence of his diaper or worry about the possibility that he could spring an unexpected leak. She drew him closely to her chest, being careful to support his head and neck. Margo would then inhale the most wonderful smell she knew, the smell of a baby.

He smelled of baby powder, formula and something so magical that she couldn't tell just what it was. His hair was blond and curled gently around his face and the back of his neck. She would gently nibble on his ears and cheeks before placing him back down on the blanket to resume changing him. Once he was redressed, she would scurry to the kitchen to make his bottle while he waited on the living room floor.

There was a small plastic container in the refrigerator filled with enough formula for two or three feedings. After filling a coffee mug with hot tap water, she would dig out a bottle, a cap, and a nipple from the wire rack that sat next to the sink. She'd carefully fill the bottle with formula and secure the lid. She then placed it in the cup of hot water in order to take the chill off of it. That is how he liked it the best. Sometimes, when she was in a hurry, Mom would skip this last step. (Margo didn't understand why she did that because she would inevitably end up having to warm it up. Owen would squirm around and pop the nipple in and out of his mouth to show his displeasure with the cold meal.) Margo would return to the family room and slide into the soft, broken-down armchair and gently cradle Owen in her arms. As she fed him his breakfast, the two of them would lock eyes just as they did that first day he was brought home. Margo would hum very softly and begin to sway back in forth in the chair. Shortly, Little Owen's eyes would begin to grow heavy and his long lashes would flutter.

It was when his mouth formed a perfect "O" and the sweet formula began to trickle down his chin and pool into the folds of his neck, that Margo knew that he had fallen back to sleep. She wiped his chin and neck and made her way back to our parents' room. She returned him to the safety and security of his crib. Before she left, she would reach into his crib and touch his chubby little hand. He would release a small sigh of contentment and sleep for another hour or two before the rest of the house woke. Margo would slip back into bed with Patty and she too would fall into a deep, peaceful sleep.

If a person were speaking about either Patty or Margo, they would inevitably start speaking about the other one. They were eleven months apart, but people always assumed they were twins. They would say, "You two are twins, right? Not identical, but the other kind." This drove Margo nuts. They didn't look a lot alike and Margo was quite a bit taller than Patty. The best she could figure is that people thought they were twins because they were in the same grade, they were both girls and Mom dressed them alike. Danny and Ellen never got mistaken for twins even though they too were in the same grade. Danny started school late and then was retained the year that Little Owen died. Whatever the reason people had for thinking they were twins, it really made Margo angry. It didn't really bother Patty. Nothing ever really bothered Patty. Secretly, Margo was envious of Patty for that very reason. Patty never worried about anything and nothing made her too upset.

If Margo failed a test, she would cry and stew over it for days. If Patty didn't do well on a test, she would act surprised and say something like, "Really? I didn't pass it? That's interesting, because I studied. Oh well, I guess I'll have to study a little more the next time."

Like most kids, from time to time Margo and Patty would misplace something. Margo would search for hours for her missing item and would make herself sick with worry about not being able to find it. She would get sick to her stomach, sometimes even throwing up. Her head would hurt so badly that she would have to lie down and she would fall asleep with exhaustion and worry. The minute her eyes reopened, she would go back to frantically searching for whatever it was that she couldn't find. Most of the time, she never found what she was looking for. Patty was just the opposite. If she lost something, she would simply say, "I am sure it's bound to show up at some point," or she would recite the *Saint Anthony* prayer four or five times and then go back to doing whatever it was she was doing. She didn't even continue looking for it when she was done reciting the prayers. Nine times out of ten, it would just show up somewhere or someone would say, "Hey Patty! Is this yours?" holding up whatever item she had lost. Patty would then say, "Oh, yeah. I was looking for that."

One time Patty lost the gold cross that our Aunt Janice, who was her godmother, gave her for her first communion. While eating breakfast she casually mentioned the misplaced cross to Mom. Mom was furious and told her not to stop looking for it until she found it. Patty promised that she would, but once she was done eating, she just ran outside to play. A little later in the day, Mom took Patty and Margo over to our grandparent's for the afternoon so that she could take us younger kids for our shots.

After playing for a little bit, grandma suggested that they eat some lunch. She was always suggesting that we eat something. That was one of the reasons we loved going to Grandma Maddie and Grandpa Will's house. On the rare occasion that all of us kids (or even just one or two of us) spent the night, food was the center of our visits.

If we were watching television after dinner our grandma would say,

"Wouldn't some popcorn go good with this show?" When it was raining and we couldn't play in their backyard, she would pull out the deep fryer and say something like, "There is nothing better than doughnut holes on a rainy day."

Our Grandma Maddie always had the best food. We couldn't wait for her to announce that she was going to lie down for a little nap. Once we knew she was asleep, we'd go into her kitchen and marvel at all the food in the pantry. The pantry was always filled with chips, store bought cookies, crackers and candy. We hardly ever had chips at our house, only on special occasions, and she often brought them out to eat when we were playing board games. "I don't eat a lot of chips," she would explain, "but I like to have them when I have company. You've got to have chips when you play *Parcheesi* or *Monopoly*. Don't you agree?" We never understood the connection between eating chips and playing games, but we didn't care.

So while Margo and Patty were eating lunch that day, our Grandma Maddie wiped her mouth and asked, "Would either of you girls be interested in this?" She placed a gold necklace with a little cross attached to it on the kitchen table, "I found this on the sidewalk a couple of weeks ago and thought one of you girls might like it."

Patty said, "Grandma, I think that necklace is mine. I was just looking for it this morning. I remember now that I wore it over here a couple of Sundays ago when I came home with you after church." Patty was excited to have it back, but not overly surprised that Grandma found it.

"Now imagine that. What are the chances?" Grandma said shaking her head in disbelief. "Be sure to put it on or put it in your pocket, Patty, so you don't lose it again," she suggested.

"I will, Grandma. Thanks for finding it for me. Mom will be so happy," Patty wrapped her arms around our grandma's thick waist. When she was finished eating her lunch, she wiped her mouth, pushed in her chair and took off from the table, leaving the necklace right where Grandma had placed it.

Food wasn't the only reason Patty and the rest of us loved going to our grandparents' house. We liked going there because their house was calm. Grandma and Grandpa always took the time to explain things to us. They were always so patient and hardly ever got mad about anything. Grandpa was retired and was content doing a whole lot of nothing.

Everyday after she ate lunch, Grandma Maddie would go into her bedroom to say a rosary. No matter who was over or what she was doing, she would stop around one o'clock in the afternoon to complete her daily prayers. If we were over she would ask, "Who wants to go with grandma and say a quick rosary?" Most of the kids would decline the invitation, but Patty never did.

"I will, Grandma," Patty would dutifully respond.

"Well, come on. Grandma would like to get a little nap in before it is time to start making dinner," she'd explain. Patty would follow her into the room and wait while she grabbed one of her many spare rosaries out of an old shoebox, where she stored her jewelry and important documents. She would draw the curtains and dim the lights. Then she would take a pillow off the bed and place it on the floor to kneel on. She'd turn to whichever grandchild was with her that day and say, "Grandma has old knees. You are young enough that you don't need a pillow." If you protested, she would calmly remind you of the ultimate sacrifice that Jesus made and then you'd feel like a schmuck for not only disappointing Jesus, but more importantly, disappointing Grandma by being so selfish.

Before she began, she would acknowledge all of the people for whom she was praying. Sometimes this part would take five to ten minutes because not only did she acknowledge each person by name, but she would also explain why she was praying for him or her. She prayed for people who were sick, for those who had lost a job and were trying to find work, for people who no longer went to church and for those who did go to church but didn't take the time for daily prayer. Sometimes she would stop and go into great detail over why a particular person needed her prayers. It was all very interesting, especially to Patty. Grandma always took the time before the praying started to ask the person who was with her if they needed to pray for anyone or anything in particular. Patty's response was always the same, "I am praying for my dad to stop drinking." Grandma never commented, but just offered that request up as well.

From a young age, Patty never underestimated the power of prayer and like her grandmother, always looked for the good in people. That was another way Margo and Patty differed. Margo believed in holding people accountable; Patty naively believed that people always tried to do their best and when they fell short, that you should cut them some slack. Margo would argue, "Yes Patty, we should accept that people are not perfect and that they are doing their very best, but when they're not, we shouldn't make excuses for them." Patty didn't agree with Margo, but that was because Patty didn't always do her best and she knew it. Patty liked whatever was easy, even if it didn't yield the results she wanted. She would then try to rationalize it by saying, "I guess it was not meant to be."

Margo would shake her head and say, "It's not that it wasn't meant to be, it is that you didn't try. You didn't give it your all."

"Que Sera, Sera, whatever will be, will be," Patty would sing and go on her way. Even after Little Owen died, Patty never gave up on prayer. As a matter of fact, she prayed even more. She prayed so much that she forgot that she too had some say in her prayers being answered by the effort that she put into things. If she had a big test, she prayed, but didn't bother studying. If she felt that she was looking a little chubby, she wouldn't diet; she would pray that she would lose weight and then keep eating everything she wanted. What angered Margo the most about Patty was how she made excuses for our dad.

TWENTY

By the time I'd finished talking about my sisters, it was starting to get dark. Jana didn't want to upset my mom by keeping me out for too long. We had only just met and she didn't want to be overstepping her boundaries.

"I think we should be getting you home, Suzanne, but I had a really nice time today. Other than Clyde, you're the only friend I have here in Michigan," Jana said. I loved that Jana referred to me as a friend.

"I like having you for a friend, too," I replied.

"The next time we get together, you'll have to finish telling me about the rest of your family," Jana suggested.

"There's not much more to tell," I said.

"Well, you didn't tell me anything about your mom and dad or your other brothers," Jana reminded me, "and most importantly you didn't tell me anything about yourself."

I looked down and pretended to brush imaginary crumbs off the front of my shirt. I felt there wasn't much to say on that topic, because my life was pretty boring.

"Well, I'm ready to go," I said.

The sounds and smells of the carnival a few blocks away followed us home. Jana stopped in front of my house and, in the middle of our goodbyes, Clyde pulled up in his truck. When he got out, Jana let go of the wagon and ran over to him. She jumped on his back and kissed him several times on the cheek.

"Hey! That's my kind of greeting after a long day of work," he laughed.

"Hi Clyde! How are ya?" I called over.

"I'm great, Suzanne. Where have the two of you been?" he asked.

"We spent the afternoon in the park, getting to know one another," Jana explained. Clyde smiled because he knew sitting in the park and shooting the breeze with someone was right up Jana's alley.

"Are you hungry?" she asked Clyde.

"A little bit," he answered.

"Well, I still have some snacks in the basket here. Shall we?" she offered.

"Yeah. How about I grab a couple of beers and we enjoy this front porch - soon the Petersons will be moving in and we won't have it to ourselves," Clyde said.

"Well, good night then," I said as I began searching for our hidden key, which was stashed under one of the creek rocks that lined either side of the stairs.

"You don't have to run off, Suzanne. Stay and hang out for a little bit," Clyde said.

"Okay!" I decided. I ran over and joined Jana on the front porch while Clyde grabbed a couple of folding chairs, a few beers and a pop for me. None of the other kids were home and I really didn't want to hang out with my mom at my grandma's.

We sat on the front porch, while I filled them in on all of the different neighbors. "Have you met the people who live in the green house on the corner?" I asked referring to the "hippie house," as all the kids called it.

"Yeah, as a matter of fact we did," he said. "They're cool people. They've invited us over for a cookout. You should come. There are a couple of kids living there that you might enjoy hanging out with."

I knew who Clyde was talking about. Spring and Wood went to my school. I thought that they were kind of weird, but I didn't tell Clyde that. Spring was in third grade and Wood was in fourth grade. They kept mostly to themselves. They too were vegetarians and brought weird food for lunch. Even stranger than their food, were their clothes and appearance. From a distance, they looked like girls. Spring's hair was long and it flowed freely about his face.

When Andrew first saw him he said, "What the heck! What's that kid's problem? He looks like he has a rat's nest in his hair." Andrew was not a fan of hippies. Wood also had long hair, but he wore his in a ponytail. He never wore jeans and football jerseys like other boys. Instead he wore pants that looked like they were made out of potato sacks. He also wore strange shirts that were made out of the same material as the Mexican blankets that all the hippies had. Every day he showed up at school wearing big, bulky shirts, even when it was warm outside. When he was gallivanting around the neighborhood, he was usually shirtless. He was sort of small for his age. Mom theorized that he was small because he was a vegetarian. She warned all of us kids that "stunted growth" was what happened when you deprived your body of meat.

He got in trouble in gym class because every time he had to run quickly, his sandals would fall off. The gym teacher told him that he wouldn't be able to participate in gym if he didn't have tennis shoes. The next day, he came into gym class wearing tennis shoes that were clearly girls' shoes. Some of the kids made fun of him. Andrew took pity on him and picked him to be on his kickball team. Later, after school, Andrew left an old pair of his shoes on his porch.

I told Clyde that I would have to wait and see about going to the cookout. I liked hanging out with Clyde and Jana, but wasn't so sure about hanging out with their new friends. Clyde plugged in a little radio that he had brought down to the porch. They stopped talking and just listened to the music. When a song came on that they liked, Clyde and Jana smiled at each other and started singing along with it. "Gosh, I love this song," Jana said. She stood up and grabbed Clyde's hands. Together they started dancing on the front porch.

I liked the song too. Danny, Ellen, and Anna listened to it over and over again when Danny first brought home the album.

"Come on, Suzanne. Don't be shy," Clyde said. He pulled me up out of my chair and spun me around a couple of times before all three of us started dancing. As we were sashaying around on the porch, my dad's truck pulled up in front of the house.

I didn't hear his truck, but I saw him getting out of it. He began walking our way and I abruptly stopped dancing. Clyde and Jana didn't notice and continued singing, "Levon sells cartoon balloons in town."

My dad reached the porch and cleared his throat, "Uh, hello! Can I talk to the two of you for a minute?" he asked. He wasn't sure if they heard him until Clyde turned down the music and looked in his direction.

"You're Suzanne's dad. It's nice to meet you," Jana said as she extended her hand to my dad. "I'm Jana and this here is my husband, Clyde."

My dad shook both of their hands, "I wanted to come over and apologize about last night. I had a little too much to drink and things got out of hand." Not sure what else to say he asked, "So, what parts are the two of you from? How do you like the upstairs apartment?"

"We like it just fine, thanks," Clyde answered. "It needs a little work, but you know how it is - we hate to invest in the place too much since we're just renting."

I wished Clyde hadn't said that. My dad was probably thinking, "Yeah, I know how you hippies are. You move in, trash the joint and then move on and do the same thing somewhere else."

Instead he said, "I get it. But if you need anything, I've got a lot of tools and am pretty handy."

"We've really enjoyed getting to know Suzanne. She's a real sweetheart and your wife, Joyce is really nice too," Jana added.

My dad looked at me and gave me a questioning smile. He had no idea how much time I had already spent with them. "Yeah, she's a quiet one, but she's a good girl. I never have any problems with Suzanne," he explained. That was probably the nicest thing that I had ever heard my dad say about me.

"What do you do for a living, Clyde?" my dad asked.

"Well, right now I'm working on the assembly line at Ford. I'm going to be taking some night classes to get my boiler's license," he explained. "School has never really been for me, and so it'll be a challenge. I am good with my hands and just don't think all that 9-to-5 office stuff is for me."

"Ain't nothing wrong with a little hard work," Owen assured him. "I'm a welder myself. Sometimes I have to work in the shop, but on most days, I'm outside enjoying the fresh air. If you ever have any questions about welding, I'm the man to ask," Owen said proudly.

"I will, sir, thanks," Clyde said shaking his hand.

"Call me Owen," he told him. He walked back over to Jana and shook her hand again.

"Well, Suzanne, we'd better get on home," he said.

I didn't want to leave, but figured things had gone pretty smoothly so far and I didn't want to jinx it. Before we left, my dad turned to Clyde and said, "No offense, but you might want to rethink that long hair of yours. I don't want to tell you what to do, but those union guys aren't going to appreciate you wearing your hair like a girl. Plus, it gets a little hot with your welding hood on."

Clyde just smiled and said, "No offense taken. I'll take your advice into consideration." Jana waved goodbye as my dad and I headed home.

"He doesn't seem too bad," Clyde said once we were out of earshot.

"No he doesn't, Clyde. Everybody has his or her problems. At least he and Joyce are willing to stick it out for the sake of all of those kids," Jana said. Clyde knew that Jana's last comment was more about her own parents and not so much about Owen and Joyce's relationship.

When Danny, Ellen and Anna came home later that night from the carnival, my dad was already in bed. He knew that he was in the wrong and the fact that he did not confront them was tacit admittance of his guilt. They were thankful just to be able to come home and go to bed. They had managed to get through the day, but they were exhausted. Once home, each of them privately recalled the unpleasant events of the night before. They took a cue from their parents, however, and didn't discuss it amongst themselves.

When Mom came home the next day from her parents' with Andrew and Robbie, no words about the incident were exchanged between her and Dad. We all went about our business as usual, until later in the evening, when Dad dropped a bombshell.

"I know that we usually go home in July, but I think we should go home now," he said. He always referred to our yearly summer trip to his family home as "going home." "My dad isn't doing well. Susie called earlier today and she's afraid that he doesn't have a lot of time. He just can't seem to shake the pneumonia he got earlier in the spring. I'm afraid if we wait until later in the summer to go see him, it might be too late. Besides, I think we could all use a little break."

Anna rolled her eyes and said under her breath, "All thanks to you." The older kids were outraged. There were only two weeks of school left and it was Danny and Ellen's senior year. They objected, and to their surprise, Dad suggested that Danny, Ellen, and Anna might be old enough to stay home by themselves. At first, Mom said that they couldn't stay home alone, but Dad assured her that between her parents and sisters, his sister and brother-in-law, and Clyde and Jana that there were enough people around who could check in on them.

Margo and Patty didn't want to go either, but Dad wouldn't hear of leaving them behind. He argued that we really didn't do anything the last few weeks of school and promised that we'd be back in time for the last week. It was settled; it would be a short trip. We would leave early Tuesday morning and come home on Sunday. Andrew and Robbie were excited to go, but I wasn't so sure. I didn't want to leave Jana and Clyde. When mom walked over to talk to them about keeping an eye on the oldest three, I went with her. Jana said that she would be more than happy to help out and tried getting me excited about the trip.

"Suzanne, it'll be an adventure. You'll be able to see your family and, look on the bright side, you'll get to miss a few days of school," Jana said.

"But what will you do without me?" I asked.

"You're sweet! I'll be fine. Let's see, what will I do? Well, I've been wanting to put in my garden. I've also been thinking about looking into taking some classes myself, and now that we're pretty much settled, I need to look for a job," Jana said.

I felt conflicted. I loved spending time with Jana, but I also enjoyed spending time with my dad's family. Visiting them was like traveling back in time. We only got to see them once a year, unless someone in the family passed. The last time we had gone to see his family, other than our annual summer trip, was when his sister, our Aunt Donette died of cancer. That was a horrible trip.

Funerals down south are so different than funerals up in Michigan. I don't know if it's because we're Catholic and they're mostly Baptist, but whatever the reason, they're not at all alike. Catholic funerals are quiet and subdued. Baptist funerals are loud and dramatic.

I felt real sad that my aunt died, but after one night at the funeral home, I was a nervous wreck and couldn't wait for the whole thing to be over with. There was no rosary, just a lot of talking and sobbing and people kissing her while she lay dead in the casket. Several people passed out in the midst of telling her goodbye. I thought it was because of the heat, but Ellen said it was because they were so overcome with emotion.

I'd never been at a cemetery where you actually got to see the casket getting lowered into the ground. That part was a little scary. Just as the casket began to descend, my aunt's oldest daughter lunged forward and tried hopping into the grave along with it. Several people had to pull her back. No sooner had the pastor gotten her quieted down than my Aunt Donette's no-good husband who hadn't been seen since the summer of '61 showed up drunker than a skunk. I had never met him before and had to ask my mom what his name was.

"I don't know what his Christian name is," she said after thinking about it a second or two, "everybody just always called him Boney because he's always been so skinny."

I found out later that he was also called that because he could never hold down a job, so he was always hanging around and looking for handouts, content with just the scraps. "He's always been like a nasty, old scavenger bird," Aunt Susie said later. "Too darn lazy to hunt himself, content to pick the bones clean of another animal's discarded carcass."

"Well I'll be," our Aunt Martha cried, "What the hell is that fool doing here?"

The funny thing about my dad's family is that the men manage to keep their cool during a crisis a little better than the women. Once my aunts get riled up, look out. When they saw Boney come stumbling across the cemetery to show his respects, a couple of them took off after him. One of them pulled a gun out of her pocketbook and threatened to blow his head off if he didn't clear out. Thank goodness someone convinced her to put the gun away for the sake of all the children present. They had him licked pretty good before my dad and our Uncle Sam pulled them off of him and told him to just get on home.

On Monday after school, I stopped over to say goodbye to Jana. We usually left at about four in the morning, which meant we arrived in the hills just in time for dinner. Jana was in the kitchen putting away groceries when I knocked on the door.

"Come on in, Suzanne," Jana yelled from behind the refrigerator door.

"Hey, Jana," I said as I walked into the kitchen and made a beeline to the kitchen table, where fresh bread was cooling on a wire rack.

"Are you hungry? I just pulled a couple of loaves of bread out of the oven," Jana offered. I was hungry, but I didn't want Jana to think that I was a little pig.

"No thanks," I said hesitantly. "I already had a snack."

"Are you all packed for your trip?" Jana inquired. I hadn't packed, but packing was a breeze. The family only had one suitcase, which Mom used for her and Dad's clothes. None of us had a lot of clothes, so packing for a trip didn't take long. We just threw three or four pairs of underwear, a few shirts and pairs of shorts and a pair of jeans in a brown paper bag that Mom brought home from the A & P. The only toiletries we packed were our toothbrushes that we tossed in the bottom of our bags.

"Yeah, I'm packed," I answered. It was easier to say that than to reveal the embarrassing truth about our lack of clothing and suitcases.

Jana finished putting all of the food away and retrieved the toaster from the cupboard next to the sink. She sliced a few pieces of bread and placed them in the toaster. She reached into the refrigerator and pulled out a container of strawberry freezer jam that she had brought with her from Baltimore. When the toast popped up, she slathered each piece with butter and jam and placed the toast in front of me. I didn't object and started eating. "Wow, Jana, this is the best bread I've ever had," I told her.

Jana smiled and asked, "Are you getting excited about leaving for your trip in the morning?"

"I am, but..." I started to explain, but wasn't sure if I should tell Jana. She might think that our family was even weirder than she already did. I decided to trust her. "Jana, remember when I told you how my brother died in an accident? Well, he died in North Carolina. It was when my family was down there for the decoration."

"What's a decoration?" Jana asked.

"Well, it's something that people in the south do. It's when all of the family gets together and they put flowers on the graves of their loved ones. After everyone gets back from the cemetery, they eat. It's kind of like a family reunion," I explained, the best that I could. "Anyway," I continued, "he died during one of those trips. I'm thinking about asking my Aunt Susie to tell me what happened. What do you think I should do, Jana?"

I felt so confused. I wanted to know what happened to my brother, but in a way, I was afraid to know the whole story. Death scared me. Once I had asked my grandma, "If dying and being in heaven with God is such a wonderful thing, why do all of the people who are still living feel so sad that the person has died?" My grandma was always so patient when responding to her grandkids' questions. When she explained death to me, it all made perfect sense. Death didn't seem so scary. But later, when I was alone, my grandma's explanation no longer comforted me. Death seemed like a punishment. Not for the person who died, but for all of the people who were left behind.

Jana sensed my anxiety. "Suzanne, as scary as it may be for you to know the truth, I think that you'll feel much better once you do," Jana said.

Jana never had the opportunity to talk to her dad about her mom leaving and she shared that it was one of her biggest regrets. I didn't comment, but kept eating my toast. When I finished, I placed my plate in the sink and told Jana goodbye.

"Suzanne," Jana called, "come here and give me a hug goodbye."

I wrapped my arms around Jana and she kissed the top of my head. "You take care of yourself and have a good trip. I want to hear all about it when you get back," she whispered.

TWENTY ONE

The next morning, Mom woke us at 3:30. We threw on our clothes, grabbed our pillows and piled into the station wagon. Margo, Patty, and Andrew sat in the back seat. The third row of seats folded down flat and that is where the cooler and anything else that couldn't fit in the stow-away section was kept. Mom covered the hard plastic with a thick down blanket for Robbie and me to lie on. It didn't take long for Andrew to flip over the seat and join us. The three of us fell back asleep quickly.

Dad never turned the radio on for the first couple of hours of the trip. He smoked cigarettes and drank coffee while Mom enjoyed the silence and looked out the window. By the time the sun came up, the three of us were awake. Margo and Patty were finally able to get comfortable sitting straight up and fell asleep.

Robbie brought with him a little tote bag filled with dinosaurs, toy soldiers, and his *Matchbox* cars. He rested on his stomach and played a game in which soldiers were attacking dinosaurs. Andrew brought along all of his baseball cards and a little notebook, which held all of his favorite players' stats. He flipped back over to the middle section and wedged himself back in between Margo and Patty and thumbed through his notebook.

I brought a few small things to entertain myself, but the thirteen-hour car ride was the perfect time to daydream and make up stories about me, Clyde and Jana. I imagined what it would be like if we had an excursion at the beach. I envisioned Jana wearing a bright yellow bikini and large, round sunglasses. She'd also wear a big, floppy hat because she was fair and didn't want to sunburn. I would wear a bikini too, but mine would be bright pink and covered with polka dots. Mom didn't let us girls wear bikinis. She thought they were immodest.

In this scenario, I wouldn't have my chubby stomach and I'd be thin and tall like Jana. Jana would pack an extra special picnic basket with all of the food that I loved. Our favorite songs would come on the radio and we would sing and dance along with the music right on the beach. I remembered that Clyde and Jana were vegetarians, but in my fantasy, the three of us wouldn't be able to resist the delicious hotdogs that a man on the beach was selling. The vendor wore white pants and a red and white striped shirt. His cart would be parked right next to where we were sitting. After eating, Clyde and I would bury Jana in the sand up to her neck. When we were finished, Jana would do the same thing to Clyde and me.

We would be having so much fun that a woman walking by would ask Clyde and Jana, "Would you like me to take a picture of the two of you with your little girl?" Nobody would correct her and say that we weren't really a family; we would just let her take the picture and assume that Clyde and Jana were my parents. I loved these long car trips and never grew tired of making up stories in my head.

At about noon, Dad suggested that we stop at a rest area to eat and stretch our legs. When he opened the back hatch door to the wagon, Robbie and I climbed out so he could get the cooler. We found an empty picnic table and sat down. Andrew and Robbie ran around a little bit waiting for Mom to pull out the sandwiches and chips she had bought especially for the trip. Patty and Margo went to the restroom only after promising Mom 100 times that they would be careful, "Perverts hang out at rest stops, girls. You always need to keep your wits about you," she preached.

Mom poured us each a cup of Kool-Aid and began opening the sandwiches that were wrapped in wax paper. "Andrew, I made a ham and cheese and for you, Robbie, a bologna with nothing on it," she explained. "Suzanne, honey, what kind would you like? I have bologna, ham, and peanut butter and jelly. You pick."

"Well, I am trying not to eat as much meat, so how about the peanut butter and jelly," I proudly answered. Mom let out an exasperated sigh and handed me the sandwich. Margo and Patty picked out their own sandwiches. Dad crushed out his cigarette and sat down at the table. Mom handed him a paper plate with two sandwiches and a handful of plain potato chips.

"Hey, can we have some chips?" Patty asked.

"Once you've all eaten your sandwich. I don't want you filling up on chips," she scolded.

"Fat chance of that happening, there are only two small bags of chips and seven people," Andrew complained.

"Just eat, Andrew," she responded.

I was still hungry after eating my first sandwich. "Can I have another sandwich?" I asked. Mom handed me another peanut butter and jelly, but I hesitated. "Maybe this time I'll try a bologna." Mom smiled, because she knew that my dedication to not eating meat would be short lived.

"Well, everybody go to the bathroom one last time before we leave," Dad instructed. Nobody was ready to get back in the car, but we knew the sooner we left, the sooner we would reach our destination. I could see that Dad was eager to see his family. After all, he only saw them once or twice a year.

I liked our dad so much more when we went on these trips. He was always calmer and even a little playful. When we got in the car, he turned on the country radio station and said, "Now this is real music." Once in a while when a song came on that he knew all of the words to, he would sing along.

"Dad, can I come up and sit with you and mom?" Patty asked.

"Yea, you can come up for a little bit," he answered. Patty carefully slipped over the seat and sat next to our parents. Patty liked country music too and the three of them sang together. Margo hated country music and tried wedging her head between her and Patty's pillows to block out the noise. Finally she gave up and started writing in her diary.

The rest of the trip was pretty uneventful. We slept on and off throughout the day and found ways to stay entertained. As soon as we reached the mountains, Dad rolled down all the windows and slowed down significantly.

Margo, who was prone to getting carsick, quickly grew nauseous from the winding hills. Andrew and Robbie loved the snaking road and viewed the curves as the best part of the entire trip. When we crossed the bridge that extended over the creek to our Aunt Martha and Uncle Sheldon's property, all us kids closed our eyes. We always feared that somehow Dad would misjudge how narrow the bridge was and we'd end up going off the side.

I had been thinking about my decision to ask my Aunt Susie about Little Owen's death, and finally committed to it just as we crossed over the Tennessee border. Jana was right, I could spend several more years trying to piece the story together or I could come out and ask the one person who I knew would tell me the whole truth, no matter how sad it was.

TWENTY TWO

Every summer Dad made the thirteen-hour trip home with our family to see his brothers and sisters and aging father. He was never particularly close to his dad, but he clung to the hope that some day they could reconcile the past. By the time we were all born, our grandpa was a tired old man, too beaten down by life to fight with his son anymore. He was no longer full of the "piss and vinegar" he was when our dad was a boy. The two of them eventually settled into a cordial relationship even though no apologies were made and no forgiveness was ever formally extended.

Grandpa no longer drank, so when Dad went back home, he didn't drink either. By leaving the mountains and being able to achieve a little monetary success, my dad gained perspective on life. By staying put, his family's life was never altered and as a result their world stayed small and they grew more and more bitter about their past, which wasn't that much better than their present.

Dad had been born and raised in a log cabin that was now over a hundred years old. It had been moved three times before permanently settling in the spot where he and his siblings were raised. Nobody had resided in the cabin for years, but it was still habitable.

In the corner of the large living space was a potbelly stove. In the winter it burned steadily, keeping all the rooms toasty warm and leaving the contents of the house smelling like a campfire. A good size bedroom and kitchen made up the rest of the lower level. The cracked linoleum floor, which was once dirt, was covered with a thin worn rug. Sheer white curtains covered both the front window and the other larger window behind the rickety old couch.

Layers of newspaper and faded wallpaper covered the interior exposed logs and gave the walls a spongy texture, like papier-mâché. The outside logs were packed with mud from the creek bank. In this mud is where the mysterious mud bees lived. My family in the mountains called them mud bees, but they were also known as miner bees or chimney bees. Their constant thrumming was the soundtrack of cabin life.

A handmade ladder rested against an inside wall and was used to reach the loft, which housed four queen-sized beds. There was one window in the loft area. In the hot, summer months it provided some relief for those forced to sleep up there. The cabin did not have a bathroom, but there was an outhouse and a chamber pot for when nature called in the middle of the night. There was running water in the kitchen and, miraculously, the old stove and refrigerator still worked. A white metal Hoosier Cabinet rested against the wall and was the only real storage in the kitchen.

Years earlier our Aunt Martha and her husband, Sheldon had a new house built down in front of the creek. Our Grandpa Doward had refused to move into the house at first, but eventually conceded. After about a year he grew tired of having to walk down to the new house every time he wanted to eat or engage in a little conversation.

When the entire family congregated at the old homestead, there wasn't enough room for everyone to be put up in the new house, which is where most of the adults preferred to stay. One or two families always had to bunk in the cabin. The adults weren't too crazy about staying in the cabin because it was hot and musty and there was no privacy. They were also leery of the snakes that took up residence whenever people were not staying there.

Over the years we heard so many stories of our dad's encounters with copperheads and rattlesnakes when he was a boy that we always tried to sleep with one eye open. My brothers and sisters and I viewed staying in the cabin as an adventure. There wasn't a boy who stayed in the log cabin that didn't pretend to be Davy Crockett or Hawkeye or any other character (real or make believe) that lived during the days of the early frontier. Of course every little girl was Laura Ingalls or one of her sisters.

After dinner the adults would congregate on the front porch and talk late into the night. This was always my favorite part of every trip. The sky was always pitch black and the only light was the light that cascaded down from the moon and the stars. The sound of the swarming mud bees, chirping crickets and water flowing in the spring box and over the rocks in the creek, served as background music. The spring box was built years ago and collected the spring water that ran down the mountain and pooled in the reservoir. A couple of times we were surprised when we pulled off the lid that was placed over it to keep any unwelcome visitors from contaminating the water and found a salamander or toad resting there. If any unwelcome visitors were occupying the box, we just pulled them out and filled up the dipper, taking a long swig of the freshest water around.

The adults talked mostly about their mom or "mommy," as all the aunts so lovingly referred to her, and about their childhood. No modern woman possessed the skills or had the stamina their mom had. Nobody could fry a chicken like their mommy and nobody could put up as many jars of canned vegetables and preserves the way she could. They bragged about her hand-stitched quilts and each recalled that one special picture that she had painted just for them.

They shared funny anecdotes from the past and occasionally shared a story that was sad or more serious, though those stories were never about any of them directly. To hear them talk, nobody would have suspected the tragedy that surrounded their childhood. The cruel times were only talked about in private. A collaborative recollection of the past would have been too painful for any of them to bear.

Our Aunt Susie, for whom I was named, was the first to remind anyone who attempted to recall an unpleasant childhood memory that, "The past is in the past and that's where it'll stay."

Aunt Susie was a wonderful storyteller and though she was getting older, she could still tell a story better than anyone else. What she couldn't remember, she made up.

Everybody knew that sometimes she embellished her stories, but the details were never too outlandish, so we forgave her. I figured she would be reluctant to talk about Little Owen's death at first because that would be a story that she and everybody else deemed should remain in the past, but I was confident that I could persuade her.

I had a speech already memorized if she refused to talk about it. Anytime I broached the subject with my mom or any of my brothers or sisters, I got only part of the story. Mom would begin to explain what had happened, but then would get too upset to finish. My older brothers and sisters would scowl at me and ask, "Why do you want to fill your head with all of that? You didn't even know him and all you're gonna do is upset mom. Stop being so selfish, Suzanne."

In a way they were right. He had died before I was born, so why did I have such a strong desire to know him and know the details of his death? I often stared for hours at a picture of him standing in front of a Christmas tree. His picture sat alone on the shelf that hung on our parent's bedroom wall. Although there was more than enough space to display other pictures or knick-knacks, it was his solitary picture that decorated the shelf.

He had just turned two when this photograph was taken. A friend of the family snapped the picture just as my family was about to leave church after Christmas Eve mass. Little Owen had stopped in the vestibule to admire the Christmas tree, which was modestly decorated with a string of white lights. He wore a red wool coat and a matching red hat. The hat was snug and secured under his chin by a big gold button. The fitted hat accentuated the fullness of his cheeks and his perfectly round, blue eyes. His expression was of total wonderment as he stood pointing to the brightly wrapped presents tucked underneath the tree.

There were a few other pictures taken of him shortly before he died, but it was this image of Little Owen that people imagined whenever his name was mentioned.

The back door of the cabin creaked as I opened it. My Aunt Susie was standing at the sink washing some dishes left over from lunch. The two open windows at either end of the kitchen created a welcoming cross breeze, but the circulating air couldn't completely mask the rich aroma of the cabin. To me it smelled like wood and the land that it was built on. It smelled of the past.

I loved everything about its smell and often thought if I could take a bite out of the cabin that it would taste like *Grape Nuts* cereal. Every now and again, after an early morning rain, I could taste and smell that cabin all the way back in Michigan. As always, my Aunt Susie was happy to see me.

"Girl, you sure are a sight for sore eyes. How are you darling?" Aunt Susie was blessed with the gift of making people feel at ease. No matter who she was talking to, that person felt as if he or she was the most special person in the room.

"If you have a minute, I would like to talk to you about something," I stated matter of fact. My Aunt Susie just smiled. She was so proud of me and my brothers and sisters. She bragged about how smart we all were and loved how grown up we always sounded. We would be leaving for home in the morning and I didn't have any more time to waste. It hadn't seemed right bombarding her with questions when we first got there, so now was my chance. I needed to be quick because I knew that at any moment someone would be coming in to find something to eat or to lie down.

"Okay, but let me just dry off my hands and we'll take a squat out on the porch. I'd love to have a private moment with my namesake," she responded giving me a playful wink. She dried her hands off on an old dishtowel and snatched a cherry tomato off the table before heading out the front door. She sat in the large rocking chair while I remained standing. "What's on your mind, Suzanne?" she asked.

I gathered my courage and asked, "Well, I was wondering if you could tell me about the day that Little Owen died? I know that you and pretty much most of my dad's family were there the day it happened."

Aunt Susie began rocking in her chair and I worried that she was avoiding my request. She looked past me, intently studying the mountains as if the story was somewhere hidden amongst the trees and the rocks. I released a tiny cough to remind her that I was waiting.

"Yes, I was there," she finally answered. "That was a terrible, horrible day and I try my hardest not to think about it."

While waiting for her to answer, I had grown restless and was studying something moving on the porch floor. "Oh, look!" I cried, "I think this sweet little bee is dying." I wasn't standing anymore, but was hunched over the bee that was loudly buzzing, spinning in circles, no longer able to fly.

The mud bees, which cohabitated the log house, resembled bumblebees - fat, yellow and black, and perfectly harmless.

"Oh, why can't we be more like those mud bees?" Aunt Susie proposed.

"How so?" I asked as I gently scooped the bee up into my hand to get a closer look. There was nothing visibly wrong with it, but it was struggling.

"When I was a little girl and didn't know any better, I thought that the same bees lived in that mud year after year. I figured when the weather turned cold they flew back into one of their holes and hibernated for the winter," she explained.

"Well that's not so silly, some bees do hibernate," I informed her.

"I never knew that, but then I wasn't as smart as you are, darling." Aunt Susie smiled and continued, "It wasn't until I was much older that I learned that they live for only about six to eight weeks before dying and being replaced by a fresh, new crop. After the first cold snap they all disappear for good until the following spring."

I looked down at the now silent bee that lay in my hand, "Sad," I decided.

Aunt Susie corrected me, "Honey, that's not sad, that's their life." I guess she could feel my heart breaking over the thought of these little bees dying. "Don't fret, honey. They actually live a very charming life."

I looked at her skeptically.

"They do, honest. They do nothing but fly around all day visiting with each other and being entertained by all the human stories they witness. Well just imagine all the stories these bees have collectively heard over the years. Most folks assume that they just buzz around looking for flowers, oblivious of the world they live in, but they're so much smarter than we give them credit for. They bear witness to it all. "

I gently placed the bee back on the floor of the front porch and gave my complete attention to her.

"They might not live long, but at least their short lives are carefree and filled with nothing but joy, not like us humans." Aunt Susie said. She stood from her chair and rubbed her left hip, "I reckon my old hip hurting is an indication that it's gonna rain."

"If they bear witness to it all," I said, "wouldn't they have seen what happened to my brother? That must have been something they didn't want to see."

"I reckon they must have. They witness life unfolding and life is filled with both living and dying, laughing and crying, but it's the good times they choose to remember. If they witness some kind of tragedy, they keep it to themselves. They dare not speak of it to anyone, not even each other. They forget the bad stuff and only remember the good."

"I wish people could do that. It's the pain that most people remember. When I'm older, I'm gonna try to remember only the good times," I announced.

"Now you're talking honey," Aunt Susie said smiling. I sat down in one of the chairs next to her and observed a dozen or so bees swarming around the walls of the cabin. They did appear to be conversing with each other. One or two would fly into a hole and then just as quickly as they flew in, a few more flew back out. It was a beautiful day and the two of us enjoyed watching the mud bees share their stories for a while.

Aunt Susie was the first one to break the silence. "Your mama and daddy probably don't talk about Little Owen much around you last three youngins. I reckon that's because they want to spare you the pain and heartache. Suzanne, knowing isn't going to change what happened. All knowing is gonna do is make you long for something that can never be."

"But I have a right to know, Aunt Susie. He was my brother too," I insisted. "Ya know, Margo sees him. She wakes up almost every night screaming her fool head off, but then like everyone else she gets up the next day and pretends that nothing is the matter. She never says a word, but she writes about it in her diary and once I read it. I know that wasn't right, but I guess I was just curious."

My cheeks burned with the shame of knowing that I had invaded Margo's privacy. "One day, when she wasn't home, I read it and do you know what it said?" Aunt Susie was silent, so I continued. "She writes down the conversations that she has with him," my voice sounded shrill and I struggled to keep from crying. "With Little Owen," I clarified. "How do you converse with a dead person? Can you tell me that?"

"Oh, darling. I'm sorry. You're all hurting so bad and your mama and your daddy can't help any of you because they can't even help themselves," she said.

Aunt Susie pulled me into her soft, large lap. I buried my head in her chest as she gently rocked me and hummed a song that I didn't recognize.

After a couple of moments, she lifted up my face and wiped away my tears, "I suppose sometimes the past can't stay in the past if it prevents us from living today. If you're really sure, Suzanne, I'll tell you about that horrible day. Just remember, God is good, and we can't always understand why he does what he does," she preached.

With her last statement, I couldn't help but think of Anna and her cynical views concerning God. She'd say, "When a door opens for this family, God quickly shuts another," or "God only gives us what he's sure we can't handle." Was she right? I didn't want her to be, but why did it seem that God let so much unhappiness rain down upon my family?

I knew my Aunt Susie would come through for me. She recalled the events surrounding my brother's death, as if they had happened just yesterday. Every now and again she would stop talking, sometimes for several seconds, at which point she would sigh deeply and smooth down her hair. I was patient though. I had waited my entire life to hear this one story, the story that nobody else had the strength to tell.

She could only tell part of the story though. Only the parts that she bore witness to - the parts she had first hand knowledge of. She didn't have the faintest idea of the events that Mom and Margo experienced later that horrible night. She couldn't tell Little Owen's story either.

Their stories belonged to only them. Neither of them ever told another living soul about what transpired later that fateful day after everyone else had finally collapsed into a restless heap.

The mud bees knew, but of course they would never tell.

TWENTY THREE

The day began before the sun came up. Since there was no privacy, once one person woke, everybody else felt obligated to get up and start the day. Everyone wanted to make the most of the time they had together. The kids stayed in bed listening to the men talking in the front room and the women rattling around in the kitchen. The smell of bacon frying and biscuits baking filled their dreams as they dozed until they were officially called to breakfast.

The adults ate first, but there was always more than enough food. One by one, each cousin waited patiently for his or her turn to climb down the ladder from the loft. The kitchen was small, so the first four or five kids to wake up were allowed to eat at the table and the rest of them either waited for an open spot or fixed a plate and ate on the porch.

There was debate amongst the adults on whether they should drive into the Smokey Mountains for the day or stay and let the kids swim and fish in the creek. If they stayed home, the men could lend Sheldon a hand bringing in the ten cords of firewood that had been delivered the previous week. He had been lucky because it hadn't rained since being delivered, but the news was calling for some rain in the next day or two and he didn't want to deal with wet wood. Most of the men really weren't crazy about an all day trip with kids anyway, so they decided to work on the wood. The women began preparing food for the decoration, which was going to be the next day. They would clean and snap the beans, make the potato and macaroni salads and make the banana pudding and other desserts. They would save frying the chicken until first thing in the morning before it got too hot.

"With all you youngins it won't take no time at all to stack up that wood," one of the aunts chimed in. The boys were less than enthused because their fishing gear was already packed up and ready to go. There was no point in arguing, so they carried their poles and buckets down to the creek and then came back up to the house to get started on the stacking.

By noon they were finished with the wood. The humidity was high and the temperature had already reached ninety degrees. Nobody felt like eating and it was a good thing because the women were just finishing up the dishes and putting the food in the refrigerator. The older kids took turns waiting for the bathroom or one of the bedrooms in the new house to open up so they could put on their suits. The younger kids had to wait for their moms or an older sibling to help them get ready.

"I'm going to fish a little further down the creek with Tommy, Mike and Brad," Danny said to Mom. "The fishing is better down there 'cuz the fish won't be spooked by all of the splashing and noise." He was already dressed and shoving the last bite of his ham sandwich into his mouth. Danny never found it too hot to eat.

"Okay, but leave your shirt on. You're already burnt to a crisp. A couple hours in that sun and your back will be blistered," Mom answered. But it was too late, Danny was already out the door and his shirt was in a pile of clothes on the floor.

Ellen and Anna were able to get themselves dressed and were helping Patty and Margo with their suits. "You've got to take your underwear off, Patty," Ellen urged. "Nobody is looking. Now hurry up."

Just then our Aunt Sarah walked by, "Miss thing, there ain't nobody here who wants to look at your little butt. Now stop acting a fool and get that suit on."

"Yeah fool, get that suit on," Anna teased as she pulled down Patty's underwear. Patty let out a scream and, after pulling up her underwear, she ran by Anna and kicked her. Patty grabbed her suit and slipped into the bathroom before her Uncle Ray could find his newspaper and camp out in there for the next half an hour.

"Put your own suit on, you little baby," Ellen hollered in Patty's direction. She motioned to Margo to come. Margo wasn't shy. She ripped off her clothes and stood in front of Ellen waiting to be helped. Ellen, Ann, and Margo laughed like crazy trying to put on Margo's suit. First, they put it on backwards. Then Margo put her leg through the arm strap instead of the leg hole. Once all the legs and arms were put through the correct openings they pulled it up and somehow the straps were all twisted and they couldn't get it to lay quite right.

"What the heck! This is the most idiotic suit I've ever seen," Ellen roared. After the third try Margo threw her hands up, "Oh well! I don't care if the straps are twisted, I just want to swim."

"That's the spirit, Margo!" Anna cheered.

"Hey monkey," Margo called out to Little Owen who had grown tired of waiting for Mom and had begun to unbutton his own shirt, "wait for mom. She'll be in to help you in just a second."

"Otay Margo," he answered, still messing with his shirt. Just then Mom came over and scooped him up into her arms.

"Who wants to swim?" she asked.

"We do, we do!" cried Little Owen and our cousin, Jiffy who was a year older. She got them both in their suits and yelled out to her sister-in-law Grace that she would take Jiffy down to the creek with her and Little Owen. She grabbed the jug of lemonade and a stack of Styrofoam cups and walked down to the creek with the boys. The creek was high that summer and the water was ice cold, but the kids didn't care. The men were already down there and some of them didn't even bother putting on their suits. Dad had his suit on, but still wore his shirt.

"You older ones, keep an eye on the little ones. That current is strong," he ordered. He threw a large stick in the water to prove his point as it quickly traveled down the creek.

"Make a chain," one of the kids then yelled and they pretended to pull Anna out of danger. They all laughed as Anna went to the end of the chain so it could be somebody else's turn to be saved. They swam for almost an hour before the kids started to complain that they were getting hungry. By that time the older boys had given up on fishing and thought that it would be more fun to torment the girls. Mom and a couple of our aunts went up to the house to make some sandwiches and to grab some bags of chips. When they came back with the food, all of the kids got out of the water. There weren't enough towels for everyone, so the older kids stretched out on the larger rocks and dried in the sun.

"Why does food always taste better after a day of swimming?" Danny asked as he reached for his third sandwich of the day.

"I know, I could eat the ass end off a barn," Brad said not loud enough for any of the adults to hear. The older boys laughed.

The adults continued to visit as they watched the kids gobble down their bologna sandwiches and soggy chips. Mom went back up to the house to make a few more sandwiches; they had already gone through four loaves of bread.

"I guess I underestimated how much some of those older kids could eat," she said, shaking her head and smiling. After a few minutes, she came back down to the creek and set the tray on the large rock that was now serving as a table. She began asking who wanted another sandwich and had many takers.

Ellen declined but said, "I don't think Little Owen has had a sandwich yet." Mom grabbed a peanut butter and jelly off of the tray and called for Little Owen. As she waited for him, she decided to eat a half of a bologna sandwich herself. She was in her first trimester of pregnancy and found if she ate little meals throughout the day, she didn't have as much morning sickness.

When Little Owen didn't come, she called for him again. Jiffy was sitting on a towel ignoring his sandwich but was munching away on his "tator chips," as he called them.

"Jiffy, where is Little Owen?" Mom asked.

"He's trying to get the boat," he answered with a mouth full of chips.

"What boat? Jiffy, what are you talking about?" she asked again this time with a little more urgency. Jiffy set down his sandwich and ran off saying that he didn't know.

TWENTY FOUR

It had only taken a few shy moments for Little Owen and Jiffy to become friends. The previous summer they had both been too young to actually play with one another, but this summer they were the perfect age for friendship. As the families piled out of their cars to convene for the summer visit and slowly got reacquainted, the two youngest cousins kept themselves entertained by playing a rudimentary yet thrilling game of climbing up the incline of the hill in front of the creek and then running back down. For generations the kids in the family had been playing the same game. They could play for hours, only stopping when they were thoroughly exhausted. It didn't take long for Little Owen and Jiffy to reach that point. Just when they thought they were too wiped out to go any further, they mustered up the energy to reach the top of the hill once again. They rested briefly in order to catch their breath. Jiffy then counted to three and the two of them ran back down, full steam ahead. For a few fleeting seconds they looked as if the momentum they had gained on their descent was going to cause their feet to disappear out from under them. Jiffy imagined that their feet were suddenly replaced with a thick set of white wings, which had magically sprouted from their shoulder blades. Their wings would allow them to soar high into the air and right over the water. The threat of going too fast and running straight into the creek made the game even more fun and exciting.

It was while playing this game that Jiffy first spotted the mysterious little sail boat cascading down the creek that ran in front of Aunt Martha and Uncle Sheldon's house.

"Look!" Jiffy cried as he helped Little Owen up off the ground, "a boat!"

The two of them ran down closer to the water's edge to get a better look.

"Where did it come from?" Little Owen asked excitedly. It made him feel special seeing that boat, as if someone had placed it in the water just for him.

"You kids get away from the water," Jiffy's mom cautioned.

The two of them joined the rest of the family as they collected their belongings from the car and made their way up to the old house.

TWENTY FIVE

Margo stood up and called, "Little Owen, come on. Let's eat and then we'll swim again." He still didn't answer. By now a few of the other kids jumped up to look for him and Ellen ran to go see if Little Owen had gone with Danny and the other older boys who had decided to give fishing another try.

Dad stopped talking with his brother-in-law and looked over to see what the fuss was about. "Joyce, what the hell is going on?" he asked.

"We can't find Little Owen. He was down here with all of you and then he just disappeared." By this time she was getting panicky.

"Well, he couldn't have gotten too far. Where are the rest of the kids?" he asked.

"Owen, they were all right here except for Danny," she explained.

Danny came running over with Ellen and said, "Mom, he's not with me. We split as soon as we were done eating."

"Of course you did. It would be too damn much for you to keep your ass still for a minute and lend a hand, wouldn't it Danny?" Dad yelled.

"Well, he's got to be somewhere, everybody start looking," she ordered. "Now!" she screamed when people didn't move quickly enough.

They looked everywhere. They looked in the new house and up at the old house. They checked the barn, the smokehouse, the canning house and back by the dog kennel. He was nowhere to be found.

"Where is he?" Mom pleaded, shaking her hands in the direction of the sky. She remembered what Jiffy had said when she first asked him where Little Owen was and ran back to the new house to inquire about the boat that he had mentioned.

"Jiffy, where did you say Little Owen was?" she asked again.

Margo didn't wait for him to answer, "He said that he was looking for a boat." She ran over to Jiffy and asked, "Jiffy, what boat are you talking about? There is no boat here."

"Yes there was. It was floating down the creek. It was white and it had a red stripe on the sail. I seen it," he happily answered.

"Oh my God! The water!" Mom screamed, "Little Owen went in the water by himself."

Dad, Sheldon, and Dad's older brother, Sam took off back to the creek. Our Aunt Martha turned in the direction of the police scanner that ran 24/7 in the kitchen and picked up the phone and called the sheriff's office. Aunt Susie grabbed some of her grandkids and Patty and urged them to get down on their knees behind the couch and begin to pray. She and Dad were the only two siblings of the thirteen who practiced any kind of religion.

"What shall we pray?" Patty asked innocently.

"Darling, it don't matter. Any prayer you know how to pray," she answered. Danny, Ellen, Anna, and Margo also knelt down next to Patty and together they started saying *The Lord's Prayer* over and over again. Mom sat in a kitchen chair with her rosary beads pressed in her hands. A couple of policemen were there within minutes and after talking to our Aunt Martha and Mom, they were outside also looking for Little Owen.

Almost an hour later, Dad came into the house carrying Little Owen's limp body. Tears were streaming down Dad's face and his shirt and swimsuit were wet and covered in mud. He placed Owen on the table and began wiping his body off with a towel that was draped over the back of a chair. Our Uncle Sam was standing next to him holding onto a white sailboat that had a red stripe across the sail. Dad yanked it out of his hand.

"This damn boat was stuck in some mud on the other side of the bank not more than a hundred yards from where we were. Where in the hell did it come from?" he asked, but nobody knew. "He was trying to get this stupid, fucking boat!" He threw the boat against the wall, but it didn't break. It bounced off the wall and landed at his feet.

"We found him not too far down from the house. His body had gotten tangled up in some branches of a tree that fell into the creek last winter," the police officer said. Margo stood up and walked to the table.

"Owen, wake up now. Open your eyes, you're scaring me," she whispered. She picked up his small hand and held it up to her face. It was cold, not at all warm like it was when he wrapped his fingers around hers as he drank his bottle. He no longer had that sweet baby smell that belonged only to him.

"Margo," Dad said as he walked over to her, placing his hand on her shoulder, "honey, he's dead. He drowned in the creek."

"No he didn't, you're a liar! He's just sleeping! Wake up, wake up this instant!" Margo grabbed our brother's arm and tried pulling him up off the table. Owen reached for Margo, but she swung around and hit him in the chest. "Stay away from me! You're a no good liar and I'm getting my brother and we're going home!" she screamed at the top of her lungs.

Mom was standing near the table in shock. She grabbed Dad's shirt and pleaded, "Owen do something. Fix this and make him wake up!" He just stared at her in disbelief. "Does anyone know mouth to mouth?" she asked.

"Joyce, honey, it's too late. He's dead!" he cried. He cupped her face in his hands and repeated, "Joyce, Little Owen is dead."

She could hear his words, but was unable to comprehend their meaning. He pulled her into his arms and hugged her, "He's dead, he's dead, honey," he said over and over again. They sobbed in each other's arms.

Margo sat down in the corner of the kitchen floor, with her arms wrapped around her legs and rocked back and forth, chanting over and over again, "No, it's not true, it can't be true."

After Margo, it was Danny who acknowledged the reality of the situation and wrapped his arms around our parents.

"Danny, oh Danny, he's dead! Your little brother has been taken from us," Dad cursed.

"Dad, why did this have to happen? I hate God for letting this happen," Danny screamed.

Ellen, Anna, and Patty were still on their knees and praying frantically. For years, when Margo closed her eyes at night, when she could no longer fight sleep, the image of Little Owen's lifeless body covered in leaves and mud was all that she could see. From that day on, her dreams were cruel and she remembered each one in great detail.

Partway through her account, Aunt Susie stopped. I had moved away from her and to the edge of the porch, facing the direction of the creek.

"Don't stop," I said. I turned around and faced my aunt, "Then what happened?"

"Suzanne, I think that you've heard enough for today," my Aunt Susie pleaded.

"But I haven't heard the whole story and if you don't tell me, I'll probably never know all that happened."

She went on to explain how Dad had to fly back from Asheville Regional Airport with the body while our Uncle Sam drove Mom and my brothers and sisters back to Michigan. The rest of his family drove to Michigan as well.

"At first your daddy wanted to bury him up at the old cemetery with our mommy and our other kin, but your mama wouldn't have anything to do with that," she explained. "She wanted to take her baby home and give him a proper Catholic burial. She wanted to do right by him and the rest of your family. She made the right decision by taking him home."

My Aunt Susie described that week after returning to Michigan as the most pitiful time she could recollect. Mom had temporarily lost her mind with grief. The doctor wanted to admit her to the hospital, but Dad wouldn't allow it. Mom's younger sister came and stayed with them to help out. Father Daniel and our grandparents came and spent a couple of hours with my mom the day she got back. When Dad arrived a couple of days later, he refused to meet with the priest.

Mr. Grossbach, who owned the local funeral home, took care of all of the funeral arrangements. His family had owned the funeral home for several generations and he and his four brothers went to school with Mom and her siblings. He picked out the casket, wrote the obituary and set the times for the viewing. When it was all over, he never sent our parents a bill. The women at the church organized a luncheon that was held in the church hall after the funeral.

The funeral was a blur for all of them. They somehow got through it, but then they were on their own. The day after the funeral, Dad's family packed up and headed home. Everybody left; giving them space and time to heal, but they didn't take it. Their emotions hung in limbo as they forced themselves to carry on.

Dad managed not to drink a drop throughout the duration of Little Owen's funeral, but as soon as the house cleared, the drinking resumed, even worse than before. He went back to work the day after his family left. Nobody expected him to come in so soon, but they knew staying home and doing nothing would kill him.

Mom took to her room and did not come out for days. Everyone worried about her pregnancy. She forced herself to eat a few bites every day, but that was about all that she could handle. The neighbors were a godsend. Each day one of the ladies came over with more food than any of them could possibly eat and tidied up the house. They made sure that the dishes were done and that the laundry wasn't piling up. They came only when Dad wasn't home. He never questioned where the food came from, but was thankful that it was there.

My brothers and sister wandered around the house aimlessly. Patty prayed, while Margo remained silent and in a state of shock. Anna took to the streets and hung out with the kids in the neighborhood. Her friends' moms took pity on her and allowed her to stay at their houses until they saw that Dad had returned from work each day.

Danny and Ellen took charge of the household as best as they could. Danny made sure that the grass was cut, the garden was weeded and watered, and that the trash was taken out each night. Ellen made sure that the girls were bathed and that they were brushing their teeth. She got them all ready for church when our grandma came to pick them up on Sunday.

A few times Ellen visited Mom's room and brushed her hair and helped her change into a fresh nightgown. When Mom was sleeping, she snuck in and fluffed her pillow. Ellen was exhausted, but never complained. She knew that somebody had to make sure that everything was being taken care of. When she closed her eyes at night, she quickly fell into a deep sleep.

"Suzanne," my Aunt Susie paused in her telling and called my name for a second time, "Darling, are you okay?"

She walked over and placed her hand on my shoulder. "The rest of the story you know because you're living it. I reckon most folks see your parents and think that they've somehow managed to pull it together and move on, but I know better," she added. I wanted to tell her that she didn't know the half of it. "You know, Suzanne when our mama died, I think that your daddy took it the hardest. We all loved her and our hearts ached something fierce, but something changed in him when she died. It was just too much for your daddy to bear. He was just a little boy, younger than you are now."

Aunt Susie had been recently married and was expecting her first child when their mom had died, but she came back with her husband to help her dad with the younger kids. "Shortly after our mama passed, I came home to help pa. Late one night, I woke up because I heard someone rustling around in the kitchen. It was pitch black in the house and I couldn't see a darn thing, so I grabbed the flashlight that I always kept next to my bed. As I got closer to the kitchen I figured out that the voice I heard was your daddy's. I found him sitting on the floor in the corner talking his fool head off."

"Who was he talking to?" I asked.

"Well that's the part that prit near scared me to death. Nobody else was in the room. I asked him what he was doing and he said just as plain as day, 'I'm talking to mama.'" Aunt Susie's eyes filled with tears. "At first, I didn't know what to make of it and was afraid he'd lost his mind. I didn't dare tell anyone because I was scared that Pa would send him away to the loony bin. Well, his talking with mama went on for months. Then one day, it just stopped. I hadn't heard him do it for several days, so I asked him why he wasn't talking to mama anymore and he said that it was time for her to leave." Susie's voice cracked before adding, "At that moment I knew that my baby brother wasn't gonna be truly happy ever again."

I sat quietly, making sure that she was really done with her story and not just taking one of her breaks. "I'm sorry that your mama died," I said solemnly.

"Dying is easy, Suzanne. It's the living part that's hard. I pray every day for your mommy and daddy to start living again, and you need to do the same. I know living with your daddy can't be easy, but he's hurting in ways that I pray you never have to hurt." I promised her that I would pray for my dad.

"Well, all this talking has made me hungry again. Do you want to fix a sandwich with me, Suzanne?" she asked.

"No thanks," I answered, "I kind of want to be alone."

I decided to walk up to the old cemetery behind the log cabin. I'd been up there many times before, but never by myself. The walk up the mountain was hard, even for a healthy kid like me. Once I reached the top, I looked back down at the cabin and the creek. It was so beautiful in the mountains and sometimes I wished that I could live there. I opened the rickety gate of the fence that enclosed the graves and walked in. I went from one headstone to the next reading all the names and dates, even though I had long ago memorized them.

I wasn't the least bit scared to be up in the family cemetery, but I was terrified of the church cemetery that we visited only on the day of the actual decoration. That cemetery was a couple of miles down the road and was much bigger.

A headstone of a little girl who died at a very young age was enclosed in a structure that resembled a large, white playhouse. An adult couldn't stand up in it, but a child could, and although it was cheery looking with its windows and flower boxes, it scared most of the kids. Over the years I had developed an irrational fear of being trapped in the little house. Danny and Anna often teased us younger kids saying that we would have to come back at night and sleep in it because there wasn't enough room for us up at the new house or the old cabin.

I forced the image of that little house from my mind and contemplated what my Aunt Susie had told me about my dad wanting to bury little Owen up here. Too bad they hadn't. I liked to think that he would have liked it.

I was exhausted. Actually I was more groggy than tired. Kind of the way I feel after sleeping too long on a rainy Sunday afternoon. Sometimes in the midst of a long nap, I feel myself struggling to wake myself up, but I can't move. My body is paralyzed, as if I was drugged. I felt overwhelmed by everything that I had learned. I decided to sit on the bench and rest before walking back down. I wished more than anything that Jana was here so I could tell her about my brother. I still had so many questions, but knew that my Aunt Susie would have no way of knowing the answers to them. I felt guilty about revealing Margo's secret. It wasn't mine to tell, it was my sister's and it was obvious that she wasn't ready to share it. We all had secrets we guarded from each other, but I was beginning to understand how some secrets weren't meant to be kept. The longer we kept them, the further it distanced us from reaching the place where we could begin to heal. It was time for us to share them.

TWENTY SIX

The afternoon of Little Owen's passing, Margo remained curled up in a ball, shivering in the corner of the kitchen floor for over an hour. Her suit was dry, but her body was covered in goose pimples. Our Aunt Sarah eventually noticed her and brought her into one of the spare bedrooms. She placed her on the bed and covered her with a quilt. The windows were open and the sheer curtains gently swayed back and forth. The sound of the creek that took our brother's life now seemed louder than ever. Our Aunt Sarah turned on the small lamp that sat on the nightstand by the bed. She leaned down and kissed Margo on her cheek, "Close your eyes baby girl and try to get some sleep. You're gonna make yourself sick if you don't. Your mama don't need any sick youngins now, ya hear?" Her voice sounded curt, but she hadn't meant it to.

She lifted Margo up off the bed and cradled her in her arms saying, "I'm sorry! I'm so sorry, Margo, you poor, sweet girl. Your little heart is just a-breaking. I wish I could make it go away, but I can't. Nobody can." She took this opportunity alone with Margo to allow herself to mourn. She too was in shock, but was trying to keep it together for the sake of our mom and dad.

After a few minutes, Margo detached herself from our aunt's body and got back underneath the quilt. She rolled over onto her side and said, "I think I'll sleep now." Margo loved our aunt, but desperately wanted her to leave. Our Aunt Sarah stayed in the room for another minute or two and then left quietly.

Margo lay there with her eyes wide open and her fists and body clenched. Several hours passed, but somehow she managed to drift off into a brief, yet deep sleep. Several times she woke to the sound of people crying and a few times even heard people shouting. Mom was screaming at our dad wanting to know why he wasn't watching Little Owen when she went to make the sandwiches. He defended himself by saying that he assumed that Little Owen was with her. Someone else was pleading with the two of them to stop, assuring them both that it was an accident, not anyone's fault. Margo couldn't tell who it was, but thought maybe it was Grandpa.

The smell of food cooking on the stove didn't wake her, but made Margo nauseous even while she slept. She had no idea where the rest of the family was and she didn't care. She longed for real sleep and prayed that she would wake up the next day and discover that she had only been dreaming. She hoped that Patty was praying for the same thing. Patty seemed to have her prayers answered more than she ever did.

It wasn't the sound of his voice that woke her, but the dampness that accompanied his body that caused her to jerk awake. She had eventually drifted into a deep sleep. It was the kind of sleep that most people only achieved with the help of drugs. Margo did not experience this type of sleep often, but when she did, she was certain to experience the sensation of flying through the house or across the night sky.

Once in a while, she recognized the places that she passed over but more times than not, the places were foreign to her. Her flights usually ended abruptly and she would wake up someplace in the house other than her bed. That night, she woke up in one of the beds up at the cabin. A gentle rain was falling and raindrops hitting the tin roof sounded like a symphony. The rain grew heavier, and Margo noticed beads of water gathering on the ceiling above the bed that she was in. She watched as the water pooled into a large, singular raindrop. The weight of it eventually caused it to fall. It fell as if in slow motion, finally landing on Margo's face. One dropped turned into several and before she knew it, her hair and clothing were drenched. As she pulled at the blankets to try to dry herself, a bright light filled the room. As her eyes passed over the room, she became aware of a presence. It took a minute for her eyes to adjust to what she was seeing. Little Owen was hovering directly above her. He wasn't in his swimsuit anymore, but was wearing a long, white gown that clung to his damp body. He was covered with leaves and mud and he smelled of the creek.

"Owen!" she whispered as she reached up and touched his foot, "I knew that you would come back. I prayed that you would, and you did." Owen looked lovingly upon Margo and their eyes locked, just as they had the first day their mother brought him home and placed him in Margo's arms.

Margo couldn't remember him leaving, but when she woke up, she was dry and back in the bed of the spare bedroom. She pulled the quilt back and sprung from the bed in search of him. The bedroom window was still open and she ran to it, checking to see if he was now outside, but he wasn't there. She caught a glimpse of something white and quickly slid the window open and pushed out the screen. She was ready to jump out, but stopped when she realized that it was only our mom.

She was coming from the direction of the creek. Her wet nightgown clung to her body much the way Owen's had up at the old house. Margo was unsure of what exactly was happening and a wave of panic washed over her. Her heart began beating sporadically in her chest and she had a difficult time catching her breath. She felt light-headed and dizzy, like she had just gotten off the merry-go-round at school. She shifted from one foot to the other trying to steady herself, but the room continued to spin. She struck her head on the corner of the bed when she blacked out and fell to the floor. She remained in the same position until morning.

TWENTY SEVEN

Shortly before sundown, Owen's body was picked up by the county coroner's office. His absence solidified the reality of his death. Mom accepted the moonshine fresh from our grandpa's still when it was offered. She threw it back, ignoring the burn as it made its way down her throat. Just as her extremities began to numb, she sank into an incoherent stupor. After a few more swigs, she completely passed out.

When she woke two hours later, her head was pounding and the sour contents of her stomach made her regret drinking so much. Dad was asleep next to her. She longed to reach out and touch him, but the physicality of the act was too exhausting. Her arms were heavy as cinder blocks. She was no longer in her clothes, but had no memory of changing. After much effort, she was able to slide her hand down into the front pocket of her nightgown. She was in search of her rosary, but it wasn't there. She moved her hand to her other pocket, but it too was empty.

The empty space in her pockets transported her to another place and time. She was only a young girl when she first heard the story of her Great Grandma Adeline. Our family on our mom's side was also originally from the south. They migrated up north around the turn of the century, first to Wisconsin and then later to Michigan. Her great grandfather, William was a soldier in the Confederate army. When the war ended and the men from those parts returned home one after another, Adeline was confident that her William would return also. She waited for months, never giving up hope that he was making his way home.

One afternoon she received a letter from a soldier who fought alongside him in the battle at Appomattox. He spoke of William's bravery during those final days of the war and of his desire to return home to his family. The man promised to return William's pocket watch that held Adeline's picture if something should happen to William. In turn, William promised to deliver a letter to the man's brother who hadn't spoken to him ever since making the decision to fight for the Confederate. Some folks in those parts said that Adeline was never quite right in the head and weren't the least bit surprised by her eventual death. Those who romanticized every aspect of the war claimed that it was her broken heart that really killed her.

Whichever the case, she was unable to recover from the loss. Early one morning while her children slept, she dressed in multiple layers of clothing and walked to the well. She heard a faint cracking sound as the bucket hit the water and broke through the thin layer of ice that had formed overnight. She filled her pockets with the heaviest rocks she could find and jumped in.

As a child, this story terrified Joyce. She grew fearful of the water even though she was a strong swimmer. She now understood the desperate act of her great grandmother. Here, all of these years later the water had betrayed her family again. "The hell with you," she yelled defiantly in her head.

She rose from the bed and tiptoed out of the bedroom. She stopped in the living room and checked in on the kids who were snuggled together on the floor, sound asleep. Anna's breathing was jagged and accompanied by a small hiccup every few seconds. Patty and Ellen were holding hands, and in Patty's other hand was Mom's rosary. Danny was curled up alone, without a blanket, clutching the shirt that Little Owen had worn earlier in the day. Joyce covered him up and smoothed his hair. She buried her hands deep in her pockets and made her way down to the water.

Once there, she removed her nightgown and crossed over the slippery, moss-covered rocks until she reached the deepest part of the creek. She completely emptied her lungs of air and submerged herself in the water, sinking to the creek floor. The light from the moon danced across the water, and for a brief moment, she thought she saw Little Owen's face looking down on her. When she could no longer hold her breath, she let her body float back up to the surface. As much as she wanted to die, she could never take her own life. She put on her nightgown and ran back to the house.

TWENTY EIGHT

When the snake slithered across one of the headstones, I took it as a signal that I should probably head back. If someone noticed that I was gone and they had to come looking for me, I'd be in big trouble. Traveling down the mountain was faster than walking up. When I reached the bottom, my rumbling stomach served as a reminder that I hadn't eaten lunch. I rarely skipped meals.

I had a hankering for a tomato sandwich, a delicacy eaten only when down south. There wasn't much to it, but there was nothing else like it. Two pieces of thin, white bread. The store bought kind – the kind that sticks to the roof of your mouth when you're chewing it. Mayonnaise slathered on both sides and stacked high with thick slices of fresh tomatoes. If there's cheese, I'd top the tomatoes with it, but if not, just a generous sprinkling of salt, pepper and crushed up potato chips. Heaven!

I walked through the back door of the old house and into the kitchen. The familiar smell of my dad's cigarette smoke wafted into the room. I quickly turned to leave, but it was too late, he heard me.

"Suzanne, come in here," he called out.

I walked into the front room expecting to be chewed out for going up to the cemetery by myself. My dad's fear of snakes was irrational. Snakes are pretty scary – I don't blame him for that – but he acted as if they had a personal vendetta against him and us children. As if they sought us out just to mess with us.

He was sitting on the couch holding onto an old *Detroit Tigers* pennant that for years had been displayed on the back of the bedroom door. I walked to where it used to hang and traced the outline that it left with my finger. It's funny how you never notice how dirty a wall or a door is until you remove something from it. By next summer, the evidence that it once was there would be gone. The door looked naked without it. Nothing left but faded flowers. I spun the oblong piece of wood that served as the door handle and watched it swirl around.

"I'll never forget that game," he said. "I bought this for my dad as we were leaving the stadium. It'll be worth something some day if it remains in good shape. 1968 – the year the *Tigers* won The World Series."

I didn't like baseball, but Patty did, and so did Danny and Andrew. Once in a while Dad was able to get his hands on some free tickets from work. The only ones who ever went to the games were my dad, Danny, Andrew, and Patty. Mom went occasionally and a few times he had enough tickets to let one of the boys bring a friend. I wished that he would get tickets to some place that I wanted to go, like the zoo, but he never did. He's never even been to the zoo and it's not even that far from our house.

"That's nice," I responded. "What are you doing with it?"

"I'm gonna bring it down to the new house and hang it on my dad's bedroom wall. He wants it with him," he answered. "I never figured him for the sentimental type, but I think his mind is slipping and this old thing reassures him that he hasn't forgotten everything from the past."

"His life has been pretty horrible. You'd think that he'd want to forget the past," I reasoned. My dad let out a little chuckle.

"What do you know about it? But yeah, you're right. His life hasn't been the greatest, but there's been some good. Look at this beautiful land he lives on. He doesn't get around a lot any more, but when he was younger he'd get off into those mountains and be gone for hours. He'd come back with a sack of squirrels or rabbits and a bucket full of huckleberries. Fishing ain't worth a shit now, but when I was a boy it was pretty good. No, if you got land, you've got something. Land matters quite a bit."

Now I was smiling because his comments about land reminded me of the big speech Gerald O'Hara gives his daughter, Scarlett O'Hara about land in *Gone With the Wind*. Every year when it came on T.V. our entire family watched it, including Dad. When it was over he always said the same thing, "Well, that's the last time I'm watching this movie. Aren't ya'll sick of it?" We'd always agree that we could never get sick of it. "Well I've watched it too many times to count." But the next time it came on, he watched it right along with us.

My dad lifted the pennant up to his nose and inhaled deeply. "It smells like a campfire and this musty, old house. Maybe the smell will stink up his new room and make him feel like he's back here, which is where he wants to be."

My dad was a sentimental guy too, but he'd never admit it. That's the reason he kept Little Owen's wooden train all those years. The train could no longer move. The long piece of string that he used to pull it around got all knotted and stuck in one of wheels, but there it sat in the bottom drawer of the nightstand next to my parents' bed. There were all kinds of things in that drawer: boxes of pictures, letters Dad wrote to his family when he was in Korea and a blue oil can that had never been used.

My mom bought it for my dad for Christmas when Little Owen first began to walk. When my dad opened it, Little Owen started playing with it and carried it off, so my dad just let him keep it. Little Owen had carried that blue can around with him wherever he went. I guess my dad got a real kick out of that. I wondered if he ever got a kick out of anything I ever did.

There was also a corsage all smashed up in the corner of his drawer. It was so dry and brittle that little pieces of flowers flaked off of it any time I picked it up. Nobody ever told me, but I think my dad wore it on the lapel of his suit jacket the day of Little Owen's funeral. All those things, including the painted picture his mother gave him, kept my dad connected to his past I supposed.

"I was just up at the old cemetery," I admitted.

He set the pennant down and said, "You shouldn't go up there by yourself. That place is crawling with snakes. I usually bring a hoe up there with me, just in case I see one. Why in the Sam hell would you want to go up there anyway?"

"I don't know. I kinda like it up there. It's real peaceful and pretty," I said.

"You're a lot braver than I was when I was your age," he smiled. "That old place always scared me."

I was feeling brave so I said, "Dad, Aunt Susie told me the story about Little Owen, about the day he died."

He didn't react the way I expected him to. He wasn't surprised and didn't seem bothered by me knowing. When he spoke, his voice was soft and calm. A tone I had never heard before, almost as if he was speaking in a foreign language, "Well, I suppose it was time you knew." He looked exhausted and his voice was filled with resignation. "I'm sorry that we've never really talked about him with you younger kids. It's just too damn hard still." He dropped his head in his hands. I walked over to where he was sitting and sat down next to him.

"I wasn't at home the day my mother died," he finally said. "Nobody came and fetched me from school to let me know. I just walked home like I always did, by myself. Your aunts always hung around the school as long as they could before the principal shooed them away. I guess they were never in a big hurry to get home. I didn't like school and my pa would have skinned me alive if I wasn't home within twenty minutes of being let out."

I noticed that our dad called his dad "Pa" only when he was talking about the past. At home he just called him dad. All of his brothers and sisters, however, still called him Pa.

"Anyway, when I got home, I saw Oats and Ollie hitched up to the old wagon. They were our mules growing up. You've seen a picture of them haven't you?" he asked. I told him that I didn't know there was a picture of them. "On the back of that wagon were shovels, hoes, and ropes. I heard my Granny Elle fussing inside. She hardly ever came around, and especially not in the middle of the week. I walked in the front door of the house to find my grandparents sitting on the couch with the doctor, and my dad sitting in the chair across from them." He pointed as he explained where they were all sitting. "My Grandpa Joe seemed real busted up. He had no color in his face and wasn't saying a word, which was unusual for him. He was always cracking jokes or singing some silly little song. He had a dog that was named Jack Rabbit that followed him around everywhere. He was nuts about that little old dog, he even let him sleep with him. He would sing and that crazy dog would dance and howl as if he was singing with him."

A smile spread across my dad's face when he spoke of his grandpa. "I asked my pa what was going on and he just shifted his eyes to the direction of the bedroom. When I walked in, I could see my mom stretched out on the bed. I knew she wasn't sleeping because I'd never seen that woman asleep a day in my whole life. She was always up working or doing something. I knew what it meant, but I walked over to her anyway.

I shook her real soft like just to make sure. Of course she didn't move and I knew. I began to shake her again because I didn't want it to be true. My Granny Elle walked over and struck me so hard in the back of my head that I actually saw stars. She told me to show a little respect for the dead and continued arguing with Pa. She wanted to take her back to her house and bury her up with her kin, but Pa wouldn't have anything to do with it. My poor Grandpa Joe, he just sat there with his heart breaking. He loved my mother. He was the one who taught her how to love and how to see beauty in things."

My dad stopped talking and wiped a single tear from his cheek. I had never heard my dad talk this way. "Suzanne, my Granny Elle was a terrible woman," he explained. "She practically forced my mom to marry my dad because she couldn't stand that Grandpa Joe loved her so much. She was his only baby girl, but Granny Elle was filled up with so much hate and jealousy that she would rather see her married to some old son-of-a-bitch than to be on the receiving end of Grandpa Joe's love and affection."

I couldn't understand why he was telling me all these things about his mom and wondered if my own mom or any of my brothers and sisters knew this story.

He continued, "When my dad married my mom, he already had my three oldest brothers and sisters by a woman who was considered his common law wife. She was killed when a wagon carrying tobacco flipped over and crushed her. My dad was anxious to find someone who was young enough to have the energy to raise his three children and who was fertile enough to have several more. My mom was a beautiful girl. Her hair was long and black and when not up in a bun or tied in braids, it hung to the middle of her back."

I always thought my grandma looked like a Native American princess, like Pocahontas.

"Apparently she was sweet on a boy in her class," he further explained, "but didn't see him much because she was hardly ever in school. My Granny Elle kept her out most of the time so that she could help around the house and tend to her younger brothers.

As soon as my mom got to the age for marrying, my granny wanted her gone. Not in a million years did Grandpa Joe want her gone, but Granny Elle was a force to be reckoned with and he knew he'd never win."

My dad claimed that his dad never laid a hand on his mother. The restraint he maintained when interacting with his wife was absent when engaging with his children. My dad and his brothers and sister received beatings on a regular basis. My grandpa's short fuse was even more explosive when he drank.

He sipped from his jar of moonshine here and there when my grandma was alive, but she was always able to limit his consumption. She'd hide the jar or add a little water to it when he wasn't looking. When he came home drunk as a skunk, barely able to walk, she tended to him like he was a baby. She fed him, burped him and put him to bed.

After my grandma died, his drinking spiraled out of control. He drank steadily, around the clock, and by early evening, he was ready to raise holy hell. He was a functioning drunk and still managed to work the fields and manage the kids.

Half the time the kids never saw him coming; he didn't really need a reason to go off on one of them. They tried to steer clear of him and when they couldn't, they took their licks and didn't dare fight back. My dad and Uncle Sam were in the barn hanging tobacco one day, when dad grew bored and began showing off by climbing up into the rafters. My Uncle Sam began to protest, but changed his mind, yelling, "You're gonna fall down and get hurt and Pa's gonna tan your hide."

"Am not," he yelled defiantly, "I'm like an old mountain goat; I can climb and climb and never fall." My dad continued climbing higher, higher than he had ever climbed before. "Look at me! Look at me!" he yelled.

The next thing my Uncle Sam remembered was my dad losing his footing and falling to the ground. When he landed, the floorboards shook, sending straw and dust into the air. My dad let out a blood-curdling scream and his brother ran over to hush him up before their dad could hear him crying. With his hand pressed firmly over my dad's mouth he tried to assess the damage, but my dad was squirming around so much that he couldn't get a good look. When he was finally able to pull up the pant leg of his overalls, he discovered my dad's shinbone sticking out through the skin. There was no hiding that accident.

Within minutes my grandpa was in the barn. His interrogation began and Sam knew better than to try to explain. My grandpa ignored my dad's cries and searched the barn for something to hit my Uncle Sam with.

A long strap used for sharpening blades was hanging on the barn wall. He grabbed it and proceeded to beat my Uncle Sam repeatedly with the strap until my uncle lay in a heap on the ground. When the doctor came to set my dad's leg, my grandpa had a heck of a time trying to explain why my Uncle Sam was the one passed out when my dad was the one who fell from the rafters.

Only when they got old enough and strong enough to fight back, did he stop. In his own way, my grandpa loved my grandma and his kids, but he had a strange way of showing it.

The only decent thing his dad ever did for my dad's mother was to refuse to let Granny Elle bury her somewhere else.

My grandpa laid my grandma out for only one night before taking her up to the cemetery to be buried. Before shutting the lid, he tucked her book of postcards into her casket. As each child said goodbye, they threw a handful of dirt into the grave. My grandpa never spoke of her to any of them again. Later, one of my dad's uncles explained how she had dropped dead of a heart attack while painting a picture. My dad and my aunts and uncles were always thankful that she died doing something that she loved. My grandpa knew that he did wrong by his wife and there wasn't a day that went by that he didn't regret it.

"I can't talk to you about Little Owen, Suzanne. Maybe some day, but not yet. Maybe never."

"That's okay, dad" I assured him. "He was your favorite and I get it, I really do. When you love someone as much as you loved him, you can't love like that again."

Dad seemed mortified by my sentiments. "Suzanne, don't you ever say something like that again," he said sternly, "He wasn't my favorite. I don't have a favorite. I know that I'm not very good at telling you or showing you, or any of you kids for that matter, but I love you all more than you will ever know. You'll only understand just how much when you have your own kids some day."

I stood and looked at my dad, seeing him for what seemed liked the first time. I never noticed that his eyes were more hazel than brown, a deep amber color. His olive skin was wrinkle free, even though the hair along his temples and sideburns was already turning grey. He was very handsome. I wanted to tell him that I loved him, but the words wouldn't come out. I did love him, but I think I needed him to be the one to say it first. To say it without beer on his breath and not as part of one of his drunken proclamations of love directed at all of the children. Not his, "I love all my babies," spiel that he inevitably gave after too much drink.

"I love you, Suzanne. You're so much like her, my mother. You've got her heart," he said.

"I love you too, dad. Thanks for telling me about your mom. I'm glad I remind you of her," I said.

My dad slapped his knee and said, "Well, I'm gonna take this old pennant to my dad. Someday maybe it'll belong to one of your brothers." He smelled it one more time, taking in the smell of the cabin, which would eventually fade. "I don't know why this is so important to him, but it is. It's strange the things we allow ourselves to get attached to."

Just before he reached the door, I ran up behind him and wrapped my arms around him. He turned around and hugged me back. I felt like I was going to pop, like a watermelon hitting the cement and its black seeds spilling out. It felt good. I felt free.

TWENTY NINE

I began assembling my sandwich, but when it came time to eat it, I was no longer as hungry as I thought. I felt weird, sad. I was eight years old, almost nine and before today I'd never had an actual conversation with my dad. Of course I had talked to him, but never like this.

My chest began to feel heavy, swelling with anxiety. It wasn't just the actual stories that made me feel sad. These stories made me realize how much we had all missed out on over the years. The happiness that I had recently experienced was rapidly disappearing and being replaced with regret.

My Aunt Susie had been right. I now longed for something that couldn't be, to know my brother, and to regain a time that had slipped away. His death stole my childhood before I was even born – not only mine, but everybody's. It took from us our innocence.

Robbie was still little and it was too early to tell how the death of the brother he would never meet would impact him. Andrew was older than me and how much he knew, I wasn't certain. The only thing that I was certain of was that Andrew had not been fortunate enough to escape our brother's death unscathed. He too had been affected.

Andrew was born three-and-a-half weeks early. The doctor explained that having a premature baby was common for women who had gone through traumatic experiences. Anna, Ellen and Patty fawned over Andrew from the moment he came home. Mom was functioning by then, but barely. Dad went to work every day, but was still drinking heavily.

When they weren't at school, my older sisters made sure that he was fed, diapered and showered with attention. They took turns feeding him throughout the night, frequently falling asleep on the couch in an upright position, not wanting to wake him. He would sleep for an hour, maybe two before waking again. They were sleep-deprived and isolated from their friends, but they never complained. As a toddler he was fussy and a picky eater. He refused to eat anything that was lumpy – ice cream, mashed potatoes or gravy had to be perfectly smooth or he'd pop it out of his mouth and pucker up his face, indicating his dissatisfaction. He insisted that his sandwiches be cut a certain way and if the fruit he was given was discolored or bruised, he would refuse to eat it.

He was tender-hearted though and nobody ever got mad at him or scolded him. For all of his charms, Margo was not the least bit interested in Andrew. She helped with him when Mom asked her to, but beyond that, she did not give him the time of day. Mom, who once cherished the hours when the children were at school, now anxiously awaited their return at the end of the day. Andrew remained the apple of the girls' eyes even after I was born.

Of course they loved me too, but not like they did Andrew. By the time I came along, Mom was emotionally a little stronger and she was better able to take care of me, but not as she had the others.

Everybody claimed that, unlike Andrew, I rarely cried and had a healthy appetite. I was content to swing in my baby swing for hours at a time or to stare intently at the mobile that hung above my crib. I was the only baby in the family to ever have one. My Aunt Susie had sent it shortly after I was born. My family reminded me of this fact all the time, as if having a mobile made up for the fact that everybody ignored me.

I was told that my face lit up anytime anyone entered the room. Most of the time I got a quick hello or a pat on the head. Margo says that she was the only one who would stop and take me out of my swing to play. Eventually her interactions with me would feel reminiscent of her interaction with Little Owen, and the memories of his death would come rushing back. Margo would then return me to my swing or crib. It was a wonder that I never cried. I probably knew it would be pointless.

When Andrew and I were old enough to really begin interacting with each other, Andrew was a good big brother. He shared his toys and always wanted me to play with him. I would play for a while, but I quickly grew bored of his games and toys. Andrew loved cars and trucks and anything that he could take apart and rebuild. When it was time to start kindergarten, he was ecstatic. He couldn't wait to go to school like our brothers and sisters. He played school with Margo and Patty and he imagined that school was going to be just like it was when they pretended.

The first day of school was a dream-come-true for Andrew. Everything was so bright and colorful. There were blow-up letter people hanging from the ceiling and the walls were covered with posters of kids smiling and having fun. For the first week of school, Andrew was the first one up and ready to go. He couldn't wait to get to school. His teacher, Miss Green was young and energetic. The children explored the classroom, played, painted, took naps and ate snacks. Andrew couldn't believe his luck and wished he could have started school sooner.

When the second week of school started, everything began to change. The kids were no longer allowed to just play all day. The teacher began teaching them the letters of the alphabet and how to write their names. They did the calendar each morning and practiced counting and writing their numbers. Andrew struggled with holding the pencil correctly. Miss Green was patient and worked with Andrew as much as she could, but when she worked with small groups of students, the other students were required to complete work on their own in stations. Andrew couldn't do the work by himself. Cutting was laborious because he was left-handed and he had a hard time remembering all the directions that she gave and so often times he started his work, but was unable to finish it.

By the end of kindergarten, Andrew had made very little progress. He was not ready for first grade, but because he was already so much older than the other kids in his class, it was decided to move him on anyway. Miss Green assured

Mom that he was a delightful child; just a slow learner and that he would catch up the following year.

Andrew never caught up. By the third or fourth month of first grade all of the kids were reading, but Andrew wasn't. He still couldn't recognize all of the letters of the alphabet or make the sounds each of them made. His first grade teacher was Mrs. Strohs and she too was patient and willing to work with Andrew. She gave him extra help and tried pairing him up with kids who were academically further along. Andrew struggled, but with the help of his, "study buddies," he got his work done. His classmates liked Andrew and so did his teacher.

Hanging on the wall of his classroom was a large pocket chart with a spot designated for each student. In the morning after the students hung up their book bags and coats in the coatroom, they put their money in their assigned pocket if they were ordering a school lunch or milk for morning snack. Andrew desperately wanted to order a school lunch, but Mom never let him. She packed our lunches and everyday it was the same thing – a bologna or fried Spam sandwich, an apple or, if we were lucky, an orange and a bag of carrot sticks. Sometimes if there was leftover popcorn from the night before, we would get a little bag of it in our lunch.

Andrew hated eating his bag lunch while the other kids got to scarf down spaghetti, goulash or pizza puffs. Ordering the school lunch would have been sweet, but it was the milk with morning snack that he really wanted. The students had a choice of either white or chocolate milk, which was appealing to Andrew because Mom never bought chocolate milk, no matter how much Andrew and I begged her to.

Day after day he brought the same boring lunch from home and ate his snack without having anything to drink.

The custodian delivered the milk every morning just as the students were finishing up calendar activities. Most of the kids in the class ordered milk, even the kids that everyone knew were poor, but not Andrew. One day, Andrew accidently stumbled upon a way to also get milk each day.

He was walking down the hall to his classroom when Mrs. Strohs stopped him. "Andrew, would you go down to Mr. Griffin's office and ask him if he could come down to our room and mop up the floor in the boy's bathroom. The toilet must have over flowed again and there is water everywhere," she explained. Andrew followed her instructions and walked to the custodian's office.

He knocked on the door, but nobody answered. Sometimes Mr. Griffin sat in his office and listened to his radio when he was on break. Andrew opened the door and peeked his head in to see if he was in there.

Mr. Griffin wasn't in his office. Sitting on his desk was an old, empty ice cream bucket labeled *Milk Money*. Each day, when dropping off the milk to the different classrooms, Mr. Griffin collected the large envelope that the teachers placed the milk money from their class in. He would then dump the coinage into the larger ice cream bucket and turn it into the office at the end of the week. On that day, the bucket was a quarter of the way full of quarters, nickels, dimes and pennies. Andrew looked around the room again to make sure nobody was in there. He reached his hand into the bucket and pulled out a quarter. He shoved it deep into the bottom of his pocket and walked out the door. His heart felt like it was going to beat out of his chest when he walked into the room; he feared that somehow his teacher would know what he had just done. Initially he thought that he'd just take the quarter home, but when the other kids began walking up to the front of the room, Andrew did the same.

He placed the quarter in his assigned pocket on the chart and returned to his seat. He pretended to get started on the math sheet that was on his desk while he watched the rest of the kids come in and complete the morning routine. Once all of the kids were seated, Mrs. Strohs walked to the chart and began collecting the money. When she got to Andrew's pocket, she peeked in like she did everyone else's and removed his money and placed it in the large envelope. Andrew wondered if she would notice that it was the first time that he purchased milk, but she didn't say a word or even look in his direction.

When Mr. Griffin walked in later that morning with the milk, Mrs. Strohs called each row one at a time to take milk from out of the crate. Andrew went up with the rest of the students in his row and grabbed a carton of milk. His nervousness disappeared the moment he took a sip of his ice-cold chocolate milk. Washing down his graham crackers with milk made him feel like he was just as good as the rest of the students. Later when he had difficulty completing his spelling worksheet, he didn't feel quite so bad. From that day on, Andrew had chocolate milk with his snack every day.

When I started school, Andrew thought about letting me in on his little secret, but worried that I wouldn't be able to keep my mouth shut and then we'd both get busted.

One afternoon my mom picked Andrew and me up early from school for a dentist appointment. Our dentist usually gave us kids a treat if we received a good report – a report of no cavities. I didn't have a single filling, but Andrew already had three. The dentist informed Mom that he would need to have two more teeth filled. I received a sucker, but Andrew got a coloring book that demonstrated the proper way to brush teeth.

He tossed the coloring book into the trash can as we waited for the light to turn as we walked back to the car, "Man, I hate that guy. Someone needs to show him how to brush his teeth because his breath is disgusting, like he just devoured a rotten tuna fish sandwich."

"Andrew don't go getting mad at Doctor Connelly, it's not his fault that you're not brushing correctly. You're always in such a big rush every morning and you don't do a very good job," Mom reminded him.

That was the problem with our mom Andrew thought to himself, she never took our sides. When we got in the car, I offered him my sucker, but he declined, giving me a scathing look and pretending to read the *Mad Magazine* he had swiped from Danny's room.

Mom suddenly remembered that she needed a can of pineapple for an upside-down cake that she was making for her Down River Dieters Club meeting and we made a quick detour to the A&P.

Andrew wanted to wait in the car, but she remembered that she needed a few other things, so it wouldn't be a quick in and out after all. Andrew of course protested. "Come on Andrew, I don't want to hear it," she argued, "You can't stay in the car by yourself. What if someone took you?"

"Yeah, cuz that's gonna happen," he shot back.

"Oh yeah, tell that to the little girl who was taken from her tent on a camping trip with her family out in Montana," she responded. Fear was Mom's favorite technique for convincing us not to do something. She had a way of relating some tragic story to any situation. We were constantly being lectured about running with things we could impale ourselves on, putting too much food in our mouths at once, and (her all time favorite), getting our eyes poked out from something sharp.

The past Christmas, Andrew's good friend, Johnny T. – he had a Polish name that nobody could ever pronounce, so we just stuck with the first letter of his last name – got a real bow and arrow set. When Mom found out, she made Andrew promise never to be around him when he was taking target practice. Of course Andrew ran right over to his house every time he brought it out. One day, Johnny's older brother was taking his turn while Johnny moved the bull's eye from side to side trying to get him to miss. I guess all the fear that our parents instilled in us must have paid off because Andrew didn't want any part of their game. Just as he was making an excuse that he had to go home, Johnny let out a blood-curdling scream. His brother had shot the arrow and it hit Johnny's eye. It didn't poke it completely out, but he never saw quite right out of it again.

Mom had us convinced that danger was lurking around every corner. While she shopped, Andrew and I hung out at the front of the store.

"Hey," Andrew whispered to me as I stared longingly at the coin-operated machines that Mom sarcastically referred to as *junk machines*, "do you want something?" he asked.

"Yeah, but I don't have any money," I said. Andrew pulled out a handful of change from his pocket. My eyes widened in surprise, "Hey where did you get all that money?"

Andrew hesitated briefly and then confessed, "Don't tell anyone, but I got it from Mr. Griffin's office." I was confused. What did money have to do with our school custodian?

Andrew explained how he found the milk money in his office and that he'd been stealing a little bit ever since. "I only take money here and there, so I don't think he notices. Now, don't go telling anyone," he said elbowing me in the ribs, "If you want, I can get a little bit for you too, Suzanne."

I was shocked. Mr. Griffin was a good man and his son was in my class. Andrew made me cross my heart and hope to die that I wouldn't tell a soul.

Later that same week Andrew was one of the winners of a drawing that was held at school. A boy in his class, Marky Richards, was diagnosed with a brain tumor. The school decided to have a fundraiser to help the family pay for some of his medical expenses. It was a pretty big deal and several local merchants donated items to be raffled off. Kresge's Department Store sent over a bunch of toys and the hardware store even donated two bikes. The teachers sold raffle tickets every morning after the pledge of allegiance was said. Andrew and I didn't bother to ask our parents for money because we knew they didn't have it, and besides, Mom had already baked several pies for the bake sale fundraiser.

When Andrew won the 3rd place prize, which was an oversized stuffed gorilla, everyone was so excited that nobody asked him where he got the money to buy the tickets. The kids who lived on our street carried Andrew and the gorilla the entire way home as they cheered and chanted Andrew's name. I followed the crowd home, but didn't join in. When they placed Andrew and the gorilla on the front steps of our house, Andrew caught my disapproving stare. My face was bright red with shame because I knew that Andrew hadn't won it fair and square.

"It's about time one of us chumps finally won some-thing," Anna said when Andrew came through the door holding his prize. I decided that maybe Anna was right and tried to be happy for my brother.

THIRTY

My dad tiptoed into my grandpa's bedroom, trying not to wake him. He had heard him up coughing all night. He cracked the window to let in a little fresh air. The room had a medicinal smell, like a hospital, a combination of Vapor-Rub and urine.

"Son, is that you?" he called, too exhausted to roll over.

"Yeah, it's Owen. I thought I'd hang up your *Tigers* Pennant for you, Dad," he answered. He held it up for him to see even though he had not yet turned to face him. "I finally took it out of the old house."

"That's nice, son," he answered. Dad tacked the pennant to the wall directly across from his bed so that he could see it whenever he wanted.

"Do you need anything, Dad? Can I get you something to eat? It doesn't look like you even touched last night's supper."

He grumbled that he wasn't hungry. My dad sat down on the edge of his bed. "Best damn game I've ever seen. Old Lolich was on fire that season," my grandpa said. "They look pretty good so far this year. Do you still get to many of the games?"

"I imagine we'll make it to a couple this summer, once the kids are out of school," my dad explained. "Once you're feeling better, you'll have to come up to Michigan for a visit and we'll take in a few games."

He was pretty certain that his dad wouldn't live for too much longer, but it felt good saying it, planning for it. He looked at his dad lying in the bed and tried to picture him as he used to be. As a young man, my grandpa was tall, well over six feet, and strong as an ox. It always bothered him that his boys took after their mom's side of the family, who were all so short. He had shrunk some over the years and now seemed so fragile and weak.

My dad was scared stiff the first time he ever stood up to my grandpa. His sisters, Martha and Sarah were told to put some cream and butter into the spring box to keep it cold. They decided to have a race to see who could get there first. Sarah won, even though she was younger. One thing led to another and the two of them started bickering. Sarah picked up a rock and threw it at Martha, striking her on the side of the head. She wasn't trying to hit her, just trying to scare her. Well, Martha lunged at her, hoping to give her a good swat, but Sarah hopped out of the way and Martha fell and knocked out her front tooth on the cover of the spring box. Their dad had witnessed the entire episode from up in the cemetery.

He came off that mountain like a swarm of hornets and decided Martha was to blame because she was older.

He got ahold of her and striped up the backs of her legs while she howled and begged him to stop. My dad and Uncle Sam were coming up the road and heard Martha's pleas. They picked up the pace and raced toward the house.

When they were crossing the footbridge, Sam's foot got caught up in a loose board and he fell, face first. My dad kept going and reached his dad and sister first. He yelled for his dad to stop, but Grandpa just pushed him aside and kept hitting her.

My dad picked up the rock off the ground that Sarah had thrown and nailed his dad right in the center of his forehead. Blood poured down his face and began to pool in his eye sockets. My dad threw up his fists, prepared to fight his dad, even if it was inevitable that he was going to get whooped. Before his dad could do anything, Sam, Sarah and Martha were standing by his side.

"You can't beat all our asses!" Martha yelled. He probably could have, but his head was throbbing and he was in desperate need of a drink.

Sitting by his dying father's bed now, he swallowed hard, trying not to cry. Maybe it was remembering that story or maybe it was because he felt genuine love for his dad for the first time in his life, but whatever the reason, he knew that he had to tell him how he felt. "I love you, dad."

His dad didn't answer, but let out a little cough. My dad changed the subject and started talking about baseball again. He thought his dad might have fallen back asleep and began to stand up to leave. His dad reached back with his arm and placed his weathered hand on my dad's leg and squeezed it. My dad covered his dad's hand with his own and accepted his gesture as an affirmation of his love. He sat with his hand on his dad's for several minutes.

"Get some rest, dad. I'll see you at dinner," he said as he finally got off the bed.

"You're a good man, son, better than I," his dad said. With his back still turned, he was able to hide the fact that he too was crying. In that moment, with less than ten words spoken, a father and son found a way to love one another.

THIRTY ONE

It rained almost the entire way home. The stops were brief, since the rain made getting in and out of the car more trouble than it was worth. My dad tried to park as close to the rest stop doors as possible, but the rain fell so hard that we were all soaked after being outside for just a couple of seconds. My dad smoked one cigarette after another and was only able to crack the window slightly, or risk getting everyone sopping wet.

The goodbyes had been especially hard. Our grandpa was too weak to get out of bed and my parents' exhaustion was only compounded by the thought that they would probably be making this trip again real soon. My mom had only talked to Ellen on the phone once since we'd been gone.

The second night after we left, Jana had walked over to our house to introduce herself. Danny wasn't there; only Anna and Ellen were home. It took Anna a couple of minutes to answer the door. She was on the phone and attempted to stretch the phone cord from the kitchen to the front door, but about halfway there the phone snapped out of her hand and sprung almost all the way back to kitchen. "Damn it," she cried and told her friend that she would have to call her back.

When she finally got to the door, she looked out the window and saw that it was Jana. "Hold on a sec," she called and grabbed the bottle of air freshener and sprayed the air, hoping it would disguise the cigarette smell. It took a long while to get the door open, because Ellen insisted on securing all three locks once it got dark out.

"Hi! You must be Anna or Ellen?" Jana said holding out her hand once the door finally opened. "I'm Jana, from next door."

"I'm Anna and hello," Anna said.

"I just wanted to introduce myself and see if any of you needed anything," Jana said.

Anna called out to Ellen and in a few seconds, she appeared holding a book in one hand and a cup of tea in the other. She was wearing some kind of facial mask that she and Anna had concocted out of avocados and honey.

Anna smiled and said, "Ellen, this is Jana, Jana this is my oldest sister, Ellen."

Ellen was embarrassed, but quickly said hello and excused herself. She ran to the bathroom and washed her face.

"Is your brother here? Danny, right?" Jana inquired.

"Danny isn't home now. He's at work," Anna lied. She did her best not to sound as irritated as she was feeling. What business was it of hers anyway?

"Hello again," Ellen said as she reentered the living room. "Sorry about that – I was trying out a new face mask. But you don't care about that. It's nice to meet you."

"Oh, don't be silly. I shouldn't have just barged over. I just wanted to meet all of you and check in because I promised your mom that I would," Jana said.

"You promised our mom?" Anna shot back. "Well, we've been taking care of ourselves for a long time, so it's really not necessary."

"Oh, I know that you can take care of yourselves. To be honest, I guess I'm just a little lonely. I didn't mean to imply anything," Jana apologized.

Ellen slapped Anna in the back of the head, "Don't mind her, Jana. She's very angry, very immature."

Ellen invited Jana to come sit in the living room. Anna didn't waste any time and started bombarding Jana with personal questions.

"I saw your husband, Clyde. That is his name, right? He's really cute," Anna said.

"Ignore her, please. She's really impulsive," Ellen said.

Jana just laughed and said, "I think he's pretty cute too."

"So why in the heck did you move here? I can't wait to get the heck out of this godforsaken town," Anna added.

Danny came in through the back door before Jana could answer. He walked into the living room holding a tennis racket. His shirt was off and it was wrapped around the top of his head like a Swami. It was obvious that he was not coming from work as Anna had said.

"How was work, Danny?" Anna asked, figuring it unlikely that Jana had forgotten her lie.

"It's okay, Anna. I can see that Danny isn't coming from work. I'm not the police. Relax!" said Jana.

"Cool!" Danny said. "In that case, I'm going back out and will be home in a few," he teased and starting walking back in the direction from which he came.

"Not so fast, I said that I wasn't the police, but I'm not going to knowingly let you do something that your parents wouldn't approve of," she said just as playfully.

"So, how do you two like the apartment? It's pretty cool up there," Danny asked.

"We like it a lot. So far everybody's been real nice and we're hoping that we can rent from the Petersons for a while. Eventually we want to get our own place," Jana added.

She started to ask them about school when there was another knock on the front door. Ellen answered the door this time. It was Clyde. He followed Ellen into the living room and stood next to where Jana was sitting. Danny quickly untangled his shirt from his head and put it on. He introduced himself and the girls to Clyde.

"Hey guys, it's so nice to meet you all," Clyde said. Clyde was handsome and for once Anna was quiet.

They made small talk about what people did for fun around the metro area for several minutes before Jana suggested that they get out of their hair.

Clyde mentioned before they left, "Hey, if you guys don't have anything going on next weekend, our friends down the street are having a party. I'm sure they wouldn't mind if you all came."

The three of them just looked at each other before Anna clarified which friends down the street he meant, "You mean at the hippie house? Holy shit, Dad would have a fit."

Ellen didn't want Anna to put her foot in her mouth any further and tried to keep things cool, "I don't know if that is a good idea, but thanks for the offer."

"Shit!" exclaimed Danny. "I'll definitely come. I bet they have some great grass there."

Clyde just laughed and said, "I don't know about the great grass part, but there will be some good food, cool people and some righteous music. A couple of the guys who live there jam in a band. Jana and I aren't into getting high." Danny looked at him suspiciously "but that's cool if you are. It's just not really our scene," Clyde added.

"What kind of hippies are you, man?" Danny asked.

"Wow! You guys really like that word 'hippie.' It has such a negative connotation to it. Look, I am gainfully employed, I'm married to Jana and we have goals. I spent several years at Boys Town and I met a lot of kids who were messed up from doing drugs. They had no drive or ambition. Some of them turned it around, but not all of them. That's not us, man. And it's not the people who live down the street. They're all just trying to carve out a life like the rest of us." Clyde responded.

"That's cool! I'm sure that someone there will have some good grass," Danny didn't relent, but he was just trying to be a smartass. Clyde understood and laughed.

"We'd like you to come have dinner with us tomorrow night if you're up for it," Jana said, looking at Clyde who was as surprised by the invite as the kids were. "Give us a call if you need anything," she added before handing a folded piece of paper with their number written on it to Ellen.

Anna snatched it from Ellen's hand and put it in her pocket, "Thanks, we'd love to come," she said.

"Okay then. We'll see ya around 6:00," Jana said.

When the door closed Ellen said, "They're really a nice couple. Jana is so sweet and Clyde is –" she was interrupted by Anna.

"Such a fox! Did you see those eyes? I love his hair and his smile," Anna said.

"Anna, he's a married man. It's a sin to covet another woman's husband. What's wrong with you?" Ellen was usually not so preachy, but she felt that Anna was getting too old to be carrying on the way she did at times.

"Loosen up Vatican Two. I just said he was attractive. I didn't say I was going to try to break up their marriage. You're such a prude, Ellen. Right, Danny?" Anna asked. She was certain that Danny would be on her side.

"You're both acting like swooning school girls. Clyde seems alright, a little preachy, and Jana seems," he hesitated, "nice, but a little too happy. She's a little pushy. Shit, I don't know, maybe I'm just used to being around people who are miserable. What do I know? Well, good night you two. Anna, enjoy dreaming about Clyde, and Ellen, enjoy that book of yours," Danny rolled his eyes. *Ellen was always reading, never living*, Danny thought.

"You're a caveman, Danny. At least I know how to read. You really should learn, you know. You can't spend your whole life just looking at pictures of naked women in those disgusting magazines that you keep hidden in the garage," Ellen said.

"Oh, but you're wrong," Danny laughed and walked to his room.

"He's a pig," Ellen said before huffing up the steps to her room. Anna returned to the kitchen, lit a smoke and called her friend back.

THIRTY TWO

The next night, when five o'clock rolled around, Ellen and Anna began to dress for dinner with Clyde and Jana.

Earlier that day when they were getting ready for school, Anna asked Danny if he was going with them or not. As usual, Danny played it cool, "I don't know if I'll go or not. What's the big deal? It's just a dinner invitation. I'll see what I've got going on and if I have absolutely nothing to do, and I'm bored off my ass, I'll go. How's that?"

"Do us all a favor, and don't go," Anna responded. When Danny came home at 5:30 and hopped in the shower, the girls knew that he had made the decision to go with them. To keep the peace, neither Anna nor Ellen commented when he came out of the bathroom with his towel wrapped around his waist and asked, "What time do they want us to come over?"

"Clyde said to come at six," Ellen answered. They continued to get ready and the three of them walked over together promptly at 6:00. Danny was wearing some aftershave that Ellen had bought him for Christmas. It was his first time wearing it. Ellen had her hair twisted in a bun on the top of her head and wore a long dress that she had made in Home Economics class. Anna chose to wear her hair down, which she rarely did. She opted for a more casual look and went with a halter-top, a pair of jeans and Ellen's new clogs. Clyde greeted them at the door and escorted them up to their apartment. Ellen, who usually took charge, let Danny take the lead.

"Oh, good!" Jana said when she saw the three of them, "I'm so glad that you could all make it." She held a glass of white wine in one hand and several long stemmed forks in the other. Clyde was drinking a beer.

"What can I get you all to drink?" he asked.

Danny rolled the dice to see what would happen if he asked for a real drink, "I'll have a beer, thanks," he said.

"What about you two?" he asked the girls.

"Wine for me and Ellen will have a glass too," Anna said before Ellen could protest. Clyde grabbed a beer for Danny and Jana poured a small glass of wine for each of the girls.

"I guess it's okay. Nobody is driving," Jana said. "I hope you kids like fondue."

"Fun what?" Danny said. The girls laughed with Clyde and Jana, even though they didn't know what fondue was either.

"Fondue," Jana said, "It originated in France and is a Swiss national dish." When she realized none of them knew what she was talking about she stopped explaining and said, "It's delicious, you'll like it."

"Now come on everyone, sit down and make yourselves comfortable," Clyde said, leading everyone to the living room.

"Don't mind, Oscar, he likes fondue too," Jana laughed. Oscar trailed along after them as if he too was a guest. Large pillows were carefully placed in a circle on the floor. In the center of the circle was a large, elaborately patterned scarf that served as the tablecloth. Three brightly colored pots, each warmed by a small flame, rested in the center of the cloth. There were several bowls filled with various fruits and vegetables. A large, oval-shaped platter was piled high with cubes of different types of bread that Jana had baked earlier in the day.

"Okay, Clyde show'em how it's done," Jana instructed, handing each of them a long, two-pronged fork. She lifted the lid off of each pot and the steam fogged up the back apartment windows. Clyde demonstrated with a chunk of bread that he dipped into one of the fondue pots filled with a melted cheese concoction. Danny, Ellen and Anna followed suit.

"Oh my gosh!" Anna exclaimed, "This is so good," ignoring the string of cheese she felt hanging from her lip. Ellen and Danny agreed as they prepared another fork to dip. In between bites, Jana gave them a quick history of fondue. "Traditionally the pots were filled with melted cheeses, but more recently people also use oil for cooking meat. Because we're vegetarians we only dip cubed bread and vegetables." The fruit was to be dipped into pots filled with melted chocolate for dessert. They ate and drank steadily for the next hour. Danny and Clyde opened another beer, while Jana refilled the wine glasses.

When they finished eating, Jana and the girls cleared away the food and dirty dishes. Jana opened another bottle of wine and carried it into the living room. She set the wine on a side table, lit a few candles and took a spot on the couch beside Clyde. He was stretched out, but sat up to make room for Jana. He looked so comfortable that she simply lifted up his legs and sat down, placing his feet on her lap. Danny and Ellen remained sitting on the floor while Anna decided to try out the wicker chair that hung from the ceiling.

Ellen and Anna were not used to drinking quite so much and were feeling tipsy. Danny stuck with beer, but he too was feeling a little buzzed.

"So, what was it like growing up in Baltimore?" Danny asked.

"Well, I didn't grow up in Baltimore," Clyde answered, uncertain of whether Danny was directing the question to him or Jana. "I was born in Iowa. My parents were farmers and I spent most of my days, when not at school, helping my mom and dad on our farm. I loved farming. There's something to be said for raising your own food. I really miss it."

"Well, how did you end up in Baltimore then?" Anna asked.

"That's a long story, but I'll give you the quick version," Clyde answered. "My parents were killed in a car accident when I was fifteen. They were driving home from a wedding late one night. A farmer, who lived a few miles down the road from us, was working late trying to get some crops in. He was crossing the road to continue on the other side of the field and his combine stalled out. Have you ever been out in the country at night?"

Danny explained how dark it got up in the mountains. Walking from the new house up to the old house was dangerous without a flashlight.

"Well, it's like that – pitch black." Clyde took a long swig of his beer. It took him a second or two to regain his composure. "I guess it boils down to bad timing. Those exact couple of minutes that he had stalled out just happened to coincide with the couple of seconds that my parents needed to cross that stretch of the road. All three of them were killed."

Jana continued the story for him. "Clyde's dad came over from England when he was only seventeen. He was only going to stay with his uncle for a couple of months in the summer, but ended up staying permanently. His uncle was a great man, but somehow never married. He died of cancer only a year before Clyde's parents were killed. His mom was an only child, so when she and Clyde's dad died, there was no family for him to go stay with. He was sent to live at Boy's Town," Jana recited the story as if it had been hers.

"I guess because of my age, the state thought that I was too old to adopt out." "When I first got there, I was in pretty rough shape, in shock I guess you'd say. I kept to myself and was so angry." Clyde sat up. "I met a kid there who was from Baltimore and his name was –" Clyde corrected himself, "- is Jed. The best damn guy you'll ever meet. He was raised by a single mom, so he was left to fend for himself quite a bit. He had a few run-ins with the law and I guess dealing with him got to be too much for her. When the judge suggested a stint at Boy's Town, she didn't say no. When we turned eighteen and could legally leave, we split. He wanted to try to find his mom and I wanted to find myself," Clyde explained.

"But you're so normal and nice. What gives?" Ellen asked. The wine seemed to have loosened her up a bit.

"I was lucky," he said. "My parents were the most loving people you'd ever meet. When I was at Boy's Town, I was surrounded by so many caring and devoted adults who taught me that I had choices about my life and what kind of person I wanted to be. Believe it or not, I learned a lot from the other kids there. Those kids were dealt shittier cards than me, but they still had their humanity." Clyde looked at Jana and squeezed her hand.

"I would like to work with troubled kids," Anna blurted out. Unlike Ellen, Anna knew all kinds of people. It wasn't until she switched schools and met kids from the other side of town that she understood that people had even bigger problems than our family. Dad drank and our parents fought, but at least they were together. Although we were poor, we always had food and a roof over our heads. As messed up as we all were, we were still a family. Anna volunteered a couple of days a week at the community center; she wanted to be a social worker.

"That's great, honey. I bet that you'd work really well with underprivileged kids," Jana assured her. Jana could see that Anna had the same look in her eyes that Clyde did after the few times he had worked with the inner city kids of Baltimore.

Anna fought with Dad more than anyone, but in an odd way, she felt that she understood him a little better than the rest of us did. He angered easily and had an explosive, often violent temper, but at least he expressed himself more than our mom ever did. Ironically the only time he could share anything personal or give affection was when he was drinking, and then nobody wanted to be around him.

"What do you want to do Danny? Ellen?" Clyde asked.

"It's silly," Ellen softly said, "I'm too embarrassed to say."

"Come on, Ellen, you don't have to be embarrassed," Clyde urged.

"I want to be a writer," she confessed, "I know what you're all thinking, I just can't be a writer, not at first anyway. Some of the best writers of our time were something else before they actually picked up a pen. I need to be successful in another profession first, so I have a back-up plan. I'll be a stewardess for my real job and work on my novel on the side. That way I can see the world and meet interesting people who I can write about." Her plan sounded even better when she spoke the words out loud instead of just inside her head.

Danny and Anna were surprised by Ellen's plans. They had no idea that Ellen wanted to be anything other than the future Mrs. Kowalski.

"That sounds like a great plan, Ellen," Danny moved over closer to his sister. "You can be anything you want to be, sis. You're so smart and, unlike me, you've got your shit together." Ellen smiled lovingly at her brother.

"I'm going to be a Marine," Danny said in hopes that Ellen would wipe the dopey look off her face. He wasn't very comfortable with emotions either.

"Yeah, fat chance Mom and Dad will let you do that," Anna scoffed.

"It's too late, I already signed up. Last week. I'm 19 and I don't need their permission," he informed her.

"Danny, no!" both girls cried.

"Yep, I'm out of here come the middle of July and I can't wait either," Danny said defensively. "I want to be out on my own, away from all of you."

"Of course you do. You treat everybody like shit. Especially Andrew, who worships you, but you wouldn't know that because you can't give him a single second of your time," Anna said angrily.

"Oh, you're a good one to talk. What about how you girls treat Suzanne, huh? That poor little freak plays in the closet and doesn't have a single friend. You girls never include her," Danny shot back.

"That's not true," Ellen argued, "Suzanne likes to be alone and besides, she has friends."

"Really? Who? When do you ever see her playing with anyone? She's a hermit and to be honest, Margo isn't much better. She's a freak too. Do you girls ever ask her what the hell she's screaming about every night?"

"You know what, Danny, if you are so observant, why don't you talk to them? You're the oldest and yet you give the least. It's always about you," Ellen began to cry. Jana stood up in attempt to calm everyone down, but Clyde gently pulled her back down.

"Really? I give the least? You've got to be kidding me! I've been looking after all of you since the beginning of time. It's always, 'Danny do this, Danny make sure this one has that.' I don't want to take care of anyone anymore. No matter what I do, it's never good enough. Everybody blames me for Little Owen's death," he said and nervously ran his fingers through his hair.

"Danny, c'mon, nobody blames you for his death. You were just a kid yourself, you weren't in charge of him," said Ellen.

"Oh, nobody says it, but I know Dad feels that way. I can tell by the way he looks at me. He hates me. I'm sure that he wishes that it had been me instead of Little Owen," Danny was on the verge of tears. "I want to take care of me. I want to get away."

Anna hated to see her brother like this. "Danny, Dad's a shit, there is no doubt about it, but he doesn't hold you responsible for Little Owen's death. Dad's hard on you 'cuz you're the oldest, he counts on you because he wants a break. He loves you, it's just he can't show you in the way you want him to," Anna said.

Anna got more beatings than anyone else, but she knew that her dad still loved her. "His idea of showing people love is to knock the crap out of them when they do something wrong and keep them on a short leash. He doesn't want anything to happen to anyone else he loves. He's just scared," she added.

"Let's face it," Ellen interrupted, "Dad isn't going to win a Father-of-the-Year contest anytime soon, and Mom's not going to either, for that matter, but that doesn't mean they don't love us in their own warped way. And Danny, I don't want to hear how you're the only one who has been strapped with the burden of taking care of everyone. I know that mom has gotten a little better since Little Owen first died, but Anna and I practically raised Andrew the first year of his life." Danny didn't protest.

Anna sprung from the chair and pleaded, "Danny, please don't go. I'm going to miss you."

"I'll miss you too, kid, but Anna, it's time for me to go. If I stay here, I'll die," he cried. He hugged his sister for the first time in a very long time. Ellen walked over and wrapped her arms around the both of them. "Danny, I'm sorry for all the things I said."

"Don't, Ellen. I am a selfish prick, you're right," he said.

"He does have a point," Anna said jokingly.

Danny loosened himself from his sisters' embraces and cleared his throat.

"Gosh, Clyde, Jana," he said, "sorry to put a damper on the evening."

"Hey, that's okay. You don't ever have to worry about what you say around us. This has actually been a fun night. I've enjoyed getting to know all of you," Clyde said.

"Hey, if you get the chance, be sure to stop by that party next Saturday night. It'll be a good time and you'll get to meet some new people, possibly some new friends," Jana said.

"We'll see." They all agreed to consider it.

"Well, I hate to bust up the party, but I have to work in the morning and you guys have to go to school," Clyde said. He was barely able to keep his eyes open any longer.

"You're right. We should get going," Ellen said.

Once home, Ellen was the first one to mention the party. "What do you guys really think? Do we dare go?" she asked.

"I don't know. Clyde and Jana are pretty cool and seem decent, but those people down the street are a different story. Mom and Dad wouldn't be happy, they're not like us," Danny said.

"Not like us? How so? Do you mean because they're easy going and not riddled with fear and guilt like us?" Ellen asked.

"No doubt," Anna agreed.

"Mom and Dad would totally freak if they knew. Especially Dad," Danny added.

"What the hell, I think we should have our own party!" Ellen suggested.

"Obviously, you're buzzed. Are you out of your mind?" Danny asked.

"I don't know," Anna answered, "Maybe Ellen's right. Maybe we should have a party. It'll be like a going away party for the two of you, one last hurrah before my life totally sucks!"

"Shit! Maybe you two are right. Let's have it tomorrow night, I don't have to work," Danny said.

"Well I do," Ellen cried.

"Stop your belly aching, you can still come when you get off work; just tell your nerdy friends not to show up until later. But here's the deal," Danny immediately took over. "We only invite a few friends each, nothing too crazy. I'll take care of the booze. It'll be real low key. Nobody will even know that anyone is here."

Anna and Ellen agreed with Danny's plan. "Alright!" he clapped his hands and then ran his fingers through his hair, "We're doing it! We're gonna be gone soon – it's time to live a little," Danny cheered.

Anna sat on the couch staring at her older brother and sister, "I can't believe the two of you are leaving."

The mood swiftly changed when Danny asked, "Do you really think that you'll go through with it, Ellen? The writing and becoming a stewardess bit?"

"Yeah, I think so, I mean I want to. I want to move to either Chicago or New York and live in a big city for a few years. I feel like if I don't leave now, I'll be stuck here forever," Ellen moaned.

"Well, this really stinks. You two will be leaving and I'll be trapped here by myself for the next two years. Ellen, you could wait for me. I'll go with you!" Anna pleaded.

"Wait and do what? I love you, Anna, but I'm not waiting. I can't," Ellen said softly.

"Hey," Anna yelled, quickly changing the subject, "let's all sleep in the living room tonight. We can pile up a bunch of blankets on the floor like we did when we were little and pretend that we're sleeping out under the stars. Remember? We used to call it 'camp out'?" Danny and Ellen smiled as the memory returned to them.

"If I remember correctly, we should have called it, 'fart out' because of Danny and his gas," Ellen said as she threw the pillow that was on the couch at Danny, hitting him in the head.

"Alright," Danny agreed, "but you two sleep on the floor and I'll sleep on the couch. I'm feeling a little gassy." He placed his hands on his stomach and scrunched up his face as if in pain.

Ellen located the extra blankets in the closet while Anna and Danny grabbed the pillows off their own beds. Anna spread several blankets over the floor while Ellen made a bed up on the couch. Danny checked the doors one more time and turned off all of the other lights in the house. He returned to the living room and crawled underneath the blankets that Ellen had arranged for him.

"How about some music?" Ellen suggested, not bothering to ask them what they wanted to hear. Tonight she'd be in charge. Danny and Anna had a way of taking over and forcing their agenda on Ellen whenever the three of them were together. They couldn't help it really, because the two of them were so much alike. Even as little kids they were close. Ellen often felt like the third wheel, the butt of their jokes and excluded from their club.

Tired of never being able to find what they were looking for, Ellen and Anna had spent an entire afternoon trying to get the family's music collection organized. They sorted the music by genre and then alphabetized all of the albums before putting them into the milk crates. The crates didn't stay organized for too long since nobody ever put the albums back where they belonged. Ellen found what she was looking for in the only crate that managed to stay organized. Aside from Ellen and Joyce, nobody in the family particularly liked folk music. She placed the album on the turntable and carefully lowered the needle. Danny and Anna must have been caught up in the sentimentality of the evening because when they recognized the unique strumming of Joni Mitchell's guitar, they didn't object. The cool breeze blowing in from the front porch windows and the whimsical music began to lull them to sleep.

"Ellen, did you set an alarm?" Anna interrupted the silence that had peacefully settled in.

"I set it, don't worry. Good night you two," Ellen called out.

"Good night..." Anna sang out as if she was one of the Von Trap children from The *Sound of Music*. Ellen laughed, letting out an exasperated sigh.

"Good night, Ellen, good night, Anna. Sleep well," Danny said. He had run out of sarcastic comments. They had agreed to sleep in the living room "for old time's sake," but the truth was, none of them felt like being alone.

THIRTY THREE

Ellen's heart sank the next night as she turned down our street and was greeted by the sound of powerful, pulsating drums. Though the house was not yet in her sights, she knew exactly where the music was coming from. She sprinted the rest of the way home, praying that the volume had only recently been cranked up and could be silenced before any neighbors started snooping around.

Several people whom Ellen had never met were conversing on the front steps with cigarettes hanging from their mouths and beer sloshing around in Styrofoam cups. At least there weren't any extra cars out in front of the house and Ellen was thankful for that. While running up the steps, she bumped into a girl from her gym class who was cruelly referred to as "sasquatch" by some of the more immature guys.

"Watch what you're doing!" the girl yelled, as half the contents of her cup spilled down the front of her shirt.

"Oh, sorry, Kim. I didn't mean to bump you," Ellen apologized.

"Sure you didn't. I know you; you're in a couple of my classes. You walk around like you own the place," she quipped.

"I don't know what you're talking about, but this is my house and I need to get in there," Ellen shot back.

"You gonna let her talk that way to you, Kim?" another girl chimed in.

"Jesus, Anna!" Ellen said to herself as she continued pushing past the strangers and entered the house. Once inside, she scanned the crowd, trying to find either Anna or Danny. The living room was packed with people. Thank God they had at least enough sense to have locked the two bedroom doors on the main level of the house.

When she walked into the kitchen, she spotted Anna doing some sort of line dance with three other girls and two guys. One of the guys had an Afro that was twice the size of his head and the other guy she recognized from the football team. The pick that was stuck in the center of Anna's bun bobbed up and down as she attempted to copy their intricate dance steps.

Ellen walked up to her and yanked the pick from her hair. As she dragged her away from her dance partners, they began to protest, but changed their minds once they saw how pissed off Ellen looked. "What the hell do you think you're doing, Anna? Are you trying to get us busted?" Ellen screamed. "Where's Danny?"

"I don't know. He's somewhere. What's your problem?" Anna asked.

"What's my problem? Gee, Anna I don't know. Maybe I'm a little worried that Mrs. Daniels or, worse yet, the police are going to be down here any minute," Ellen screamed.

"There she is," interrupted Kim, the girl from the steps. Standing behind her was her sidekick trying to look intimidating – all ninety-five pounds of her.

"Alright Ellen, outside."

"What?" Ellen asked, obviously new to the practice of being called out for a fight.

"Whoa, hold up," Anna intervened, "I know you're not talking to my sister that way."

"Hey, I don't have a problem with you, Anna. We're cool. It's your sister that I've got a problem with," Kim informed her.

"Well, if you got a problem with my sister, you've got a problem with me, so let's go," Anna said trying her hardest to sound like a badass.

Kim and her friend exchanged a few words and decided that it was all a big misunderstanding. They didn't have a problem with Ellen after all.

"Alright everybody, it's time to go! The police have been called," Danny announced. He tried to use the most authoritative voice he could muster, since no one had actually called the police, but he had figured this ruse was the quickest way to clear out the unmanageable crowd.

"Ah, man – you've got to be kidding," was heard throughout the house. Danny stood at the door and stopped a few people here and there, informing them surreptitiously that they didn't have to leave. When the house cleared out, there were only about twelve people left.

"Anna, what were you thinking?" Danny asked.

"What were you thinking?" Ellen inquired, "Where were you when all of this was going on? You didn't see all of these people traipsing around our house?" Ellen asked.

"I was upstairs with Shelia...talking," Danny answered while motioning to a petite, fragile-looking blond to come forward so he could introduce her to his sisters. She gave them both a little wave and smile, but Anna and Ellen just rolled their eyes. "I told Anna to keep the music way down and to make sure everybody stayed in the house. I don't know how all of these people got here in the first place," Danny argued.

"Yeah, Anna. How did all of these people get here? We agreed to keep it small, just a few people we know," Ellen said accusingly.

"What can I say, I know a lot of people," Anna shot back.

"Well I sure hope this doesn't come back and bite us in the butt," Danny said, more for Ellen's benefit than his own because he wasn't really too concerned. "Ah well, let's move this party into the living room," Danny suggested.

Everybody sat in a circle on the living room floor while Danny put some music on. "What should we do?" asked one of Anna's friends. Danny's friends suggested Spin the Bottle or Truth or Dare, but Ellen quickly squashed that idea because all of Danny's friends were creepy and she knew none of the girls would participate.

"I know," said Anna, "let's have a séance." One of Danny's buddies looked around the circle and asked, "Why didn't you pick a couple of cool chicks from our class to stay?" What he really wanted to ask Danny was why he hadn't picked some girls that they might have been able to hook up with to stay.

"Ooh yeah, let's have a séance," the girls all agreed. Ellen and Anna left to gather some candles while Danny and his two buddies went into the kitchen to mix up some more drinks for the girls. They met back at the circle and Ellen lit the candles before Anna shut off all of the lights. "Who should we try to contact?" Shelia giggled, "I don't really know anybody who's died."

"Yeah, if it's really gonna work, we need to contact somebody we all know," Danny's friend concurred. "Not like Al Capone or someone famous like that, but like a family member or something. Alright guys, start giving up some dead relatives."

Danny, Ellen and Anna remained silent. Ellen's friend, Marybeth put her hand on Ellen's shoulder and said, "It's okay, Ellen."

It took a couple of seconds, but Danny's friend's face turned red. He cleared his throat and said, "Ah, Danny. I'm sorry, man." The rest of the kids in the circle began to realize what he was apologizing for. All of them had gone to school with each other for years except for Shelia who was new. She didn't have the faintest idea about Little Owen.

"What's going on? What does everybody know but me?" she asked.

Anna jumped up from the circle and ran out of the room. Ellen followed her.

"What's wrong with her?" Shelia asked.

"Her little brother died, you idiot," cried Marybeth.

"Okay, just relax. She didn't know," Danny said. He whispered something to Shelia and told the rest of them that he'd be right back. He went upstairs in search of the girls. They were sitting in Anna's bedroom window. Anna was smoking a cigarette and crying quietly. "Hey, let me have a drag on that," Danny said.

"I'm sorry for being such a downer, but when they started talking about people dying, it just hit me really hard," Anna said through her tears, "I don't know what I was thinking by suggesting a séance."

"Do you two still think about him a lot?" Danny asked, "When he first died I thought about him all the time. Sometimes I'd wake up in the middle of the night and I could have sworn that he was in my room. It sounds crazy, but I really think that he was."

"I know what you mean. One night I was feeling a little sad. Not about him, but just about life-ya know? I started praying and I kind of called out to him," Ellen walked from the window and sat on the bed. "Anyway, I closed my eyes and I could feel someone sit down on my bed. At first I kind of freaked out, but I stayed calm. When I opened my eyes, I didn't see him, but I knew he was there."

"I don't think about him as much as I used to and I feel really bad about it. Every so often I shut my eyes and force myself to recall his face. Even now when I shut my eyes," Anna squeezed her eyes closed, "I can see him so clearly. Blond hair, blue eyes, chubby cheeks." Her eyes sprung open, "But then I see him spread out on Aunt Martha's kitchen table and I..." She began crying again.

"Focus on the good memories of him, Anna. Don't think about him on that kitchen table. I never do," Ellen suggested.

"Let's not do this tonight," Danny urged them. "Whatever happened to living a little?" They never made it back downstairs, and their friends let themselves out.

THIRTY FOUR

We got home later than Dad had planned. The rain slowed us down quite a bit even though we made fewer stops. Danny was helping one of the neighbors remove a dead tree from his back yard, but Ellen and Anna were home. Jana had suggested that the girls prepare dinner so that Mom wouldn't have to cook after being in the car all day.

She was pleasantly surprised. "What's that delicious smell?" she called out as she made her way into the kitchen. Jana had taken the girls grocery shopping and helped them plan the menu. Anna had to explain to Jana that it couldn't be anything too fancy or Dad wouldn't eat it. After much discussion, they had decided on roast beef with boiled potatoes, cooked carrots, a salad, homemade applesauce and Jana's freshly baked bread.

"We made dinner for you guys," Anna informed Mom.

"Jana told us what to do and we prepared the meal all by ourselves," Ellen proudly explained.

"Well, this is a wonderful treat! Thank you, girls." She was touched by the gesture. Dad came in with the last of the bags from the car.

"Hey girls! Anything exciting happen while we were gone?" he asked.

"Not really," Ellen answered. "We had dinner with Clyde and Jana one night and Grandma had us over for dinner last night. The last few days have been pretty uneventful," she lied.

Ellen and Danny had decided that they would tell Mom and Dad their plans as soon as they returned home from the mountains. Graduation was only a few days away and they wanted to be able to share with their friends and family what they would be doing after high school.

Patty, Margo and I went upstairs to put away our things. Margo pulled her clothes out of the brown paper bag and placed them in a pile on the floor. She would take them down to the basement to be washed once she was done unpacking. She carefully tucked her diary and pen underneath a stack of shirts in one of her drawers. I walked into the room and startled her.

"Gosh Suzanne! You almost gave me a heart attack. Don't sneak up on people like that. You scared me to death," she said. Margo quickly pushed the drawer shut.

"Sorry, Margo, I didn't mean to scare you, I just wanted to talk," I apologized. Margo continued putting things away and waited for me to speak. I hemmed and hawed for several more seconds before Margo grew impatient and demanded that I say whatever I had to say.

"Okay, what do you want to talk about?" Margo asked.

"Well, let me start by saying that you're probably going to be mad, but know that I'm really sorry, okay?" I told her. Margo was curious, so she remained quiet.

"Uh, I read your diary," I said and then braced myself for either a verbal lashing or a physical one. "I know about Little Owen. I mean I know that you see him and that you talk to him."

I had rehearsed only telling her the part about reading her diary and didn't know what to say next. To my surprise, Margo didn't explode. She looked relieved. For years she had longed to share her secret, but she was afraid that nobody would believe her, that everybody would think she was just making it up to get attention. Like me, she was afraid that talking about Little Owen would upset our parents too much.

"I see him less and less," Margo began. "When I see him, he doesn't talk to me as much as I talk to him. He has spoken to me only one time. It was a year or so ago. Mom and Dad were fighting and I woke up to the sound of Dad yelling and Mom pleading with him to just go to bed. I rolled over onto my side and covered my head with my pillow. I was facing the window and the light from the street was pouring into the room.

That's when I saw him, standing in front of the window. He was perfectly still, just looking at me. It's weird, but he seemed older, still the same size, but he was wiser or something."

In such a comforting way, he said, 'Margo, close your eyes and think of a time when you were happy. That's where you need to let yourself go.' I reached out my hand to touch him, but he was too far away."

Margo stood in front of the window where Owen had been standing. "I told him that I would try and I shut my eyes."

"What else did you say? What did he say?" I asked.

"Nothing. Can you believe it? After every encounter I think of a million things to say to him, to ask him, and then when he comes, I blow it." Margo sat down next to me on the bed.

"People always think of what to say or do after the fact." I told her. "Did you think of a time when you were happy?"

"Yes, I thought about when he was just a baby and I'd hold him close. And ya know what, Suzanne? Just like that," she snapped her fingers, "I felt at peace and was able to fall asleep. I never felt so relaxed in my life."

Margo's smile drained from her face. "But sometimes, I get so scared that he's going to stop coming to me. That I'll lose him all over again, but this time for good."

"Is that why you wake up screaming all of the time?" I asked.

"No," Margo moved closer to me on the bed and looked around the room to make sure nobody else was listening. "I wake up screaming because I'm terrified. Suzanne, something strange happens to me at night and I really don't know how to explain it. I don't think anybody would believe me."

"I'd believe you Margo. You can tell me," I promised.

Margo wanted to trust somebody with her problem and at that moment, she decided that I was going to be that person. She paced back and forth across the room contemplating the best way to explain it all to me.

"At night, when I finally fall asleep, I have these weird dreams, only they're not exactly dreams." Margo quickly grew frustrated. "See? I don't know how to explain it so that it will make sense to you," she cried.

"It doesn't have to make sense to me, just say it so that it makes sense to you," I urged her.

"So, I'm sleeping and all of a sudden, I'm somewhere other than my bed. Like I'm in a strange house and I can smell it and I can touch the things that are in it. I move from room to room opening doors and sometimes I'm walking and other times I'm flying." Margo stopped talking to gauge my reaction. I guess I didn't look as shocked as she had anticipated, as she quickly began again.

"Sometimes I'm outside or in places other than people's homes. Most of the time I know where I'm at, but other times, I have no idea. What's really weird is that there've been times when I'm someplace that I am not familiar with. It's a totally new place and then a couple of days later, I end up being in the same place, only I am awake." She continued, "Do you remember last year when mom drove us out to her friend's house? Her friend who has MS?" she clarified.

"Yeah," I thought for a second, "wasn't her name Frieda? She lives on that farm and has a bunch of cats and a horse named Bobby, after Bobby Kennedy," I said.

"Ha, you're right," Margo said, "How do you do that? I mean, how do you remember every stinking detail that everyone else forgets?" Margo was impressed. "Anyway, I was in her house a few weeks earlier, you know, when I was asleep. I was walking from room to room and ended up in her living room.

I stood outside a curio cabinet and looked at her display of Hummel figurines. Then I walked over to an end table that sat next to a rocking chair and opened the drawer. Inside I found a bag of butterscotches. I wanted to eat one because you know how much I like butterscotches, but I didn't," she added. "I didn't think anything of the place at the time of my night visit. But that day when we went out to her house, I recognized her place right away. At first I thought maybe we had been there before and I just didn't remember, but mom said that it was her first time out to her new place. After lunch, Frieda took mom and the rest of you out to see her horse. I stayed back and looked around. I walked over to her end table, the one I had seen when I was sleeping. It was exactly as I remembered it, even next to a rocking chair. I pulled the drawer open and sitting there, right on top of a stack of bills, was a bag of butterscotches."

Margo let out a long sigh of relief when she was finished telling her story. "Margo, I believe you. I really do believe you," I assured her. "Dad would believe you, too. When Dad was a little boy he talked with his mom after she died. He knows what it's like to experience something that can't be explained."

"Well, I'm not going to tell Mom or Dad about Little Owen or flying around at night. What could they really do about it anyway? I don't want to stop seeing him and as far as what happens to me at night, I'll have to just deal with it." Margo, like everybody else in our family, felt no control over her life.

"Girls, come on down and eat! Your sisters made a lovely meal," Mom called to us.

"Thanks, Margo," I said.

"For what?" Margo replied. "I should be thanking you."

"For not getting mad at me for snooping in your diary and for sharing your secrets with me. Nobody ever tells me anything," I said.

"Suzanne, I hope you know that you can tell me things too. You're my little sister, and I'm sorry that I don't spend a lot of time with you, but I want that to change." Margo said.

"Me too," I agreed.

The two of us headed downstairs for dinner, but I didn't have much of an appetite. I was eager to see Jana; I missed her so much and couldn't wait to tell her about my trip.

THIRTY FIVE

The days immediately following Jana and Clyde's move had left Jana with very little time to talk with her Aunt Margie and Uncle Walter. She called them the day they had arrived safely in Michigan, but hadn't talked to them since.

One morning after Clyde left for work, she decided to give them a call before her day got too busy. Her Uncle Walter answered the phone, but was eager to pass the phone on to her aunt.

"Hello, Jana. It's so good to hear your voice. How are you, honey?"

"I'm great, but what's wrong with Uncle Walter?" Jana asked.

"Oh, you know him. The Orioles lost yesterday and today he's sulking, licking his wounds. Tell me what's been going on with you." She was excited to catch up.

Jana told her all about the apartment, Clyde's new job, and that she was thinking of starting school. Her aunt couldn't get a word in edgewise because Jana had so much to tell her.

"Jana, honey, I need to talk to you about something," she said in a voice that Jana had never heard her use before, "but I think that you should sit down."

"Aunt Margie, you're scaring me. Is everything okay with you and Uncle Walter?" she asked.

"Yes, yes, honey, we're both fine, just missing you. It's something else, and I don't know how you're going to feel about it."

"Okay, I'm listening," said Jana.

"Well, a letter came yesterday," she said.

"From who?" Jana asked.

Her Aunt Margie got a little flustered, "Well if you let me finish. I came in from shopping and was deciding whether to fry chicken or put a roast in the oven, because you know how your uncle loves both. Well I decided to take a break from all the thinking and walked outside to check the mail. I was hoping that there would be a letter or postcard from you since we hadn't really heard from you. Now, I understand that you've been busy, so don't feel bad..."

Sometimes Jana's head spun when having conversations with her aunt, because her aunt often carried on several conversations at a time – many of them with herself.

"As I was saying, I checked the mail. There was a bunch of junk mail as usual, but there was a thick envelope addressed to me. There was a return address, but no name to go with it. It was sent from Plano, Texas. Now we don't know anyone from Texas and it was a hand written envelope so I knew it wasn't a business letter or anything like that. I mean, what kind of business do your uncle and I do anymore?"

Jana's heart sank. She knew what her aunt was going to say.

"Jana, are you still there, honey?" Aunt Margie asked.

"Yeah, Aunt Margie, I'm still here."

"In the envelope, honey, was a letter from your mom." She said it so quickly that Jana asked her to repeat what she had just said.

"Jana, there was a letter, actually two letters from your mom."

"What do the letters say?" Jana asked.

"Well, I only read the one because the other one is addressed to you," Margie answered.

"Read me your letter, Aunt Margie, please!" she insisted.

"Okay, but only if you're sure," Aunt Margie said.

> Dear Margie and Walter,
>
> It's taken me years to get up the courage to send you this letter, so please forgive me if I cut right to the chase. I don't know if Jana still lives with you, but I suspect that she might not because of her age. I'm confident, however, that you both are still actively involved in her life. You owe me nothing and neither does Jana, but I am asking for your help.
>
> I beg you to do this one last favor for me and then I promise that I'll not bother you or Jana again. Give this letter to Jana for me. I am not seeking forgiveness or asking for a second chance. I just want to tell her a few things before it's too

late. So, if you can find it in your hearts to get this letter to her, I would be even more indebted to you than I already am. I've always loved and respected the two of you and I know that you've always done right by Jana and by your brother.

Sincerely,

Viv

Aunt Margie finished reading the letter and waited for Jana to respond.

"Aunt Margie, I don't know what to say or how to feel. I'm sorry that you had to get that letter after all of these years," Jana said.

"You don't apologize young lady. And you don't have to try to explain how you feel. I just need you to decide what you want me to do with her letter," Aunt Margie told her.

"What to do? Gee, I never thought that I would hear from her again. I wasn't even sure if she was alive. I need for you and Uncle Walter to know something. The two of you and my dad were my parents. You all raised me, not her. Whatever she says or doesn't say in that letter is never going to change that fact," Jana explained tearfully.

"Oh Jana, honey we know that. You need to know that your mom was a good woman. We don't know why she left, but I think you owe it to yourself to hear her out,"

"Send me the letter, please. I don't want you to read it over the phone. That wouldn't be right. Mailing it will give me some time to process everything I'm feeling right now."

As soon as she hung up the phone, Aunt Margie placed the sealed letter in another envelope and scribbled Jana and Clyde's new address on the front. She wasted no time, and promptly drove to the post office to mail it.

THIRTY SIX

After unpacking our paper bags and getting settled in a bit, everyone made their way to the kitchen. When everyone was finally seated (with poor Anna perched on the stool at the counter, as usual), we said grace and began to eat. The table was silent except for Robbie, who was pretending to be a meat-eating dinosaur. Robbie had recently become obsessed with dinosaurs. Each time he tore into his roast beef, he growled and snapped like a T-Rex.

Dad was tired from the trip and thankfully didn't drill Danny and the girls about what they had done while we were gone. Ellen and Danny sat across from each other and nervously exchanged glances, waiting for the other to share first. After several awkward minutes, Mom finally asked, "Okay, you two. What's going on? You're both acting like cats that swallowed canaries." This got Dad's attention and he put down his fork.

"Did something happen while we were gone?" he demanded.

"No, Dad! Everything was fine, we didn't have any problems," Danny answered.

"Well, that's not exactly true, is it, Ellen?" Anna called from the counter. Ellen shot her an angry look, but understood that Anna had just created an opportunity to come clean.

"What's that supposed to mean," Mom asked, placing more little bites of roast onto Robbie's plate.

"Mom, Dad, Danny and I both have something to tell you. Danny, you go first, you're the oldest," Ellen said.

"Thanks, Ellen. I know how you've always respected my seniority," he said, rolling his eyes. By then our parents were worried.

"Damn it, Danny! What the hell is going on?" Dad asked. He looked first at Danny and then at Ellen.

"I signed up for the Marine Corps. I'll be leaving in a couple of weeks for basic training," Danny confessed.

"Oh Danny, why?" Mom asked. "Why on earth would you do that?" she didn't cry, but was visibly upset. "I don't want you being sent over to some godforsaken place. This world is a mess. There are other options than the military!"

"No Mom, there really aren't. Not for me. Are you kidding? I barely graduated. I'm not like Ellen and Anna. School just isn't for me," Danny told her.

"Now Joyce, he's a grown man. That was his decision to make," Dad said. Our mouths hung open in disbelief, surprised that he would be the one to support him. "The military will be good for Danny. It'll teach him some discipline and move him in the right direction," he suggested.

"Well, I guess your dad is right, Danny. It is your decision – but the Marines? They're the first ones in whenever the U.S. gets into some kind of squabble with another country." She shook her head. "I'm going to miss you horribly. You do so much around here and you're such a good son." By now, she was a sobbing mess.

Danny got up and hugged Mom. Dad sat looking out the window.

"Since everyone is being so honest," Ellen interrupted, "I have some news of my own." The attention quickly shifted from Danny to Ellen. Danny sat back down and gave Ellen an encouraging nod.

"So, I decided that I want to be a writer. I know being a writer seems like a pretty lofty goal, but it's something that I've always dreamed about. Writing not only requires skill, which I have, but a writer also has to have significant life experiences, some real exposure to the world," she said. Our parents looked at her dumbfounded. Ellen expected that they would object at any moment, so she paused. When they didn't say anything, she continued, "With that in mind, I've decided to become a stewardess."

Dad began to rise from his chair. Sensing his disapproval she quickly explained, "I've looked into it carefully and have learned that you have to have at least two years of college under your belt before you can go through the selection process. So, I have decided to go to Wayne State for two years to study writing. Marybeth and I are going to get an apartment downtown and work there while we go to school. Her dad can get us a job in his office. After two years, I'll try to become a stewardess." Ellen spoke with confidence and decisiveness. "I've got it all figured out – I'll work and travel and write."

"I had no idea that you wanted to be either of those things," Mom said. Dad looked at Mom as if she had been holding out on him. She shrugged her shoulders, "I didn't know any of this. When did you decide all of this, Ellen?"

"I've known my whole life about the writing, mom, but the stewardess idea – Antoni helped me with that," Ellen explained.

"Yeah, well, we know how wise Father Flanagan is about the ways of the world," Danny joked.

"So much for us sticking together, Danny," Ellen cried. Danny wiped the sarcastic smile off his face and apologized to Ellen. She knew that he was only joking, only being Danny.

"I never said anything, because no one ever asked me what my plans were," she answered truthfully.

"How could we ask?" Dad demanded, "You're always holed up in your room with your head in a book."

"Did it ever occur to either of you why I'm always in my room? I'm passionate about learning and reading. It's who I am," Ellen explained.

Anna couldn't resist the opportunity to educate her parents on the other reason why Ellen and everyone else stayed hidden in their rooms, "Well, that may be true Ellen, but you can't ignore the other reasons. We all retreat to our rooms because it's a war zone around here and we fear for our lives." Our parents didn't take the bait.

"I think your plan is okay, Ellen, except for working and living downtown. That city's a mess and I wouldn't sleep at night knowing that you were living there. Why can't you just live at home and keep your job at *Kresges*?" she asked.

"You're not living downtown!" Dad was adamant.

"Damn it, dad, I want to get out into the world too. You didn't ask Danny why he wanted to leave. I've always done what you and Mom have asked me to do, and now I'm not asking for your permission; I'm just telling you how it's going to be. My counselor helped me fill out some paper work for scholarships and I qualify for several of them," Ellen cried. She was just as determined as Danny and she needed to make this clear to everyone.

"This is just great!" Dad said as he shoved his plate out of the way and stood up. "I'm losing my family. Does anyone else have anything they want to say?" he asked.

Robbie shouted out, "Who's that?" He was pointing to the back door. Nobody looked but Margo. Standing in front of the door was Little Owen.

The only time Margo had ever seen Little Owen was at night while she was asleep or dreaming (or whatever it was that she was doing). Robbie resumed being a dinosaur, but Margo jumped up from the table and made her way to the door.

"Little Owen, honey? Robbie can see you?" she asked, not expecting him to answer. She turned back towards the table to see if anyone else noticed him, standing here now, as if he had never left. Apparently no one did; only Margo, and now maybe Robbie – she couldn't know for sure. Perhaps he was a figment of her imagination, something she concocted. She had never doubted his existence before, but now standing there in the light of day talking to someone who may or may not have been there, she felt like a fool. She buried her face in her hands and began to cry. Her tears, initially silent, turned into sobs. A low, guttural cry rose from the pit of her stomach.

"Now what the hell's wrong with you?" Dad demanded, and everybody looked in Margo's direction. She pulled her hands away from her face and her brother was gone. "I said –" Dad began to ask again, but then stopped. The look on Dad's face confirmed that he felt Little Owen's presence. Her visions weren't something she just made up. He was there.

"Do you see?" Margo asked Dad.

"No," he whispered, "but I feel him. He's here." He walked over to the door, hoping for something more than just a feeling.

"See who? What do you feel?" Joyce inquired.

After his son's death, Owen had pleaded with God for months, trying to strike a deal, negotiating. He would settle for seeing him just once if that were all God could spare. When his prayers went unanswered, he defiantly bypassed God and prayed to his mother instead, asking her to intervene on his behalf. He was angry with God, no longer willing to ask him directly.

Since her first encounter with Little Owen after his passing, Margo had lived in fear that someday he would go away for good – that he would stop revealing himself to her, but she knew now that she didn't need to fear. Owen was always with her, with all of them, only they didn't always know it. The noise, the emotional turmoil that defined their lives made it impossible for them to embrace the entirety of life that surrounded them. She knew then that if they could find a way to silence the noise, everyone could feel peace, could feel Little Owen's constant presence. They needed to crawl out from under the fearful past in order to live in a confident, honest and peaceful present.

Feeling defeated and scorned by God once again, Dad reached for the door. He needed to get out of there; he needed a drink. Patty jumped quickly out of her seat. Her chair crashed to the floor. She felt wobbly in the knees, so she used Danny's shoulder to steady herself.

Dad yelled, "Patty, what in the Sam hell are you doing?"

Patty's heart and mind were racing. Just praying wasn't enough right now. It was now or never, she figured. "Don't go, Dad!" she yelled, "You can't just leave and get drunk every time you don't like what you're hearing or when something doesn't go your way! You just spent the last several days without drinking! You didn't have a drop and you were happy. We were all happy. Why can't you just stop, dad? Can't you at least try?"

The room was silent. Mousey little Patty had finally found her voice. "Enough is enough," she cried.

"What...did... you say?" Dad asked Patty.

Patty didn't back down. "You heard me, Dad. You need to stop drinking. You're destroying our family and killing yourself and we're all sick of it."

Dad looked around the kitchen table at all of us and for the first time in a long time he seemed to actually see us. From the expressions on all our silent faces, he knew we all felt the same way. How could we not?

When he was a boy he had hated his dad and promised himself that things would be different with his own kids. He so wanted a different life for his family. He used to think that he was doing a little better than his dad did at parenting. At least his kids were better off than some of his nieces and nephews back home. Several of them were on dope or had run-ins with the law.

Ellen was off to college and he was confident that the others would go too. Danny was a good kid. He'd serve his time in the military and then maybe go to college himself. At the very least, he'd be able to get a good paying job in one of the manufacturing or automotive plants. There would have been no jobs and no future for his family had he stayed back in the mountains.

Now he felt ashamed. The realization that he had provided for them financially, but let them down in all the same ways his own dad let him down came flooding into him. His family was barely hanging on emotionally, including him. He was exhausted. The emotional baggage he'd been carrying around his entire life had finally become too heavy to carry. He was tired of being sad, tired of being angry all the time, and tired of worrying about what would happen if he didn't think about Little Owen every single day.

He had let his guard down when he married Joyce, but it had been hard to let her in, to be open with her about his feelings, because he couldn't be honest about them with himself. The memory of his mom and childhood faded a little more with each passing year. He would allow himself to hope and then life would knock the chair from underneath him again. He didn't want to be happy if it came at the cost of betraying Little Owen's memory, but he realized now that he couldn't go on sacrificing the others for the sake of one.

"Alright then, I'll try!" he conceded. The weight of this long hoped for statement hung in the room, as we sat amazed and silent.

Drinking had always seemed like a good idea, especially after emptying his first can of beer. The anxiety that needled him throughout the day would magically begin to fade. By the third or fourth beer, he felt great, still able to have a rational conversation, but a little less anxious. Past that, he knew he was a mess.

After a night of binge drinking he felt remorseful and vowed not to drink as much the next time, but he had never committed himself to just out-and-out stop.

"Oh Dad, that's so good," Patty said in disbelief.

"I said I'd try. Don't lose your head over it."

"That's all you can do, Owen, is try. That's the first step," Mom said.

His hands were shaking, but he managed to open the door. He walked down the steps and into the back yard, where he stood trying to digest what he had just committed himself to. Andrew slid from his chair, followed him outside and stood by his side.

"This yard looks like a jungle. We need to cut the grass and then change the oil in the car. Are you up for learning how to do that?" he asked Andrew.

"Yep," he answered, "but let me go get Robbie. He'll want to help us too." He quickly trotted back into the house to get our little brother.

Mom was the first to speak, "Pray for your Father. Pray that he can do it."

"I will Mom, you can count on me," Patty said running off to her room to get started.

Danny and Ellen sat in silence, their thoughts still reeling. Anna was ecstatic to learn that Ellen wouldn't be jet setting around the world just yet. She'd be able to see her all of the time because Detroit was just a stone's throw away. She was already scheming on how she would convince her parents to let her stay the night with her sister once she moved into her apartment.

I was sitting at the end of the kitchen table, and nobody noticed when I slipped out the front door to go visit Jana.

It had never occurred to any of us to just ask him to stop. In the early years, Mom had pleaded with him to quit drinking. She even threatened to leave him if he didn't. Only once did she act on her threat. She had left, but not for long.

THIRTY SEVEN

About six months into their marriage and with Joyce already pregnant with Danny, Owen and Joyce got into one of their most explosive arguments yet. The fight wasn't so much about his drinking as it was about how he behaved when he drank. Owen had tossed Joyce's overnight bag out the back door after she made another threat to leave. Humiliated and hurt, she grabbed a few things, stuffed them into the bag, and headed over to her parents. Grandma opened the front door to find Joyce resting on the steps. Seeing the suitcase, Grandma Maddie invited her in and listened for well over an hour to her complaints. More than anything, she just needed someone to vent to.

When she had said everything that she needed to say, Grandma Maddie rubbed Joyce's stomach, which had only recently popped out to resemble a full-fledged pregnant woman's stomach rather than just a little chubbiness around the middle.

"Marriage isn't easy Joyce. You know that you are always welcome here, but you took a vow and now you have to try your hardest to honor that vow. Get some sleep. You'll see things differently in the morning," was all she said. It was her only advice. She fixed her a bed on the living room couch and then went to bed herself.

Joyce felt like a failure as she tossed and turned on her parents' couch, unable to relax. A light went on in the kitchen. She recognized her dad's cough, but didn't call out to him. After about ten minutes he walked into the living room with a cup of warm milk in his hand.

"Scoot over, Joycie," he said. He helped her get into a comfortable position.

"Dad, do you remember how well I did in school?" she asked.

"Of course I do. You were the smartest person in your class, probably in that entire school. You weren't valedictorian for nothing" he answered. "What's on your mind?"

"Dad, why didn't you try harder to persuade me to go to school? I know that you were disappointed when I made the decision to marry Owen instead of going to college." She helped herself to a sip of his warm milk while waiting for him to respond. Our grandpa was not one to voice his opinions unless directly asked.

"It wasn't my decision to make, it was yours. I learned a long time ago that nothing good ever comes from forcing people to do something they don't want to do or aren't ready to do," he explained. He reached for his cup, which was now empty.

"Did I ever tell you kids how I wanted to be a cowboy?" he asked. She smiled, trying to imagine her buttoned-up father as a cowboy. With all of the stories he had shared over the years, she had never heard this one.

"You, a cowboy?" she laughed, "I never pictured you as the cowboy type. Was that before or after mom?" she asked.

"During, I guess," he shrugged his shoulders. "The truth is, ever since I was a small boy I wanted to be either a pilot or a cowboy. My bad ticker ruled out my chances of ever flying planes, but a cowboy was within my reach." He smiled at the thought of it and then settled in to tell her his story.

Maddie and Will had known each other since they were small children. Will's family lived only two houses down from Maddie's family. In grammar school, Maddie had an air about her. She acted as if she was just a little bit better than everyone else. She was as smart as a whip and was always trying to impress the nuns. She really got under Will's skin. By the time he reached his teens, she still got under his skin, but in a different kind of way. He felt Maddie to be the most beautiful, proud and intelligent girl he had ever met. Unfortunately for Will, Maddie was head over heels in love with Francis LeBeau, and he with her. They were destined to be together, or so everybody thought.

Will and Maddie both worked at Joe's Market, which was located at the end of their street. As Maddie grew older, her boastfulness and conceit disappeared and she and Will actually became friends. It was difficult for Will to listen to Maddie talk about Francis all of the time. When Francis stopped by the store, pretending to be running an errand for his mom, Maddie was giddy and unable to concentrate on her work. Watching the two of them was painful, but Will conceded that it was better to have her as a friend than not to have her in his life at all.

On the night of their graduation, after partaking in a little too much gin, Will decided to declare his love to Maddie. Maddie was sympathetic and tried to let him down gently. She was flattered, she explained, but was hopelessly in love with Francis. To add insult to injury, she confided in Will that she and Francis were already secretly engaged. Will swore that her secret was safe with him, but he was crushed.

Two months later Francis and Maddie were married. A year after that, Maddie had another exciting announcement to make, she was finally pregnant. Will, who still hadn't gotten over her, was trying desperately to convince himself that he too was happy.

His new job at the steel mill paid well, but he felt restless and unsettled. He was still living at home and felt that his life was passing him by. Many of his friends had already been drafted or willingly signed up to go fight in Europe or Japan. Not Will – he was 4F, medically unfit to serve because of his heart. As a boy, he had contracted diphtheria and was lucky to survive, but the illness left his heart slightly damaged, making him unfit for the military.

Doug Roberts, a buddy he went to school with, had just returned home from spending a year out in Montana. After graduation, he had answered an ad he found in the back of a magazine. The ad called for young men who sought adventure in the great west. He had spent the last year working on a dude ranch. Doug was the envy of all of the married guys who were now strapped to their jobs and wives and kids. He was an inspiration to all of the single guys, like Will, who seemed to be just biding their time until something better came along. Will was always practical and never did anything without carefully weighing the pros and cons. After hearing about Doug's adventures and consuming several pints of beer, he made up his mind. When Doug left at the end of the week to return to Montana, Will was going with him.

As he stumbled home, he noticed several cars parked outside Maddie's family home. Maddie's oldest brother was coming out the front door and called Will over. He had bad news. Francis had been killed that day in an industrial accident at work. Will was shocked and respectfully inquired about Maddie's well being. She of course was devastated and had taken to bed. Will understood that this was not the time to personally call on her and sent his condolences with her brother. For the next two days, Francis' death lay heavy on the hearts of many. At the funeral home people sat quietly whispering about the latest tragic turn of events, Maddie's miscarriage.

Doug left at the end of the week as planned, but Will didn't go with him. He had decided that he needed a few more months to tie up some loose ends. Fall turned into winter and, by spring, Maddie began getting out a little more. Will ran into her a few times, but they spoke only briefly. By this time, another friend of Will's had joined Doug out in Montana. The two of them had made it their mission to get Will out there as well. Before he would make a move to quit his job and uproot his life, Will decided he had one other very bold move to try. The timing wasn't the best, but the way he saw it, now was just as good a time as any. He was going to once again tell Maddie how he felt. He had nothing to lose. And this time around, she said that she was willing to see where their friendship could lead. Will put his dream of being a cowboy on the back burner for the time being. Six months later, when he asked her to marry him, she agreed.

Joyce had known about our grandma's first husband, but she hadn't known any of the rest.

"When I married your mother, I knew that her heart didn't completely belong to me. Sometimes it's bothered me that she didn't love me the way she loved him. But after a while, I realized that we can't help whom we love. Love is complicated, and it's wonderful, and it's always changing. Your mother and I love each other, maybe I love her a little more than she loves me, but I'm okay with that. I wouldn't want to love anyone else," he proudly stated.

"Oh, Daddy! You're so wonderfully sweet," she cried and placed her head on his shoulder.

He patted her knee, "You love Owen, Joyce and I don't think that you could love anyone else. Try to be patient. When things are good, savor each moment that you're happy and when things are not so good, know that this too shall pass."

The next morning Joyce woke early. She made up the bed, placing the sheets and blankets back in the linen closet. After getting dressed, she walked out into the screened-in porch where Grandma Maddie was saying her morning prayers. She set her suitcase down and settled in next to her. Together, they prayed. She prayed, wanting to be heard, wanting someone to listen. When they were done praying, she went back home to Owen. With him was where she belonged.

THIRTY EIGHT

As I flew from our house, with Dad's words still ringing in my ears, I felt truly happy for the first time in my life that I could remember. There was absolutely no pretending necessary. I didn't knock on the back door, but instead ran directly up to the second floor. The door to the apartment was closed, so I decided that it would be rude not to knock, though I felt I would burst with happiness. Clyde answered the door, "Hey sweetie, how was your trip?" he asked.

"It was wonderful, thanks. Is Jana home? I really need to talk to her," I explained.

"She's not here right now. She's down at the park if you want to go visit with her. A little visit from you may be just what she needs right now," he said.

"Thanks, Clyde! I think I'll go see her." I ran down the steps and headed to the park. I spotted Jana sitting on a park bench. Her sunglasses masked the fact that she had been crying. It wasn't until she spoke that I knew something was wrong. Her voice was tired and flat.

"Hey, Suzanne! You're home, welcome back," she said. She handed me a small bag of torn up bread to feed to the birds that were congregating around the bench.

"Jana, were you crying?" I asked. Jana took off her glasses and dabbed her eyes with a tissue.

"Oh, I'm okay. How was your trip?" she changed the subject.

"Jana, so much has happened since I left. I couldn't wait to get home and share everything with you," I said, bursting at the seams, ready to recap the events of the past several days, but Jana was crying again.

"Gee, Jana, tell me what's wrong?" I pressed. Jana held up the letter from her mom. I had no idea what it was or who it was from.

"What's that, Jana? A letter?" I asked.

"Yep, it's a letter and I bet you can't guess who it is from," Jana said as she waved it around in the air.

"Um, I don't know. Who is it from? I couldn't begin to guess," I answered. I'd never seen Jana act this way before. She was angry and sarcastic.

"Since you'll never guess, not in this lifetime, I'll just tell you. The letter is from my mom," Jana said. My eyes grew wide with surprise.

"What does it say? I can't believe you got a letter from your mom. I bet you're so happy," I said.

"Happy? I haven't read it. I don't know what it says and I don't know if I want to know what it says," Jana informed me.

"Not read it. Are you crazy? Why won't you read it?" I asked.

"I don't know, Suzanne. What's the point? I haven't seen or heard from my mom in years. Now, out of the blue, she sends me a letter. I'm afraid, Suzanne," she explained.

"Hmm. I remember not too long ago having a similar conversation with you about being afraid. Do you remember, Jana? I told you that I was afraid and you said – " I didn't finish my sentence.

Jana interrupted, "I remember what I said. Our situations are different, Suzanne. You knew that your brother died, but you just didn't know all of the details surrounding his death. You didn't know him and that's not to say that you weren't affected by his death, but..." Jana stopped arguing because she began to realize that our situations weren't really all that different. Jana had spent her entire life asserting that she couldn't miss something that she didn't know. She didn't really remember her mom, but she still missed her. There was a void that couldn't be filled. She had grown up without having a mom, and then later without a dad. She didn't allow herself to dwell on it too much because she had her Aunt Margie and Uncle Walter. I thought that was probably why she could understand my parents. They had eight children, but those eight children could not compensate for the one child they had lost.

"Suzanne, I need you to do something for me," Jana said. She gathered both of my hands into her own. I was embarrassed because her hands were so pretty and mine looked like little sausages – short and plump, the nails bitten down to the quick.

"You know that I'd do anything you asked me to, Jana," I said.

"Will you read the letter to me?" Jana asked.

"Me? Are you sure you don't want Clyde to do it?" I asked.

"No," Jana shook her head. "I want you to read it, Suzanne."

She placed the envelope firmly into my hands. I got up and stood before Jana. I opened the envelope slowly and carefully, not wanting to tear anything inside. It felt precious to me. I removed the letter from the envelope and looked at Jana once more to be certain that she really wanted me to read it.

"Look, Jana your mom writes just like you do," I said.

I cleared my throat and began reading the letter.

Dear Jana,

Where do I begin? How do I attempt to offer an explanation for such a cowardly and selfish act? I am not writing to you now, after all of this time, to justify what I did. There is no explanation that I could give which would excuse what I did to you and your father. I want you to know what happened and consequently, you will pass judgment as you see fit.

Your father and I were two very different people. He and his sister, your Aunt Margie, were raised by loving and supporting parents. When I first met him, he shared stories from his childhood that seemed magical, stories that I could not relate to. My own childhood was not magical nor anything that I was proud of. My parents drank, but even worse, they were careless and not very dependable. My mother wasn't a cruel woman, but she had no business being a mother. My dad could never manage to hold down a job for more than a couple of months. He bounced from one thing to the next and usually ended up getting fired. My mother did what she could to help out when money got real tight. She cleaned houses and did laundry for single men who didn't have wives to cook and clean for them. The two of them went out drinking almost every night of the week. I was the oldest of three girls and from the time I was five, I was left in charge of them, sometimes for days on end. My parents were always getting mixed up with some shady sorts. Well, one night they took off with a group of fellas that they met down at the bar. I am pretty sure they were selling moonshine in a couple of nearby counties, which were still dry at the time. People would drink gasoline if they thought it would get them drunk enough. They had left for the night and it was bitter cold out. The heat had been turned off for weeks. My baby sisters were so cold that they couldn't sleep. I decided to build a fire in the fireplace to keep us warm. I watched my dad do it a thousand times. We all piled up on the floor in front of the fire to get warm. Once they fell asleep, I carried them to the bed they shared before dragging myself to my own bedroom upstairs.

I fell asleep quickly and slept hard for an hour or so before I heard the sound of breaking glass. I woke up to a room filled with smoke. When I opened my door to run downstairs to get my sisters, the heat and the flames that traveled up the steps pushed me back. I made my way to the window and looked out.

There was a row of bushes on the ground below and even though it would hurt like the dickens, I knew that I had to jump. I knew that I could survive the fall and then I could bust open their bedroom window and get my baby sisters out. I jumped and landed safely. Before I could get up on my own, a fireman was picking me up and carrying me to an ambulance. I told them that my sisters were in the bedroom and they promised me that they would get them out. They asked over and over where my mom and dad were, but I didn't have an answer for them. The firemen weren't able to completely keep their promise. They got them out of the house before it burned to the ground, but they were already dead. The two of them were found in the closet huddled together.

My parents didn't come back that night or the night after that. As a matter of fact, they never came back. I don't know whatever happened to them. I was sent to live with my dad's brother and his wife. They were nice enough people but they had five kids of their own to look after. I stayed with them until I was seventeen and then left. As you know, your father was a police officer. I was working as a waitress in a little café when he came in one night after his shift. I don't know what he saw in me. He claimed it took two months and ten pounds of café food weight gain before he could muster up the courage to talk to me.

I never knew that a person could be so kind. We spent hours talking and when I finally told him about my mom and dad and my sisters, he cried. Oh, Jana,

I should have known better than to let a man like him fall in love with someone as damaged as me. I experienced bad spells where I couldn't get out of bed and I did nothing but cry. He made me happier than I'd ever been. In the beginning I thought that his love could somehow save me. I was so naïve. Some things just can't be fixed. Love cannot conquer all. I shouldn't have done it, but I married him.

I wanted to feel safe and secure and loved and he made me feel that way. We were happy for a while and then you were born. God knows how I loved you. You were blond and beautiful and created out of love. But shortly after you were born, I retreated to a dark place. I couldn't look at you without thinking of my baby sisters and how I let them die. Why did God spare me, but take them? I hated him for that. When I held you or rocked you to sleep, my heart yearned for them. I was sick, Jana, in every sense of the word. I couldn't sleep, I couldn't eat, and it got to the point where I could barely take care of you. Your father and Aunt Margie tried to help. God bless Margie, she didn't know what was wrong with me. All she wanted was for me to be better and for you and your father to be happy.

I suffered Jana, in a way that no person should have to suffer. But I finally saw a light at the end of the tunnel and knew what I had to do. I decided to take my own life and yours as well. You see, even in my darkest hour, I wanted you with me. I wasn't thinking about your father or how it would affect him, I just thought of myself. Once I made that decision to take our lives, I felt euphoric. Why hadn't I thought of that before?

All of those years of being sad I could have avoided if only I had thought to take my life sooner.

I woke one morning and the sun was shining and the birds were singing and I knew that that day would be the day that I would do it. I bathed you and dressed you in a pretty little summer dress. My plan was to have your picture taken so that your father would have one last picture to remember you by. It's strange how the mind works. I was suicidal yet I could make a strange almost rational decision like this, to have your picture taken. It was like I shifted in and out of sanity. I drove us to the photographer's and decided to take some pictures of you on the carousel that sat out in front of the shop. Jana, you were just so beautiful and precious. You smiled and laughed as you went round and round. And as I watched you, I had a moment of clarity. I felt as if someone socked me in the stomach and knocked the breath out of me. How could I ever have thought of taking your life or taking you away from the only person who ever truly loved me?

I took you off that horse and brought you into the studio to get your picture taken. When we were finished, I drove you home, packed my bags and left. Your father was such a good man. He knew my heart and he finally understood what I had been trying to warn him about before we were married. I was too damaged to ever really share a life with someone and deep down he knew it. He hired someone to try to track me down. Once he found me, he didn't try to persuade *me to come back. He just wanted me to know that he forgave me and that I was always welcome to come back, if I was ever able to forgive myself. I had left him, alone with a baby and had completely destroyed his world, and all that man could think to do was to let me know how much he loved me.*

Oh, how I wanted to come back, Jana, but it wasn't until recently that I was able to forgive myself. I read about his death in the paper. I even attended the funeral, though nobody knew I was there. I saw you with Aunt Margie and Uncle Walter and knew that you were where you belonged.

Jana, I am not asking for your forgiveness. I just want you to understand how truly blessed your life has been. Your father was a wonderful and selfless person and so are your aunt and uncle. You are my miracle and because of you, I have come to know that God is good. People are the ones who make the choice to turn away from him. He is always there for us and thankfully he waited for me to ask him for help. If you choose to read this letter, I thank you. If you have decided not to read it, I understand.

With all of my love,
Your Mother

Jana sat quietly and listened while I read the letter. When I finished, Jana was crying. She was devastated. "I had no business asking you to read that letter. I should have known that there might be things in that letter that wouldn't be appropriate for you to hear. I was being a selfish coward."

"Jana, it's okay. How could you know what she was going to say? I know most people think that I am just some strange little girl, but I understand a lot more than people think," I said.

"Did she include a telephone number or an address where I could find her?" Jana inquired.

"As a matter of fact, she did. She wrote both her address and telephone number at the bottom of the letter. Are you going to contact her, Jana?

Jana shrugged her shoulders. "I don't know what to think. I need a little time for my heart to catch up with my brain. All these years, I assumed that she didn't care about us. I didn't allow myself to miss her," said Jana.

"I'm sorry, Jana." I couldn't think of anything to say that could make her feel better.

Jana dried her tears with the back of her hand and asked, "How was your family's trip? Did you talk to your aunt? Did you find out about your brother?"

When I was down south I could hardly wait to get home to confide in Jana. But now, in light of Jana's revelation, all of my news didn't seem as important.

"I'm going to leave you alone for a while," I told her, "you need to think and talk to Clyde. He'll help you sort all this out."

"Suzanne, you sound so grown up, not like a little girl at all." Jana smiled in spite of herself.

"I think you're right. Let's go home and we'll talk when we're both feeling a little better," Jana agreed.

THIRTY NINE

Before leaving for school a few days later, I decided to check in on Jana. She had been in a funk ever since receiving her mom's letter and was keeping a low profile. Several times, over the last couple of days, I had gone to Clyde and Jana's apartment hoping to speak with her, but ended up only talking with Clyde. He'd open the door, shaking his head no even before I inquired whether Jana was home or not.

"She's just not up for company yet," he'd explain. I was going stir crazy all cooped up in the house, and so was our entire family. It had rained nonstop for the last three days. Dad had assured everyone that all the rain was good for the grass and garden, but Mom didn't care a thing about the grass or the garden at this point and prayed that the rain would end and everything would dry up in time for the graduation party.

I was starting to believe Anna's mantra about one door opening and another one closing. I had so much to be happy about, but now Jana was so unhappy.

So much had changed with our family recently. Danny and Ellen were leaving soon, and our dad had remained true to his commitment to try to stop drinking.

He was pretty ornery, but he hadn't had a single drop. His craving for alcohol was replaced with an insatiable sweet tooth. One day he taught us how to make molasses taffy, which we all thought was gross, but we didn't tell him because we didn't want to hurt his feelings. Another day he made a black walnut cake from the walnuts we'd brought back from the mountains. The cake wasn't a big hit either, but it was his mom's favorite, so he talked about her the entire time he was putting it together.

One night after dinner, our parents made my Grandma Maddie's caramel popcorn balls and we watched old home movies. It took a while for Dad to drag the old screen from the basement and to set it up, but it was worth the wait. Most of the footage was taken before Andrew, Robbie and I were born. Everybody looked so young, including our parents. In one clip our mom was in a two-piece swimsuit and was wading into the creek with Danny. My dad let out a little whistle when he saw her. I felt embarrassed when he did that, but I also thought it was kind of sweet.

"Hey, why did you get to wear a two-piece and we don't," Ellen and Anna protested, but my mom said her two-piece was practically a one piece and the suits that young girls wore today looked like nothing more than bras and underwear.

"Bras and underwear," Robbie screamed, "Yuck!"

Everybody got quiet when Little Owen came on the screen. He was a sweet little guy. In one clip, he and Margo were taking a bath together. Margo was so skinny and Little Owen looked like a fat little cherub.

"I remember how hard it was to hang onto him. He was like a slippery little seal," Margo said.

"At least he didn't poop in the tub like Andrew did when mom forced me to take a bath with him," Patty complained. Andrew stood up when Patty said that and starting shaking his butt in her face.

"That's enough, Andrew. Sit your ass down," my dad instructed him.

The film began to fly off the reel and my dad had to stop the projector and thread it back through. When it came back on, I was on the screen.

"Hey look, it's you, baby girl," Dad shouted.

I was pretty cute even though I was wearing the most hideous outfit. I was wearing a Detroit Zoo t-shirt and a pair of orange and brown striped leggings that accentuated the folds of fat that ran up and down my legs. My bangs were short and crooked and plastered to my fat face. The back of my hair came down to my shoulders and was poker straight. I was trying to get on Andrew's rocking horse that one of our uncles had made for his birthday. Andrew appeared on the screen and you could tell that he was mad and didn't want me riding his horse. He was naked except for a cowboy hat.

"Turn it off," Andrew screamed when he saw himself, "Turn it off!"

"Oh, come on Andrew you were just a little squirt, nobody cares," Mom teased.

The night we watched movies together was one of the best nights of my life. We were a family, and I had a rightful place among us.

FORTY

It was the last day of the school year and though the other kids in my class had been moping around the last few days, I couldn't wait for the year to be over. I was eager for summer vacation to begin so I could spend more time with Jana.

I watched as Clyde left for work. I waited a couple of minutes before calling on Jana. This time when I knocked on the door, Jana answered. She was still in her pajamas and her hair was twisted up into a knot on the top of her head. "Hey there, Suzanne! How've ya been?" she asked.

"Good. Just a little worried about you, that's all," I answered.

"Well, that's sweet, but I'm fine. I just got a lot on my mind," Jana said. I stood there hoping for Jana to say something about her mom's letter.

"Hey," she said instead, "today is your last day of school!" She grabbed my hands and did a silent clap with them. I smiled.

"Well, maybe I'll see ya after school," I said.

"You bet! I'll be here," Jana assured me.

I walked to school in the rain, which had thankfully slowed down some and was settling into a soft mist. The last day of school seemed like it was never going to end. Mrs. Burns gave all of us our report cards and tearfully told us goodbye. She presented each student with a book that we could read over summer break. We were all given the same book. While the rest of the kids were saying their goodbyes, Mrs. Burns called me over to her desk.

"Mrs. Row and I know how much you love to read. It would be a shame for you to go all summer without reading," she sweetly said. She handed me a small package wrapped in paper, which was decorated with zebras, elephants and other zoo animals. A bright red ribbon was wrapped around it.

"It looks so pretty! I don't want to tear the paper," I said.

"Here," Mrs. Burns said taking the package from my hands, "if you want to keep the paper, let's just peel off these two small pieces of tape. Thank goodness I ran out of tape while wrapping it." She handed it back to me and watched me slowly remove the paper. It was a hardcover book and taped to the front of it was a public library card. I removed the card in order to read the title.

"To Kill a Mockingbird," I read. "I love that movie. It's one of my favorites." I opened the book and discovered that both teachers had signed the inside of the cover. I turned the library card over in order to examine my name and account number.

I felt so important seeing my name in print. I raised the book and the card to my chest and said, "Thank you so much, Mrs. Burns. I'll be sure to thank Mrs. Row before I leave."

"We didn't know if you had a library card. Now you can go and check out books whenever you want. We also enrolled you in a summer reading program. It's a lot of fun and it's free," Mrs. Burns added.

I hugged her and thanked her once again before lining up. When the bell rang, I made the familiar trek down the hall to Mrs. Row's room instead of leaving the building. Mrs. Row was standing at her door saying goodbye to the other students as they walked down the hallway. She smiled when she saw me.

"I see you got your present," she said.

"Yes, thank you, I love it!" I couldn't stop smiling.

"You're welcome, Suzanne. I'm glad that you stopped by. Mrs. Burns and I have decided that you won't need to come to my room next year," she said.

I stopped smiling, "Why? Did I do something wrong?"

"Of course not. Suzanne, you're a smart girl. You probably didn't need to see me in the first place. We were just worried about you. You seemed so unhappy, so disengaged. I think what you needed more than anything was silence. Time to collect your thoughts, time to read and dream," Mrs. Row answered. Her voice was always so reassuring, never cross or loud.

I walked home with my book in one hand and my library card pressed firmly into the other. When I turned onto our street, I noticed Wood and Spring walking on the other side. Wood gave me a quick smile and I managed to say hi before looking back down at the ground. As I approached our house, I noticed Jana and Oscar sitting on the front porch of the Peterson's house. The rain had finally stopped and the sun was trying to peak out. When Jana saw me, she waved me over. "Come sit with us on the swing," she said.

"Hey, where did that swing come from?" I asked. I plopped down next to Jana and started petting Oscar.

"Mrs. Peterson, I mean Kathy. She and her husband Frank are moving in next weekend. She came by to make sure the delivery went smoothly. She's really a nice woman," Jana said.

"Who's really a nice woman?" I asked.

"Aren't you listening to me? Kathy Peterson. You know, I just met her this morning." Jana nudged me in the side.

"Oh, oops, sorry. I guess I was too busy seeing what old Oscar was up to." When he heard his name, he lifted his head and looked around before resuming his nap. I filled her in on Danny and Ellen's plans, not knowing they had already revealed them to her. I also told her the exciting news about our dad and his efforts to stop drinking. Jana was pleased to hear that things were going so well for our family.

I decided that it was best not to mention her mother's letter and to let Jana bring it up when she was ready. Jana said nothing about the letter, and instead began inquiring about our trip. I was telling Jana about Grandpa's health when Mom called me over to help with the preparations for Danny and Ellen's graduation party.

"What time should we get to the school?" Jana called out to my mom.

"Be there by five if you want to get a good seat," Joyce suggested. I wasn't certain what the two of them were talking about.

"Oh, Danny and Ellen asked if we would come to their commencement ceremony tonight and your mom invited us over for ice cream and cake afterwards," Jana explained. I was excited to hear that Clyde and Jana were going to be there.

"Well, I better get home to help my mom. Some family is coming over and she gets stressed out if everything isn't just so," I gave a quick kiss to Oscar and skipped back over to our house.

After the graduation ceremony our grandparents took a family picture of all of us, and we went back to our house. Later, when the house began to fill up with more and more family, Jana and Clyde decided that they should probably say their goodbyes. Before they left, they reminded Danny, Ellen and Anna about the neighbor's party. Jana, feeling giddy from too much cake and pomp and circumstance, even invited our parents to come along. We knew she was pushing her luck, but didn't want to burst her bubble. Everybody was in a good mood. It was Danny and Ellen's big day and one of the last times, at least for a while, that we would all be together.

It was nice to finally have a family event where Dad wasn't drinking. Danny announced to all the guests that he had joined the Marines, and the room filled with congratulations from all of the men and a bunch of, "Whys?" from all the aunts and female neighbors.

Danny didn't really care what any of them had to say, he was just so happy that after 19 years, he was finally able to pick out the type of cake that he and Ellen would share. Of course when Ellen shared her plans to attend Wayne State, everybody was pleased. They were shocked to hear that she would be living downtown in an apartment with her friend. Detroit seemed like a completely other world to most of the people in our circle of friends and family.

"We're not worried, Ellen's a smart girl, she'll be fine," Dad told them all. Since everybody was making speeches and proclamations, Antoni decided to share his news. He had made the difficult decision not to enter the seminary, at least for the time being. Instead he was going to attend U of M in the fall, where he would double major in philosophy and psychology.

His decision worried his parents, who viewed his plans as impractical. Anna overheard Antoni's parents expressing their concern over his change of heart to our mom and Ellen.

Antoni had shared his plans privately with Ellen the night before. Everyone assumed that Ellen would be overcome with joy to hear his news. She was, but not for the reason people assumed. Ellen did love Antoni, but lately her love for him was different. Ever since they were kids, he had looked after Ellen. Antoni was quiet and reserved and she viewed him as her tower of strength. But the truth was that Antoni never had to fight a day in his life to survive. From the time of his birth, his parents created a safe, warm cocoon for him.

While our family seemed to have no expectations, Antoni's family had too many. Ellen gave him a relationship that was safe, one with little pressure. Being devout and living your faith was not easy for a high school student and while most kids were rebelling and turning away from the church, Antoni was embracing it with the enthusiasm of a child. Kids liked him well enough at school, but he didn't have very many close friends. He had been content surrounding himself with books and keeping company with Ellen and the Lord, but not lately. He too wanted something more.

Later when the topic of Antoni and school came up, Anna commented on what she had heard. "Well, if you ask me, his parents are big hypocrites. What are they thinking? They act as if Antoni was going to be making money hand over fist as a priest."

Mom was not amused by Anna's cynicism. "Darn it, Anna! Why do you always have to be so negative? You're always so critical about the church and God, and quite frankly everything as of late."

"The way I see it, if you want something or need something done, you have to take matters into your own hands. Patty was the one who asked Dad to quit drinking, not God. And if dad really wants to stop, he'll have to do it, all on his own. How can you continue to believe in someone who repeatedly lets you down? Your faith is pathetic."

"Oh, Anna, it's all I got," she cried. She realized that Anna wasn't angry with God, she was angry with her. "I'm sorry that I've let you down over the years, and maybe I didn't always do my best as a mother, maybe I gave up, but I can't take any of it back. Please forgive me."

"What are you talking about? I'm not talking about you," Anna said defensively, "You haven't let me down," Anna lied. For the first time Anna did not look defiantly in the face of her mother.

Mom walked over to Anna and lifted up her chin, "I haven't been much of a role model for you kids. Please don't ever give up on life. You ask why I still believe in God. I still believe because, look at all that I have. I still have all of you."

"Oh, Mom, you're hopeless." Anna promised herself in that moment not to be so angry all of the time.

FORTY ONE

I woke the next morning bright and early. While walking to the bathroom I looked out the back window and noticed Clyde, my dad and Andrew walking back over to the Peterson house. Clyde was installing some new lighting in their kitchen that morning and had asked my dad if he could lend him a hand. Andrew happened to look up at the window and caught me looking down at them. He gave a wave and a little smile.

I never remembered my brother looking happier. Seeing Andrew this way made me hopeful that Andrew wouldn't continue stealing milk money, or anything else for that matter. I blamed his stealing on being unhappy, but the truth was I wasn't sure why he did it. I was beginning to understand that people had very good reasons for behaving the way they did, though sometimes those reasons were unclear to the people they share their lives with.

I still retreated to my make-believe world, but not as much as I had in the past. I didn't seem to need to anymore.

At about 6:30, Danny and all of us girls announced that we were heading over to the neighbors' party. Andrew and Robbie were sitting on the floor flipping through Andrew's book of baseball cards.

"Andrew, aren't you coming with us?" I asked.

"To the hippie house?" Andrew replied.

"Don't call it that," Dad scolded him, "I met a couple of the guys who live down there when they helped Clyde and me with the electrical work. They're decent people; they just need haircuts, that's all." He winked at Andrew when he said it. He did believe what he said, but he wasn't quite ready to socialize with them yet.

"Nah, I'm going to stay here and watch the game with Dad and Robbie," Andrew said. I didn't blame him. Andrew had stuck to Dad like glue ever since returning from our trip.

Mom was getting ready to go to our grandma's house to visit some aunts who were in town. Before she left, she handed a chocolate Bundt cake to Danny and instructed him to give it to one of the women who lived in the house that was hosting the party. Danny started to protest, but there was a knock at the door and he wisely made the decision to answer the door instead of arguing with Mom.

"Holy shit! What's up with the hair?" Danny asked in disbelief. Clyde walked into the living room sporting newly shorn hair.

"With all the change that's been going on around here, I thought it was time for me to make some changes too," he laughed "and besides, I didn't want you being the only one with no hair," he added ruffling the top of Danny's head.

"Thanks, bro!" Danny said.

"It looks good, leave him alone," Dad said and he got up and gave Clyde a pat on the back.

"Where's Jana?" I asked when I realized that she wasn't with him.

"She's coming, kiddo! She'll be down in a couple of minutes," Clyde said. "Owen, I wanted to return these tools that I borrowed from you and to thank you.

I won't make it a habit. I'll get my own as soon as I can save up a little money."

Dad assured him that it was not a problem and that he could borrow them any time he needed them. Clyde went with Dad out to the garage.

We decided to head out to the party, knowing that Clyde would catch up with us when he was ready. Danny, Ellen and Anna led the pack, with Patty and Margo trailing behind as usual – only this time, I was walking between them.

The smell of the grill and the loud music greeted us before we could even set foot in the backyard. Mrs. Daniels was sitting on her front porch and glared at us as we walked by.

"Hey, Mrs. Daniels," Danny called out, "are ya coming to the party?" She shook her head in disgust, stood up from her chair and walked into the house, slamming the door behind her.

"Boy, I'm gonna really miss old Mrs. Daniels," Danny joked.

"Oh, we'll keep you updated on the old hag," Anna said. We all went around to the back of the house and joined the party. The yard was packed with people. It was hard telling the guys from the girls.

"It's a good thing Dad didn't come," Danny said, "This might have been too much for him to handle. He'd shit his pants."

Jana came into the backyard wearing a long sundress, a big floppy hat and glasses that covered almost her entire face. She said, "Let me introduce you to some people."

Clyde was right, there were a lot of people, and my brothers and sisters quickly found someone to hang out with. I hadn't found anyone, so I just sat at a picnic table and helped myself to some chips. A few minutes later, Jana approached, accompanied by two boys that I recognized from school.

"Suzanne, you know Spring and Wood, don't you?" Jana asked. She wasn't going to be happy until everybody had made some new friends.

"Yeah, sure," I said. Spring said hi and then took off with a few boys who came running by with a football. Wood stood there by himself with Jana and I, not sure of what to do.

"Wood, why don't you show Suzanne the puppies," Jana suggested. She was trying to break the ice.

"You have puppies? Oh my gosh-how cool! What kind?" I asked.

"Well, they're mostly Husky, but they're mixed with a few other breeds, so basically, they're mutts," he laughed.

"Oh, don't call them mutts. That makes them sound like there's something wrong with them," I cried.

Wood quickly apologized, "Oh, sorry. That's not how I meant it to sound. I actually like them for that reason. I mean c'mon," he said. "Look at all of us. We're not exactly what most people would call normal."

I liked how easily Wood laughed. I imagined that Clyde was probably much like Wood when he was a boy.

"Well, do you want to see them or not?" he asked.

"Of course," I answered, "lead the way."

We went into the house where the puppies were kept. All of the dogs were in a large box in the kitchen, and the puppies were nursing. The two of us sat admiring them. When they were done eating, Wood and I reached into the box and each took out a puppy. The mom let out a little growl of disapproval, but Wood quickly calmed her down, "It's okay girl, we won't hurt them."

"You know," Wood said after a couple of minutes passed, "my mom would probably let you have one. We need to find them good homes," he said.

"Oh, really? I absolutely want one. I just need to convince my mom and dad," I answered.

"Hey, Wood. Grab your guitar," his dad called from the back yard, "and come out and play for us." Wood excused himself and got his guitar as his dad instructed. I walked back outside after spending a few more minutes alone with the dogs. Jana was sitting on a swing, listening to Wood play.

"Are you having fun yet?" she asked. She got off the swing and let me get on.

"I am." It was strange how I didn't feel the least bit uncomfortable around these people. I felt more at home at the hippie house than I did at my own, though my feelings about my own home were slowly changing. Jana and I listened to Wood sing and play his guitar. After a few songs, Byron and John's band took the makeshift stage and began to play.

Several people got up and danced, including Jana, but I was content to just watch. I looked across the yard and noticed Ellen talking to a guy who looked about her age. He had sandy brown hair and was tall and thin. He looked quite normal, not at all like a hippie. I thought he was pretty cute and was happy to see Ellen talking with him bravely.

Jana took a break from dancing and walked back over to where I was sitting.

"A penny for your thoughts?" she asked. She pulled back the swing and then sent it sailing into the air. I held on tightly as I soared back and forth, higher and higher.

"Hey, remember, I don't really like rides," I screamed. Jana slowed it down and eventually the swing came to a complete stop.

"I know things have been crazy since you've gotten back, but you still need to tell me about your trip," Jana reminded me. Wood came running over to us to share some good news.

"My mom said that you could have one of the puppies. Let's go back to your house and ask your parents if it's okay," he said.

"Okay!" I eagerly agreed. "Sorry, Jana, but I'll have to tell you about my trip later." We headed for the gate and I glanced back at Jana, who had taken my place on the swing.

"What do you think your mom will say?" Wood managed to ask as he struggled to keep up with me. I was moving along at a steady clip, sprinting down the sidewalk right over the cracks that I ordinarily tried to avoid out of fear of "breaking my mama's back."

When we reached the house, I tried the front door, but it was locked. I would only knock if I absolutely had to, because the sound of knocking doors at night freaked my dad out.

"C'mon to the back," I urged, "My parents probably left that door unlocked." As we rounded the corner of the house, I threw up my arm, preventing Wood from going any further. I practically knocked the wind out of him.

"Shh!" I said to Wood. Mom did the same thing to us kids when we were driving in the car and she had to brake suddenly.

"Oh, you'll thank me someday when I prevent you from flying through the windshield," she'd preach.

Mom and Dad were sitting on the back steps talking, but I couldn't make out everything they were saying. Dad was rubbing his hands across the stubble on his face as if he were trying to rub away the urge to have a drink. Mom got up from her spot beside him, moved directly behind him and began kneading his back.

"We're all so proud of you, Owen. It's got to be hard, but keep your eye on the prize. Think about how good you feel?" she assured him.

"It's hard. I've been drinking for more than half my life," he confessed. He hadn't had a drop in days and it was killing him. It was a hard habit to break. He had been eight or nine years old when he secretly began to cipher moonshine from his dad's still.

I didn't want Wood to hear anymore, so I cleared my throat, walked into the light, and quickly popped the question about the puppy. After being subjected to a twenty-minute lecture from Mom on the responsibilities of dog ownership, I was given the green light on the dog. My family seemed to grow safer, and more normal, with each passing day.

FORTY TWO

The next day, Mom didn't wake us for Mass. The older kids hadn't rolled in until well after two in the morning and Andrew, Robbie and I had stayed up late playing with the new puppy. Mom was not thrilled about having a dog, but I promised her that I would be the one to take care of him. Mom started a pot of coffee and sat at the table, waiting for it to brew. The house was eerily quiet and the silence that she had longed for for so many years now left her feeling melancholy. It filled every corner of the room and reminded her that Danny and Ellen would soon be gone.

Her solitude was brief. Danny entered the kitchen looking sleepy eyed and slightly hung over. "What are you doing up, Danny?" she asked. "You're never up this early. I practically have to beat you out of bed every Sunday for church."

She retrieved two coffee cups from the cupboard and filled them with coffee, adding a little bit of milk to one.

"You might need this," she said handing it to Danny. He accepted the coffee, hoping that the caffeine would rid him of his pounding head; he had drunk too much at the party.

"Clyde and I are going for a run," he told her. Mom disliked the red bandana that he had tied around his head, because she thought it made him look like a pirate. She wanted to tell him to at least put a shirt on, but she didn't. Danny flexed the muscle of his left arm and then tightened his abs before pounding them a couple of times. "I really need to get into better shape, or basic training is gonna completely kick my ass."

She raised her eyebrows in protest of his language. "I really hope you don't go into the military and become a foul mouth like your second cousin, Jimmy." She leaned in real close to Danny when she said it, as if her cousin was in the room and might hear. "His parents had to ask him to move out because of his vulgar language. They were afraid that he was going to corrupt his younger brothers and sisters."

Danny rolled his eyes, but didn't say how shitty he thought it was that Jimmy had been kicked out, considering his circumstances. Jimmy wasn't quite right in the head when he returned home from Vietnam. Danny was certain that there was more to the story than his cursing, but their family never liked to talk about things that were the least bit unpleasant. Danny took another swig of his coffee before setting the cup on the counter.

"My stomach can't handle this right now," he said. He opened the refrigerator in search of something else to drink and settled on milk. He took several swigs from the container while standing in front of the open refrigerator.

"Believe it or not," Mom's voice cracked, "I'm actually going to miss seeing you do that, Danny." Danny closed the milk carton and set it back on the shelf. He smiled and promised Mom that he would teach Andrew and Robbie how to do it before he left. He leaned into the wall and did a couple of push-ups. Then he grabbed his right ankle, pulling it in towards his back to give his hamstring a quick stretch. He did the same with his left leg and then touched his toes a couple of times.

"Well, I'm off," Danny announced, trying to sound enthusiastic.

Before he could make a clean get away she said, "It hasn't been all bad, has it? We've had some good times."

Danny stopped. He understood full well what she was referring too, but sort of resented her asking. "What hasn't been bad, Ma?" he asked.

"You know what," she said, and waited for him to answer.

Danny considered all of the possible ways he could answer Mom's question. His first option was to be honest, but at this point, the truth seemed unnecessarily cruel. There had been some good times over the years, but those good times were few and far between. He showed a little restraint and gave her a more diplomatic answer.

"Nah, ma, it hasn't been too bad. Shit happens," he said, "It's just that we've seen our fair share of shit." Danny wrapped his arms tightly around her and kissed her on the cheek.

"Oh, you're such a liar, but thank you for humoring your mother. You have a real gift, Danny. You always know what people need," she said. "You're what you'd call a real bull shitter."

"Language, mom. Don't become a foul mouth," he warned her. He squeezed her shoulders one last time and left to meet Clyde for their run.

The creaking of the stairs leading from the upstairs signaled that someone else was now awake. It was me. I had been sitting on the steps waiting for Mom and Danny to finish their conversation. I walked into the kitchen with the puppy securely wrapped up in a blanket.

"I think he misses his mom," I explained. "He's been crying for the last hour."

Mom looked at the dog and smiled, "Poor little guy, he's so sweet. Have you decided on a name?" she asked.

"Yep, his name is Finn," I said proudly.

"What the heck kind of name is Finn?" she asked.

I had recently finished reading The *Adventures of Huckleberry Finn* and now considered it one of my new favorite books. I had discovered the book one day while rummaging around in our grandparent's basement. My Grandma Maddie was concerned that it was too advanced for me and handed me a copy of *Old Yeller* instead. She thought that it might be an easier read. I thanked her, but explained that I had already read that book.

I was already familiar with the story because I had watched the movie about Huck Finn with Mom when I had stayed home sick from school with strep throat. One of Mom's few pleasures was watching *Bill Kennedy at the Movies* every weekday afternoon. Bill Kennedy was a former actor and retired staff announcer at one of the local radio stations before hosting a daily TV program that featured old movies. She was almost never able to sit down and watch the entire feature, but she enjoyed having it on in the background while she folded laundry or scrubbed the kitchen floor. His old movies somehow made the work more bearable.

When Ellen discovered that I was reading the book, she was so proud of me. She tried explaining to me the many themes of the story – themes of slavery, racism and the oppressive social climate of the time. Ellen could have written a dissertation on the topic, but most of what she said went right over my head. I thought that it was just about two friends on an adventure.

The friendship between Jim and Huck is what had piqued my interest. I imagined what it would be like if Jana and I had floated down the Mississippi River on a raft. I would be Huck and Jana would be Jim, only not black or a runaway slave. I would have to figure out a way to get Clyde on the raft with us, but I hadn't gotten that far in my fantasy. Instead of running from something, I had decided we would be searching for something, something wonderful.

I placed Finn on the kitchen floor and sat down at the table with Mom.

"Well, he's your dog sweetie, name him what you want," she told me. She watched the puppy wiggle out of his swaddling and begin chewing on a flip-flop that someone had left on the floor. "He's such a rascal," she laughed.

I took a bowl from the cupboard and filled it with cereal. I ate slowly, hoping to kill some time. It was too early to take the puppy over to show Clyde and Jana. My mom pried the flip-flop from the puppy's tiny mouth and scooped him up on her lap. She let Finn nibble on her finger much the same way the children did when they were cutting their first teeth. I stopped eating and watched as she interacted with Finn.

She still looked tired, but she also looked lighter, less stressed and more content. She caught my stare and gave me a little wink. "Puppies are sweet," she said, "not as sweet as babies, but they're still sweet."

We shared a comfortable silence for several minutes before I took advantage of the rare opportunity of having Mom all to myself.

"What was I like as a baby, mom?" I asked.

"Oh, Suzanne, I can't remember you as a baby," she answered. As soon as the words escaped her mouth, I knew she regretted them. She knew how horrible they must have sounded.

I stopped smiling, but did not express my disappointment out loud. I dutifully swallowed my feelings. Like the rest of my family, I had successfully mastered the art of denial years ago. "Yeah, I guess that was a long time ago."

She tried to make me feel better. "I didn't mean for it to sound like that. Of course I remember you as a baby." She didn't sound very convincing. "You were, well, easy. You hardly ever cried and when you were older, you kept yourself entertained. I never worried about you, not like I did the others. You were self-sufficient and not very demanding."

Her second response felt even worse than the first. Mom was not at all like Danny. She couldn't just lie and say what she thought someone wanted to hear.

She searched my face to see if I too realized how sad her recollection of my early years was. "Did you know that you didn't speak until you were almost four years old?" she asked. "Everyone-my mom, my sisters, all of my friends-we were so worried about you. They were certain there was something wrong with you. Well, you know me. I panicked and took you to the doctor as soon as I could make an appointment."

I sat and listened intently to yet more new information about my past. "After thoroughly examining you, Dr. Lee assured me that you were fine. He said that you would talk when you were ready. Can you believe that?" she threw up her hands. "I'd never heard such nonsense in my life. Well, right there and then I made up my mind to take you to someone else, a good American doctor. When Dr. Lee left the room, I started collecting all of our things to leave. You were sitting on the carpet playing and when I bent over to pick you up, I noticed something in your hand. It was a little book and the cover had a picture of a kitten batting at a ball of yarn. Do you know what you did?" she asked.

"No," I answered.

"Well, just as plain as day you said, 'Mom, will you read me this book? I like kittens.'"

I felt elated, "I said that? Just out of the blue I asked you to read me a book? And those were the first words I said?"

Nobody ever told stories about me. I wasn't even sure there were many to tell. There were always plenty of stories about Andrew. Stories about how round his face was or how cute he looked in the little Santa suit he wore to get his first picture taken. There was endless film footage of Andrew as a baby as well: Andrew pulling himself up onto the couch, Andrew taking a bath, and Andrew dancing while wearing only a diaper. Most of his major milestones had been recorded, captured permanently on film. The stories about Andrew were endless, and because Robbie was still considered a baby people commented daily about the cute things he did.

"Just like that," my mom answered her. "You've always been my smart little girl." I think my smile eased my mom's guilt.

Her first response to my inquiry had been accurate, but her second recollection was more personal, and that felt good. Mom confessed that she did find it more than a little odd that I didn't really have friends. She worried about me sleeping in the closet, but told herself that it was just a phase. All in all, I was not a difficult child. Though I did keep to myself, I rarely complained.

"I like that story," I announced and continued eating.

I emptied the bowl, eating only one soggy square of cereal at a time, and placed it on the floor so Finn could lap up the remaining milk. When he was finished, I carried the bowl to the sink and then glanced at the clock once more. It was still a little early, but definitely a more appropriate time to call on Clyde and Jana.

As I was walking upstairs to dress, I heard a light tapping on the glass of our back door. It was Jana. I held up one finger to signal that I would be down in a minute. I continued up the steps and quietly entered our bedroom in search of something to wear. I changed out of my nightgown, brushed my teeth and made my way back to the main level of the house to locate Finn. Finn was in the living room gnawing on the head of one of Robbie's dinosaurs. After freeing the dinosaur from Finn's mouth, I buried the now headless creature in the bottom of the trashcan and hoped that my little brother wouldn't notice that it was missing.

FORTY THREE

I scooped up Finn and pulled open the door. I expected to find Jana waiting, but instead almost tripped on the flowered suitcase perched on the second step. Jana was standing in the middle of the garden admiring my dad's tomato plants. I glanced at the suitcase and then back at Jana. "Are you going somewhere?"

Jana answered, "Yes, Suzanne, but don't worry, I'm coming back." She bent down to extract a weed from the ground before casually adding, "I decided to go ahead and meet my mom. I couldn't do it without Aunt Margie and Uncle Walter with me, so we're meeting in Baltimore."

"Really Jana? That's great!" I exclaimed.

Jana had struggled for days over whether or not she should contact her mom after all of these years. In the end, it was Clyde who persuaded her to give a reunion a go. She'd never get back the years that her mother was gone, but the chance of a future together was worth exploring. It was true that she had abandoned Jana, but she was opening the door for a return, and that had to count for something.

"Will you do me a favor, Suzanne? Will you keep an eye on Clyde and Oscar for me while I'm gone?" Jana asked. "They'll be terribly lonely without me."

"You know I will," I answered her. "We all will."

"Now there's just one more thing you have to do for me before I go. Tell me about your trip," Jana said throwing her arms into the air and looking exasperated.

The two of us sat on the bottom step and I contemplated telling Jana everything that I had learned while visiting our family and since being home, but decided against it.

It occurred to me right then that my Aunt Susie might have been right all of these years. Maybe the past should remain in the past. Today I decided I would follow the example of the mud bees and remain silent, keeping my stories to myself.

The past no longer seemed as important. I had something bigger to share with Jana. "Remember that night when we talked in the park? You told me that everybody has a story and that our stories don't necessarily begin or end with ourselves. Do you remember explaining all of that to me?" I asked.

I guessed that Jana could see the wheels in my head spinning. "Yes, of course I remember. I'm not that old yet," she joked.

"I told you that I didn't have a story, but I was wrong. I changed my mind, I do have one."

"I knew that you did," Jana said smiling. "We all do, sweetie."

"All this time I thought that my story started and ended with my family, but it doesn't. They're part of it, but they're not all of it. I guess stories don't need to begin or end with just one person, unless of course you want them to."

Until recently I had believed that the death of Little Owen was the start of my family's story. But now I wasn't so sure. Was it possible for people to have false starts? Could people's stories begin the same, but have different endings at different times? I had never viewed my mom and dad as anything other than my parents. Not once had I considered that long before any of us were born, their stories had already begun. I had thought of my family as one singular, solid unit instead of identifying each of us separately, as individuals.

Jana had asserted that each person had to decide what role their past would play in their future. Over the last few weeks, I had witnessed our family struggling to do just that. Dad, it seemed, had spent almost his entire life trying to recover from losses. From the loss of his mother to the loss of his son, sadness had attached itself to him. As for our mom, she had been a relatively happy person until Little Owen died.

Our parents fought horribly, but even now I could see that there was still love between them. Losing her child was the single worst thing that had happened to Mom and she struggled to recover. Unlike our dad, she didn't find comfort in mementos of times gone by. She could easily dispose of most things, but not the pain. That, she hoarded, planning on disposing of it at a later date.

Jana interrupted my thoughts, "Ya know I used to think that I had my story all figured out too, but then out of nowhere, my mom was back in the picture. I guess now my story will need to be revised. I should feel happy that my mother has reentered my life, but more than anything, I feel so uncertain. Meeting her will probably be the easy part. It's what comes next that I'm worried about."

I understood what Jana was feeling. My own family had most recently turned a corner and life appeared to be getting better, but for how long? When was the bottom going to fall out again? I pushed those negative thoughts to the back of my mind before standing up.

"I love my family, Jana, but I don't want my story to be like theirs," I said. I picked up Jana's hand and placed it on my heart. "I want my story to be different. I want it to be happy and hopeful, because I'm tired of being sad."

Jana's eyes were brimming with tears. I continued, "I want my story to begin on the day that I met you."

"Me?" Jana whispered placing my other hand on her heart.

"Yes, Jana, you. My story begins with you," I said with a smile that wasn't forced, a smile that finally seemed to fit my face.

I looked once more at the suitcase that would soon lead Jana to the next chapter in her life. Though uncertain of my future, I was finally ready to begin reconciling my past.

Though it was far from perfect, it was mine, despite the pain and imperfections. I would cherish each story just as my dad cherished that last picture he received from his mom. Like his picture, my painful memories would begin to fade, becoming softer around the edges. The bad memories would slowly disappear. Not right away, but gradually, over time.

In the meantime, I would focus only on the good. Maybe people were more like the mud bees than my Aunt Susie realized, capable of remembering the good and discarding the bad.

My story began long before I was born and it would continue long after I died. I closed my eyes and for a brief moment I could hear the sound of the mud bees thrumming. They refused to waste a single moment pondering past hurts or how much time remained, but focused only on living in the midst of what was good. I pressed my two fingers to my lips and tasted my family's old log cabin. I inhaled deeply, savoring the memories of generations, and recalled the first day that Jana and I met.

THE DROWNING
(as told by the bees)

He longed to feel the cool creek water passing over his feet. Catching another glimpse of the tiny vessel that had sailed past him a few nights before was what his heart truly desired. He was forbidden to go anywhere near the creek without an adult and so he obediently waited for his mom to take him down to the water.

Jiffy and Little Owen held firmly to Joyce's hands, one on either side of her, as they carefully waded in. The rocks were covered in a green, slimy moss, which made them smooth and slick, like pieces of glass. Jiffy quickly lost his footing and slipped, but Joyce was able to pull him up and out of the water before he knew what was happening.

"Wow, that water is c-c-cold!" he howled. His chattering teeth couldn't prevent a smile from forming on his face. "You should try it, Owen."

It did look fun. Little Owen began moving his feet back and forth like a skater venturing onto the ice for the first time. While still holding onto his mom's hand, he slid his feet straight out in front of him until he was sitting in an upright position on a large rock. He giggled as the water washed over his lap. "Ooh, it is cold, Jiffy!"

After a few minutes, the boys let go of Joyce's hands. They splashed and slid around on the rocks, but soon grew tired of being in the shallow water. After Joyce assured them that the water wouldn't be over their heads, they hopped off of the rock and into the deeper water. It took only seconds to adjust to the cool water that now reached slightly above their waists.

"Don't go any further, boys," Joyce cautioned, "I'm right here though, don't worry." Joyce's sister-in-law, Grace and a few of the other adults joined her in the water. They visited and cooled off while the kids swam.

Little Owen and Jiffy laughed and played for quite some time before one of the older cousins complained that he was getting hungry. Joyce wasn't ready to get out just yet, but she knew it would be only a matter of time before all of the other kids started scrounging for something to eat. She called for Little Owen and informed him that it was time to get out. He wasn't ready either, but he didn't object. Upon hearing that it was time to take a break, Jiffy tried to elude his mom by hiding behind a large rock, but Grace was fast on her feet and was able to snatch Jiffy up before he could protest too much.

Once out of the water, Joyce found an abandoned towel and draped it over Little Owen. She teased him, saying that he looked like a wet little ghost. He giggled from underneath the towel and slowly raised both arms over his head and tried his hardest to sound like a howling spook. She towel-dried his hair and then wrapped him tightly, like a butterfly in its chrysalis.

"You stay here and relax and I'll be back down in just a little bit with some lunch," she said smiling. Jiffy waddled over, wrapped securely in his own towel and joined Little Owen on the grass. They sat by the water and basked in the sun as they watched the other kids reluctantly exit the water. Jiffy heard his mom announce from the front porch that the sandwiches were ready. He ripped off his towel and raced toward the house. He wanted to get himself a sandwich before the older cousins hogged them all. Little Owen looked up to his big cousin, Jiffy and mimicked his every move. He was just about to join him on his quest to secure a sandwich when he noticed something white moving in the water. It was the boat. He watched it as it gracefully sailed toward him. He wished that Jiffy could see it with him, but he knew that the boat would be out of sight once the two of them got back down to the water's edge. He stepped back out onto one of the larger rocks to get a better look. After it passed, he looked back over his shoulder to see if anyone else had noticed the boat. Nobody else seemed to be paying any attention. Just when he thought that it would soon vanish from his sight, the boat stopped. It rested further down the creek on the opposite side of the bank on a pile of rocks, leaves and twigs.

"I'll be back in a second," he said to no one as he ran along the creek bank down to where he saw the trapped sailboat. He carefully skipped across the creek on a few strategically placed rocks, but had to stop about half way across. He looked down into the water, hoping it wasn't too deep. Maybe he could just walk the rest of the way over, but he couldn't be sure that the water wasn't over his head. He understood that he really didn't know how to swim, that he had just been pretending.

He remembered seeing a long stick as he was making his way down to rescue the boat. He traipsed back over the rocks and found the stick in the grass. It was long and skinny, but not too heavy. Once back in the middle of the creek, he extended his arm as far as he could and jabbed at the sailboat with the stick, but couldn't quite reach it. He stepped to the very edge of the rock and stretched a little bit further before he was finally able to make contact. He gave a couple more pokes and successfully dislodged the boat from its captor. It began to move away from him quickly. He could think of nothing but retrieving the boat. He stepped off the rock.

He sank rather quickly. Even with his eyes wide open, he struggled to take in all that he was seeing. His brain could not quite register what was happening. The water was crystal clear and he felt a large fish brush the small of his back as it swam by. Suddenly he was frightened. His legs thrashed wildly under him. He felt a shimmer of hope when he felt the creek's floor with his left foot. It was cool and muddy and using only his big toe, he pushed off the bottom and temporarily broke through the surface of the water. He tried calling out to Margo for help - she'd know what to do - but his mouth filled with water. "Help me, Margo! I need you," his words formed only in his mind. He was drowning.

The water around him filled with a radiating light. He stopped struggling. He became aware that the water and the plants surrounding him were more alive than he was. Several fish and water snakes swam toward him, and they were smiling. He saw his family. They were all there - his mom and dad, Danny, Ellen, Anna, Patty and Margo. They were around him, above him, below him, with him, in his heart. He saw Andrew, Suzanne and Robbie too, and he knew them by name, though they were yet to be born.

A NOTE ABOUT THE AUTHOR

Madonna Ball (b. 1970) was born in a Downriver suburb of Detroit. With degrees from Michigan State University and Eastern Michigan University, she has been teaching in the field of elementary education for the last 20 years. She currently lives in Omaha with her husband and three children. This is her first novel.